Confessions of an Average Half-Vampire

by
Lisa Shafer

Copyright 2011 Lisa Shafer
http://lisashafer.blogspot.com

Cover design by Lisa Shafer and Lynn E. Shafer.
Cover formatting by Steve Rossi.
www.srossi.net
Copy editing by Kevin McDaniel.
Scots copy editing by David Cunningham.
http://cloudworld.org

For Mom and Dad, who never have understood why I have this hobby but love me lots anyway. And also for Aunt Dawnie, who's always been there.

My thanks go to the dozens of teenage and adult beta readers who gave their input for this novel.

Prologue

The last time I bit someone was when we were still living in Denver.

I was a dweeby seventh-grader attempting to be cool at the local rec center's annual Halloween party. Except it's hard to feel cool when you can't sit down. And I couldn't sit down because I was dressed as a yellow M & M. Picture bright yellow poster board made into kind of a big, circular envelope stapled over the top half of my body so that only my arms and legs -- covered in yellow ski underwear -- stuck out. I couldn't bend or sit. I couldn't even turn my head because my face was covered in thick clown make up, and I didn't want to scrape it off accidentally on the poster board surrounding it. It was pretty annoying, actually, but I was hoping to win the costume contest with the grand prize of an Amazon gift card. There were tons of tunes and old movies to upload there, which was my idea of paradise.

"Eric, that is really clever," Mrs. Mott, my pre-algebra teacher from Edison Junior High, said as she took my four-dollar entrance fee at the door. "I'm glad you kept with the non-violent theme, as we announced at school."

I mumbled something politely unintelligible at her and headed for my neighbor Justin Skinner, who was hanging out by one of the craft booths, watching his six-year-old sister make a monkey mask out of a paper plate and brown construction paper. He was dressed in his little league football uniform.

"I thought we were supposed to be non-violent," I told him, punching him on one shoulder pad as well as I could without crunching up my costume.

"Hey, hockey's violent; football's not," he said. The black grease under his eyes made him look meaner than he really was. "What are you supposed to be?"

"I'm an M & M. Duh," I said, suddenly realizing that my nose itched and I couldn't scratch it.

"How long did it take to get stapled into that?"

"My mom did it in about twenty minutes."

"Boring."

"Yeah, well, so's watching Katie glue her eyelids shut," I told him, nodding toward his sister. "Let's go find the pie-throwing booth."

"Can't," Justin said, shrugging as well as he could under the masses of plastic padding. "Mom told me I gotta stay with Katie all night."

I rolled my eyes and walked away. I wasn't going to hang around the whole time with a little girl whose favorite activities were whining and picking her nose.

I watched the pie throwing for awhile, but I couldn't try it because I could only move my arms from the elbow down. I wandered over to the obstacle course to watch José Perez from my pre-algebra class race Kaitlyn Fitzer on tricycles around a bunch of bright orange cones. José was dressed as the Franken-stein monster with big, clunky boots that kept banging on the floor, so Kaitlyn, who had her legs free below a ballerina tutu, easily won.

"Hey, Eric! Wanna race? I'll do it again!" José called over to me.

"I can't ride a trike in this thing!" I yelled back at him.

He untangled himself from the tricycle and handed it over to an eighth-grader who was so tall he could barely sit on it. "Okay, let's go get some food then," José said. "I'm starved."

My stomach gurgled in agreement. I hadn't eaten dinner at home because food was included with the entrance price to the Halloween party. And I could smell tacos cooking somewhere. "Yeah! Let's go!" I told José.

The line wasn't too long, so we had our tacos and Cokes about five minutes later. José sat down at a table with a bunch of kids from Mrs. Mott's class, but I had to stand at the end of it in my poster board prison.

"How are you gonna eat without ruining your make up?" Savannah Kritley asked me, the beads of her long earrings bouncing into her frizzy dark hair as she spoke. I had no idea what she was dressed as, but she had more make up on than I did -- and that was saying a lot because I was coated with sticky yel-low face paint.

"Very carefully, I guess," I told her.

"Whatever." She shrugged and started gabbing to José, who'd scarfed down his taco in about two bites and was now trying to chew a way-too-big mouthful without spraying Savan-nah with corn chip crumbs and spit.

I reached for the taco on my paper plate. Oh yeah. White gloves on Mr. M & M. Problem.

I started to move my left hand over to pull off the right glove, but I couldn't. There was poster board all the way to each elbow, and I couldn't reach.

Crap!

I picked up the taco shell very carefully between just my thumb and first finger and brought it slowly toward me. Leaning my face out of the hole in the poster board as far as I could, I got my lips three inches away from the hamburger and salsa. The scent of melted cheddar was drifting up my nostrils and my mouth was watering, but I could not get the food to my mouth.

"Look at Eric!" José yelled. "He can't move right! Hey, Eric, does M & M stand for 'mutant man'?" He began flinging his green-tinted arms around in a fake spasm, and Savannah and the elf girl next to her giggled like he was the funniest thing in the building.

"Hilarious," I said. "How about some help?"

"Sure! I'll take care of your taco problem!" And José stopped flinging his arms, grabbed the taco from my hand, and shoved it into his mouth as fast as he could. Savannah had collapsed onto the elf's shoulder, weak from laughing.

"Hey! Give it back!" I said, trying to grab him. But it was too late. The fate of my dinner was sealed. I was going to be hungry until I got home.

"Attention, everyone!" a female voice said loudly over the P.A. system. "It's now eight o'clock, and we are ready to start the costume contest! We have five different age levels for the contest, with prizes in each level -- and a grand prize for the overall winner! If you have a great costume, come down to the multi-purpose room for judging now! And remember, boys and girls, only non-violent costumes will be allowed in the contest."

Even though I was considering doing some serious damage to José the taco thief, a Halloween costume just doesn't get much less violent than an M & M. Plus, I wanted that gift card, so I worked my way through the crowded hallway to the multi-purpose room to find the junior high age group. About ten kids were already there: a rabbit, a hippy, Marilyn Monroe, Elvis, a princess, a punk-rocker, and a couple of others. Savannah and her elf friend were squeezing in line behind me to sign up when one of the supervisors started shouting about something.

"No! No satanic costumes in this competition! I won't allow it!" He was a big man in a blue suit, yelling at a tall, curly-haired woman at the center table.

"Reverend Burke, the rules clearly state that *violent* costumes are the only ones forbidden," she told him angrily. "No weapons or gang affiliations or portrayals of terrorists. This girl is clearly dressed non-violently, and she therefore qualifies for the contest."

I scribbled my name on the junior high list and got into the judging area without paying much attention to the lady giving me directions. What was this guy so worked up about? What kind of costume would be satanic? A devil suit? Someone carrying a sacrificed cat?

"She is a representation of evil!"

"Kindly wave your personal, religious hang ups with pop culture on your own flagpole and get them out of this *secular* activity," the tall lady said in a voice that could've frozen a laser beam.

I stood on my tip toes to see better over all the kids in the room. The woman had her arm around a girl in a black robe and was gently maneuvering her to the fifth- and sixth-grade section of the contest. When the girl turned around, I could see she had a store-bought Hogwarts patch on her shoulder and a plastic wand in her hand. She looked terrified.

Harry Potter costumes were evil? What was up with that?!

"Who's the fat guy with the anger management issues?" I asked Savannah, who was still next to me.

"Pastor of the church two blocks over," she said, pointing her thumb over one shoulder. "He's Luke's dad. You know, the kid in Mr. Jameson's class with all the Bible verse t-shirts?"

"So, what's he got against Harry Potter stuff?"

Savannah shrugged and her earrings swung around again. "Dunno. He's tried to get the books banned from school libraries before, though. My mom's friend told us that. She says he thinks kids'll get into witchcraft if they read them. He hates *Lord Of The Rings*, too."

"Weird," I said, hoping he didn't notice me. I certainly didn't want to get yelled at for anything, although being dressed as a piece of candy seemed pretty safe to me.

There was a lot more waiting around while the judges picked their favorite costumes, but the preacher guy had walked out of the room mad after the lady'd told him off, so there were no more shouting matches. I won an honorable mention in the junior high category and got a free candy bar which I couldn't move my arms enough to eat, so I got Savannah to drop it inside my poster board costume and hoped it wouldn't melt all over before I got home.

I wandered over to the main gym because *The Creature From The Black Lagoon* was playing there, and I'd always wanted to see that one, with its black-and-white 3-D images.

It was dark, but my eyes adjusted very quickly, just like always, and I climbed over a few bodies on the floor to stand along the back wall, just behind a row of bean bag chairs covered with either piles of girls about my age or else guy-girl couples a little older who didn't really seem very interested in the movie. And it was one of these couples that turned Halloween into a real horror for me. Me and my stupid bloodlust, that is.

The guy was about sixteen and dressed as Bela Lugosi's version of Dracula with the slicked-back hair, the fancy shirt, and the long cape. I knew the girl with him; her name was Carla, and she lived two houses down from me. She was supposed to be Dracula's victim in a long, white dress and her hair all pinned up to expose a fake wound on her neck. They were both more than half asleep on the comfy bean bag chair in the dark gym, her head leaning over onto his shoulder.

It wasn't real blood on her neck; I knew that. This was Halloween, for one thing. And it didn't smell like blood, for another. But it *looked* real. Way too real.

And I was hungry.

On the screen, the plastic-suited creature swam around the bottom of a lake while a lady in white did the backstroke above him, completely unaware of her danger. But I barely noticed. I was staring at the way the tendons in Carla's neck were tense under her pale skin. Skin that was stretched tight and thin at this angle. It would be so easy to break the skin and get at the real blood.

I hadn't had any blood for almost a week. And here was a chance, right in front of me.

But I wasn't supposed to bite people. I knew that.

Dang, I was hungry.

Saliva swirled in my mouth like the tide was coming in, and I knelt down on the floor behind the bean bag. Which meant that my M & M costume made me look like a yellow moon behind two lovers on a beach.

I don't know what I was thinking right then. Geez, I was twelve. I *wasn't* thinking. Who thinks when they're twelve?

So I bit her. Fast. Poster board crunched as I bent over swiftly and punctured her throat with my teeth. I didn't numb her skin with my saliva first, and Carla woke up from her doze to find a giant M & M sucking her blood. She screamed and pulled away from me before I could lick over the wound to seal it up.

A fine spray of blood spurted up across my chest and face as she lurched toward her boyfriend, and I felt hands grab me from behind.

"And what do you think you're doing?!" a loud voice yelled near my ear.

I heard more screaming from girls in other bean bag chairs. Carla was shouting, "I'm bleeding! He bit me! That little freak *bit* me!" There was a smear of yellow make up on her throat.

And simultaneously the movie went off and the lights went on.

Argh! Bright lights! Way too fast!

Blood I didn't dare lick off was dripping from my chin and running down the big white M on my costume, making me look like the terrorist candy from Hades. Let's face it; no one likes the thought of a bloodthirsty piece of chocolate.

Squinting at the light, I tried to see who was holding onto me, smushing the sides of my costume and shaking me until my honorable mention Snickers bar dropped out a leg hole and got stepped on.

"'Only be sure that thou eat not the blood: for the blood is the life; and thou mayest not eat the life...!'" came a voice that would've sounded exciting from a pulpit but was enough to scare the spit out of you close up. And it *was* close up; it was right in my face.

It was Reverend Burke again. And this time he'd found someone he could bully. Someone violent enough to be covered in evidence: a blood-sucking M & M.

"Only a child of Satan would drink the blood of an innocent girl!" he bellowed. I squirmed and tried to pull away. His breath was warm and reeked of coffee as it hit my face in moist bursts.

"Lemme go!" I yelled in a voice embarrassingly close to tears.

"Damn it, Burke! Don't *do* that!" It was the voice of the tall lady who'd told him off earlier.

I should've stayed to thank her for making him let go. But the second she pulled his hands off of me,   I ran as fast as I could. The last thing I heard as I reached the door was the minister's voice announcing, "Sinners will burn in hell!"

Three weeks later, Mom and I moved. To Utah. Where nobody knew us at all.

Chapter One
(Two Years And Three Months Later)

Friday morning. The clock in the corner of my computer screen read 6:35 AM as I updated my profile on our school's "friendsite."

Yesterday Kacey Wolton had complained about it. "You're, like, the *only* guy in the school who doesn't have a picture on your profile," she'd told me. "That's just not *normal*."

And "normal" was what I really wanted to be. You know, the all-American, boy-next-door type. Which I'm not. Unfortunately.

I smirked and added a photo of the lead singer of Narcissistic Sarcophiles to my profile. Not that I look anything like Chris Bellamy, but girls think he's hot, so I figured it was a good photo to post.

An actual photo of myself is just one of the things I leave off the profile, since cameras tend to show what ordinary human brains "correct" for most people's eyes: my skin is slightly translucent. Without the honors English vocabulary wording, that means it's possible to see a heck of a lot more of my circulatory system than most folks want to. Also, cameras capture what my tinted contact lenses normally hide: that my irises are huge and almost clear. Which means the blood-red retina catches the light and makes it look like I have demon eyes from an '80s horror film. The honors English vocabulary word for this is "disconcerting." But most people have a few other phrases for it that are less printable.

What else do I leave off of my profile? That I sometimes faint in really bright sunlight (not to mention getting that ever-unpopular lobster skin look in about five minutes). That I have super-sharp teeth. That I have saliva that both numbs and heals. That I have to drink mammal blood to survive. That I'm a vampire. A half-vampire, actually.

Kacey doesn't leave anything off the friendsite; she has a whole photo album, playlists, and her own blog. I think that'd be cool, but it wouldn't exactly help me blend in better at school if I had a blog called "Confessions of an Average Half-Vampire," so I skip it.

The friendsite wasn't the only thing that'd been worrying me lately. Mom and I had been living here in the thriving metropolis of Emma, Utah (population 2000, except during the deer hunt, when it's more like 1300), since we'd had to leave Denver, and it'd been a couple of years since I'd had human blood. But since the beginning of January, things had started getting bad again. I was craving human blood. Maybe it was a puberty thing; hormones can really mess with a guy. But health textbooks don't cover vampire hormones, and since my vampire dad (who'd left my mom right after she got pregnant with me) wasn't around, I couldn't exactly ask him. In fact, since Mom hadn't even believed in vampires until she'd gradually discovered that if I didn't get about eight ounces of mammal blood every week I'd show signs of malnutrition, I couldn't ask her, either.

So I was both craving and clueless. And it was starting to bug me. Big time.

That Monday had been the semester change. A couple of new kids had transferred into my first period class, and that's when I'd started noticing the vampire puberty thing. Well, actually, the first thing I'd noticed was Alexis.

As Alexis stood in the front of the classroom, waiting for Ms. Nielson, our English teacher, to assign her a seat, I couldn't take my eyes off her. Her short, brown hair was scooped up into a ponytail, leaving her whole neck uncovered. Her skin was the color of carmel fudge, without a single freckle or flaw anywhere. And she had on this black, stretchy choker with little sparkly beads on it. It was so tight on her skin that I could see her pulse beating through it; with each heartbeat, the beads would catch the light.

Saliva swirled in my mouth. How was I ever going to concentrate if Nielson put her near me? Wouldn't that be --?

There was a poke in my ribs.

"Whoa!" came Scott's hoarse whisper from behind me, "Check those out! Awesome!"

Scott had noticed sparkling beads? This was *not* his style.

But I just nodded. "Yeah, amazing," I whispered back, not turning my head much in case Nielson decided to look up at me.

"Yup," Scott added, "Gotta be size double D, at least. Hope Nielson puts her real close to me."

Beads have sizes? What was he --? Oh.

I glanced down a bit from Alexis' neck and figured out what Scott had been talking about. I hadn't even noticed, but I felt myself turning darker and darker shades of red -- even though Scott had no way of knowing I'd been checking out her *neck*, for crying out loud. How embarrassing.

Even though I don't usually have to wear them inside a classroom, I put on my sunglasses to help hide my face.

But everything got even worse after Ms. Nielson had moved us all into new seats. Alexis sat at the back, out of my line of vision, but I now sat behind Tim and kitty-corner from this guy named Michael, which was not a good thing.

The next day, I caught myself staring at the way the tag of Michael's t-shirt was sticking up instead of down while Nielson was writing notes about the Victorian Era on the white board.

On Wednesday, when I was supposed to be finding all the predicate nominatives on page 64 of *Warriner's English Grammar and Composition*, I realized I was wondering what it would be like to touch the shaved-short hairs on the back of Michael's neck.

Whoa! Not good. Not good at all. Why was I staring at a *guy*? Did that mean I was gay? Crap. A gay vampire. Like I wasn't different enough already.

I shuddered and made myself look at Britni instead. She smiled and mouthed the words, "I hate grammar," at me. I felt a little better.

But the feeling didn't last.

Very early Thursday morning, I was asleep after working on Spanish imperfect verbs for a couple of hours (for one of my online classes that I take because I can't go to school in the sunlight all day). That's when I had a super-freaky dream.

It started off like a normal dream: I was half-walking, half-floating near the Emma City park in the soft light of the street lamps, except that the lamps were shining pale blue instead of the normal white. And suddenly Britni from Nielson's class was there, looking in the windows of Andy's Kite and Bike Shop. And somehow I just knew that she couldn't see or hear me, so I got closer. Lots closer.

The dream Britni was leaning right up against the long display window. I could see the bright colors of the kites beyond the glass, but I was much more interested in how the soft blue streetlights made the skin on her arms almost glow. And I could almost see the blood pulsing in her arteries right beneath the skin. I knew that if she fell through the glass, that blood would spurt everywhere. So I pushed her.

The glass broke much more easily than real glass would've, and Britni's left arm went right through a gaping hole, getting sliced from her thumb to her elbow. Awesome!

I grabbed her arm and began licking at the blood. She didn't seem at all upset. In fact, she kept stroking my hair with her other hand while I lapped up the blood like a poodle eating gravy.

Wham! Suddenly I was awake. In my room. With my face buried in a pillow that was completely soaked through with my own spit. I had drooled my way back into reality. Gross.

The memory of the dream was kind of bugging me by the time I got to school. I'd attacked a girl just to drink her blood. And I'd liked it. That was bad. Would I really do that? I shuddered and tried to focus only on taking notes for the whole fifty minutes of class.

So by Friday I was determined to have one *normal* day. Mom had left the night before to scout out locations for some fast food franchise that wanted to open a store in Scotland, and that was good. That meant I'd get to be my own boss for a few days, which is always way cool. I love my mom and everything, but I love making my own decisions about stuff while she's gone, too.

Mom travels all the time -- Scotland a lot lately, but also Canada, France, Japan, Argentina -- heck, once it was even *Kansas*. That's why it doesn't really matter that we've lived everywhere from Boston to San Francisco, as long as there's been an airport nearby. In fact, Mom's boss, whose office is in Chicago, claims he likes having his employees spread out all over so that they can find more available sites for the company's clients. He says if all his employees lived in the same city, then Internatcorp wouldn't be as successful.

So I was feeling good today. No one actually knew that I'd dreamed about drinking Britni's blood. And I'd handled Kacey's complaint about my friendsite profile. Hey, I could handle being normal. Or so I thought.

Until Ms. Nielson started handing out books, that is.

"As you've probably noticed, class," she said, plopping a large cardboard box down on Britni's front-row desk, "we've been talking about the Victorian period and the genre of Gothic horror stories."

Nielson began passing out copies of blue-and-white paperback books. "So, I'm sure you've realized that we'd be reading a Gothic horror novel for the mid-term book essay."

Ah, so that was it! What was the book? *Frankenstein* would be cool. Yesterday, Nielson had been going on and on about Mary Shelley and her determination to write a more horrible story than any of her friends could. I'd seen a bunch of old movie versions -- because, hey, old movies are my main hobby, especially old horror movies. I loved the original *Frankenstein* movie. But I'd never read the book.

"Make sure you initial on the list next to the number of the book you're checking out," Ms. Nielson was saying as I grabbed the book that Tim passed to me.

The day instantly got worse.

Dracula. Great. Really great.

Chapter Two

By Monday, the whole class was obsessed with vampires. Even Joseph Mitchell, my best friend, kept talking about them.

"So," he said, slamming his locker shut and spinning his wheelchair in the direction of Nielson's room, "what do you think of the part where Dracula drains all of the sailors' blood and that ghost ship comes into the harbor?" He craned his neck to look up at me and pull a face.

I was walking behind him because it's easier. Everybody automatically gets out of his way to avoid having him wheel over their toes.

"I can't figure out why he'd need that much blood," I said, scowling. Really, I mean they'd be about three months on the ship. He wouldn't have to have more than about a quart a week at most -- even assuming that full vampires needed a lot more blood per week than I did. But of course I didn't explain all that to Joseph.

"He's a vampire, dork! Vampires drink blood!"

Duh. Like I didn't know. But then Joseph didn't know. About my vampire secret, that is.

"A vampire wouldn't need *that* much blood to survive," I argued. "And he wouldn't need to kill people. That's evil."

Joseph laughed at me. "Dude, vampires *are* evil!" he said as we got to room 19. I winced a little, but I didn't say anything. What could I say?

The fact that Joseph doesn't have any legs (they got crushed by a tractor when he was little, long before I ever met him) makes him understand what it's like to be different. I liked that, even though he didn't know just how different I really was. He just thought I had a weird disease called porphyria that made me allergic to the sun so I could only have a couple of morning classes at the junior high while I had to do the rest online through the community college in Park City.

Still, nobody calls him "evil" just because he's different. And he hasn't had to move from city to city all his life when people found out about his "differences."

And how would I deal with the Michael problem today? It was only a problem in English, and Michael was the only guy I felt like that about. I never thought about him at all when I wasn't in the same room with him. Which wasn't true of Alexis, Britni, Kacey, and just about every other cute girl I knew; they kept getting into my thoughts when I was supposed to be doing homework and stuff. Michael didn't. Which was a relief. But why did I keep staring at him? Why wasn't he just *there*, like any other guy?

It was because of Michael, during the vocabulary review that day, that I endured the single most embarrassing moment of my ninth grade experience so far.

"Jocular," said Ms. Nielson, pacing in front of the room, listening to us chant back the definitions.

"Joking," we all said. Michael's eyes were on her, his head turned away from me, the tendons in his neck showing clearly. Suddenly, I couldn't take my eyes off his throat.

"Profound."

"Deep or insightful." Michael's hair was cut short so that his ears and entire neck were always exposed.

"Eccentric," Ms. Nielson said, pausing by the window.

"Odd, unusual, or quirky." I could see the faint purple outline of an artery through his pale skin. My stomach growled.

"Enigma." Nielson paced back toward her desk, and Michael turned his head to follow her, bringing into my view two brown moles which relaxed back into place over that artery. Two small moles spaced exactly far enough apart that they looked like teethmarks. And they were right over that artery on such thin skin. There was no fur to bite through and no animal smell to kill the appetite. And human blood is so much sweeter than animal blood. I hadn't forgotten that part.

"Eric, are you okay?"

"Huh?" The class was too quiet. I felt thirty-five pairs of eyes staring at me. Shoot! What had I done? Oh no. I was drooling, for Pete's sake! Please, God, can I just die now and get it over with?

I wiped my hand over my mouth and said, "Sorry, Ms. Nielson."

22

"Your eyes had such a glazed look, and you were leaning forward," she said, coming closer. "I thought you might be feeling faint."

Ah, ha! Nielson, like everybody else, thought I had porphyria. It was a good excuse. "Well, maybe a little," I lied. "I'm not sure. I didn't eat this morning." That part was true, anyway. I'd been in too much of a hurry.

Nielson went over to the window and closed the blind, even though it was snowing outside. She kept glancing at me suspiciously for the rest of the period. I guess she was afraid I might pass out.

After class, Kacey Wolton caught up with Joseph and me in the hall.

"So, Eric, what was up with you in English?" she asked, stepping in front of Joseph's wheelchair so he had to stop. Kacey's not intimidated by wheels or guys; her dad's a mechanic and she's got four older brothers.

"Uh, I don't know," I lied from behind Joseph. "Sometimes my medical condition makes me feel weird even when it's not sunny." Well, that part was true. But I didn't bother to define "weird."

Joseph glanced down the hall impatiently, but Kacey didn't budge. Instead, she stuck her non-bookholding hand on her hip and frowned at me.

"You were staring at Michael for about two minutes," she said, "and then you started, like, *drooling*."

Terrific. She'd noticed. There was no open locker nearby to crawl into and hide, so I decided to fake ignorance and rubbed my forehead like I was trying to remember what had happened. "I - - I was?" I asked. What would she think? Salivating over another guy is just not a socially acceptable activity in junior high. And why was I so frickin' interested in Michael? My stomach growled angrily as I wondered.

Joseph turned his torso and looked up at me with one raised eyebrow, then turned back to Kacey. "So, if you're hinting that Eric's gay," he told her, "I want you to know I'm okay with that as long as he doesn't try to kiss *me*." He gave a cheesy grin. Whew. It was a relief to know that Joseph, at least, could joke about it.

But Kacey was still scowling. "Nyah," she said, "my uncle's gay; that's not weird. It's the drooling -- like he was hungry or something."

I blinked at her mindlessly, then the little light clicked on in my head. She was right! I was *hungry*! Yes! It all made sense now. I didn't want Michael's body; I wanted to sink my teeth into those two straw-hole moles on his neck and drink. I wasn't gay; I was just a vampire.

Heh, *just a vampire.* Gay might be easier. After all, there are support groups for gay kids who feel alone. Ever heard of a support group for vampires? Me neither.

But how was I going to explain my stupid drooling to Kacey and Joseph? Somehow, "Actually, if Nielson hadn't stopped me, I would've bitten Michael's neck" just didn't seem like the thing to say at the moment.

So, in a rather less-eloquent speech, I explained, "I dunno, Kacey. I felt kind of hypnotized or something. I didn't know what I was doing." At least that wasn't a total lie.

"Great. Good explanation for my drooling buddy here," Joseph said, wheeling to the right, around Kacey. "Maybe he's teething." And we left her standing there, shaking her head.

So I wanted Michael's blood. And probably Britni's -- except that I'd only dreamed of that. But hey, at least I knew what was going on now. Things had to get better. Right?

But Tuesday wasn't better; it was worse.

Look, I *started* off just fine. I didn't even glance at Michael. Or Britni. I also didn't blush when Ms. Nielson spent fifteen minutes going over the Dracula-as-Anti-Christ theme in the book, but I was relieved when she announced that the rest of the class period would be devoted to pronouns.

Pronouns. It seemed like such a safe topic after *Dracula.* Yeah. Sure.

I took out my steno notebook and began to copy down what she wrote on the whiteboard. Nielson's a tough teacher; if she explains something, you'd better learn it because she'll expect you to know it later.

"These are the reflexive pronouns," she said, pointing her orange dry-erase marker at a chart that read: myself, yourself, himself, herself, itself, ourselves, yourselves, themselves. I copied dutifully.

"Just like the reflexive property in geometry," she stopped briefly as a couple of people groaned, "what's on one side equals the other."

Nielson stared directly at the front row. "Or like a mirror," she continued, capping the marker and walking forward in a kind of trudge. "If I look in a mirror, I see *my*self, not *your*self or *her*self." She pointed the marker at Alexis, then at Becca, who immediately started giggling.

She pointed the marker at me. "And if Eric looks in the mirror, he sees -----?"

"Himself," the class chanted automatically.

"Right. So don't let me hear you saying things like 'Please talk to Mr. Wendall or myself if you have a problem.' *You* can't talk to *my*self. You can only talk to *your*self," she explained. Most of us laughed a little, and Becca giggled even louder.

Ms. Nielson clomped back to the board, then added, "Remember: one side equals the other. So, if Eric doesn't see himself in the mirror.....?"

"Then he has a split personality?" Keith offered. Joseph and most of the class laughed. Becca giggled. Again.

I smiled nervously. I *hate* mirrors. They're almost as bad as cameras. My skin looks like that vellum stuff the ladies at church use in their scrapbooks: cloudy-clear -- but with a whole network of blood vessels throbbing slightly underneath. And my eyes. Ugh. The retina glows worse in a reflection, making the red shine right through my dark gray contact lenses. Even Mom says she can hardly stand to look at me in a mirror.

But the class didn't know any of that. I hoped.

"If Eric doesn't see himself in a mirror, then we'll know he's a vampire," finished Ms. Nielson, turning back to the board.

I stopped smiling. All the laughter sounded like it was coming from the end of a long tunnel. Maybe she was just referring to the part in *Dracula* where Jonathan Harker can't see the Count in his shaving mirror.

Or maybe she *knew*. About *me*.

I had sudden flashes of mobs outside my door with torches. Stakes for my heart. Pitchforks. That kind of thing. It was like a scene from *Young Frankenstein*. I closed my eyes.

But that was worse. Because then I saw the screaming neighbor in Seattle who'd shoved me out of her house after I'd bitten her daughter, telling me I was a beast and that she'd call the police if I ever came near them again. I'd only been nine. Mom and I had moved to San Francisco right afterward.

Then my friend Andy the next year. One night when he was sleeping over at my house, I bit his leg and drank a couple of swallows of his blood before he woke up. I'd blamed it on dreaming I was a dog, but Andy's dad had never let him come over again.

And the scariest was that minister in Denver who'd called me a "child of Satan" because my lips had touched human blood, which he'd said was forbidden in Deuteronomy. I'd been twelve then, and we'd moved to Emma because of him and his threats.

I shuddered. Please, God, not again. I don't kill. I don't even hurt anyone when I bite. I'm not evil. I don't want to drink blood, but I have to. I'll die if I don't. Literally. Please don't let them start hating me again.

I opened my eyes, expecting everyone to be staring at me like they'd done the day before. Only this time, waiting for me to admit what I really was.

But instead, everybody was looking at the board where Ms. Nielson was listing indefinite pronouns. No one had even noticed me. No torches. No stakes. No crosses. No garlic.

Not that garlic would've bothered me anyway. I *like* the stuff. Especially in Italian food or a Mongolian barbecue.

Stoker's explanation for Dracula's lack of reflection was that he didn't have a soul. That's why the crosses and holy wafers kept him away.

Was that what was wrong with me? No soul? I'd never heard anything about that at church.

But scarier than not having a soul was how everyone would treat me if they knew I was a vampire. People hating me again or thinking I was a freak, *that* scared me. Losing all my friends. Again. I just didn't know if I could take that.

As soon as geometry was over at 9:30, I put on my coat, hat, and dark glasses -- which are always necessary outside in the daytime unless it's really cloudy -- and walked home down Main Street, passing most of the town's landmarks on the way: Monty's Gas-n-Go, Central High School, the Assembly Hall, the Emma Smith Memorial Library, the J-Bar-7 Motel with its incredibly ugly turquoise doors, Frida's Cafe, and a bunch of stores. I turned down 300 South, where there's a red sandstone church that was built about a hundred years ago, and walked three more blocks to get home.

Thanks to Brigham Young's city planning of the nineteenth century, each block is one-eighth of a mile, so my round trip every morning is a mile and three quarters. But, the promise to the school that I would walk it and that I'd work out with sit ups and stuff at least five times a week at home satisfied my counselor that I could earn my P.E. credit that way, so it was all good. As long as it wasn't too sunny by 9:30 in the morning, which was kind of a problem in May. But this was only January, so I wasn't worried yet.

Mom was still in Scotland, so I sent her a quick text message while I waited for my computer to boot up. Then I did my online coursework: Spanish, physiology, and Asian culture studies.

Yeah, I know: Chinese philosophy is weird for a ninth-grader, but they don't teach geography at the community college, and I had to have a social studies credit. Biology wasn't offered this semester either, so my counselor at the junior high had said to take physiology instead. At least Spanish was normal for someone my age.

After a nap, I practiced the piano. I get music credit at school for this -- my piano teacher checks with the school every term to give me a grade. I'd do it anyway, though. I kind of go for artsy stuff more than sports. That's because of my sensitivity to light. You can't exactly golf indoors, you know.

But I don't play anything by Bach. That dude's stuff is way too Addams Family for me. Actually, my favorite songs to play are all by Scott Joplin. That's probably because ragtime music would make a lousy soundtrack to a horror movie. It's way too -- well, *perky*.

I practiced about an hour, but my mind kept drifting off. There were so many things I wanted to know. Why did the blood cravings hit me so hard sometimes? Was there any way to control that? Would control get easier when I got older?

I wished like crazy I could e-mail Dr. Simon, my online physiology teacher, and ask him. But he wouldn't know. Only another vampire would know this stuff.

Oh. *Another vampire.* I'd never really thought about that before.

I stopped playing in the middle of "Maple Leaf Rag." There *had* to be other vampires out there somewhere -- besides my dad. I didn't want to find *him*. Not after what he did to my mom; he obviously wasn't the family type of guy. But he couldn't be the only other vampire in the world. If I could just find another one, I could get some answers.

But how do you find a vampire? And how could I find one without letting anyone else figure out that's what I was doing?

Somehow I'd have to act super-normal while I hunted for other abnormal people like me.

Sure. Piece of cake.

Not.

It wasn't until I was out getting my weekly fill-up of blood at about two the next morning that a perfect solution for appearing ordinary hit me.

I was out in Hank Jackson's field next door, trying to convince a sheep to hold still so I could draw out some blood into the hypodermic syringe. It's not enough to hurt the sheep -- except maybe to make it a little dizzy the next day -- but a needle stings, so the sheep generally try to run away. Unless I talk to them and calm them down, that is.

In *Dracula*, Bram Stoker gives the vampire the strength of twenty men, the ability to change into a bat or a wolf, power to control the weather near him, and incredible night vision. I, however, appeared to have the strength of a leading laundry detergent, the ability to look amazingly like a fourteen-year-old boy, and the power to tune into the weather on the local radio station. The night vision was the one vampire-like thing I knew I'd gotten from my dad's bad DNA.

But night vision only helped me find a sheep, not hold it down. So there I was, calming the animal, talking to it until I could get its dull little brain used to me before I clamped its head between my legs and stuck the sterilized needle in its neck.

I learned a long time ago that animals jerk less if I talk to them. This is especially important if I'm going to extract blood from a cow that outweighs me by several hundred pounds. With the cows, I usually have to talk to them for a couple of minutes until they get really dozy. I don't care if the sheep stay awake. A sheep isn't big enough to trample me. So I just get them nice and calm.

Anyway, I was cuddling up to this sheep and being grateful that it was at least warm, when I heard myself telling it, "That's it, baby, just snuggle up against me like a pretty girl."

Girl! Yeah, that's it!

I smiled at the woozy sheep. "Good idea," I told it soothingly, while slipping the syringe out of my coat pocket, "I'll ask a girl to the church dance for Valentine's Day. That's a nice, *normal* thing to do. Nobody thinks of vampires on Valentine's Day."

I made a quick jab with the needle in my right hand. The sheep didn't even flinch.

"Well, a girl will sure smell better than you, anyway," I told it, "but it's too bad I can't drink her blood like I can yours."

Within a couple of minutes, the syringe was full. I let the animal go, pulled the needle off the syringe, and put the end in my mouth. Warm, salty liquid made the walk over the hoof-tracked, fresh snow more than bearable.

I was happy. I had food, and I had a plan. Yup. Operation Smokescreen for Vampire Hunting. It just might work. Now all I had to do was find that other vampire and get a date for the dance.

Chapter Three

"How long will you be at the library, honey?" Mom asked as I slung my backpack over one shoulder after I'd finished dinner: a nice chunk of raw lamb and a salad. (Yeah, I know. E. coli poisoning in the making: one of the occupational hazards of being a vampire.)

"Uh, maybe an hour?" I fidgeted with my scarf, not looking Mom in the eye. "The website said the *Scars of Dracula* DVD that I requested's in now, but if Joseph or anyone's there, I might wanna hang out for awhile."

She kissed me on the forehead. "Be home by nine, please," she said.

Yes! Nine was plenty of time. Not for the library, of course. I'd picked up the DVD this morning on the way home from school; it was in my backpack now so I could show Mom when I got home tonight.

Nope. I was not going to the library. I was off to the wrestling room at Central High. To the blood drive.

Okay, I know. A vampire hanging out with the Red Cross phlebotomy team is like Weight Watchers holding a meeting at the Hershey factory. That's why I didn't tell Mom where I was going.

But I had to start looking for another vampire *someplace*, even if it meant lying to Mom -- which I hated because Mom's really about the only person I trust. But there were questions Mom couldn't answer, so on the last Monday night in January, I nearly froze my tinted contact lenses to my eyeballs by running against the icy wind to the high school.

Central High is mostly sandstone on the outside. The oldest part was built in 1913, gutted by fire in the 1970s, and rebuilt inside soon afterward, with a new gym and a new auditorium stuck on the sides like a crab's claws. This was the third time I'd ever been in the wrestling room, which was really the old boys' gym -- untouched by the fire -- in the basement of the big, rectangular main building. Walking into it was like getting out of

Bill and Ted's phone booth into a different decade, like maybe the 1920s.

The old gym was a half-sized one with a track running around a balcony at the top. But since the school had had an outdoor track around the football field west of the building for at least fifty years, the wrestling room balcony held about the last fifteen years' worth of broken desks and other junk. It was the perfect place to hide.

I settled in between a stack of wooden chairs and a couple of crates covered in a musty, army-green canvas. The cement wall that formed the balcony edge was about two feet high, and the metal rail attached to it added about another foot, so I could easily crunch down, practically invisible from the cots, tables, and screens of the blood drive on the gym floor below. I was too far away to smell the blood, since not much of it was hitting the air anyway, and I didn't even let myself look at the deep purple liquid swishing through little tubes like mini mass transit systems for hemoglobin.

Little bits of conversations were echoing loudly off the ceiling, but I still unzipped the front pocket of my backpack very slowly to keep it quiet. I then pulled out my secret weapon: a purse-sized face powder thing my mom had thrown away last week.

Okay, pretty technologically lame, I know. But I'm not James Bond tracking down some KGB spy. (Eric Wright, Agent 707, on the trail of.... oh, never mind.) Sure, why my reflection was all funky and like something out of a Body Worlds display was one of the questions I really wanted to ask a Dracula descendant when I found him (or her, I guess), but a mirror was the best way I knew of to spot a vampire. It was a simple concept: a reflection showing normal clothes but see-through skin and glowing red eyes = vampire.

I rested the mirror on the cold concrete wall, angling my hand so that I could see blood donors and Red Cross workers without accidentally redirecting the overhead lights into flashes that resembled distress signals from a sinking ship. And that's where I squatted, eyes straining for data, for nearly an hour. I saw Joseph's parents, a couple of Kacey's brothers, Britni's mom, a bunch of teachers from my junior high school, Frida Jones from the cafe on Main Street, and about seven Red Cross workers. Not a single one of them appeared as anything other than solid and normally-colored in the mirror. Lucky snots. And not one person looked entranced and ravenous at the sight of pint after pint of human blood. Well, okay, there was a two-year-old who stared a lot at the tubes hooked up to her mom, but the only drooling she was doing had more to do with the thumb in her mouth than with the red and white cells in motion.

Splot. Fizzle. Well, this hadn't been such a great idea. I was the only vampire in the vicinity who'd risked a blood drive tonight. But that didn't mean that there wasn't another ---

"Hey! What the hell you doin' up here?!"

Note to self: never again try to move near-frozen muscles from a crouch to a full standing position in less than one second.

There was a loud clatter as the stack of chairs I fell against collapsed onto a metal garbage can. And an even louder thumping sound as my heart rate went into Nascar finals speed. I found myself looking into the flannel-covered chest of Tobias Clyde, brother of the giggling Becca and senior redneck extraordinaire. Stupid and smelly as an mule, but -- unfortunately -- stronger than a gorilla. I'd seen black eyes and loose teeth on one of Kacey's brothers who'd disagreed with him about some money last November.

"Sorry, I was, uh, just leaving now," I mumbled, with unfaked humility. I shoved the mirror into my coat pocket. But I wasn't quite fast enough.

"What? Yer up here to put on yer make up? You some kinda drag queen?" he asked, adjusting the brim of his blue trucker cap, the kind with that silhouette of a seated, nude girl on it.

Great. Just what I needed him to tell people about me. And I'd barely gotten through that episode with Michael's neck last week, too. I didn't want anyone remembering *that*, for crying out loud.

"No, I'm... uh... looking for someone," I mumbled, reaching down to grab my backpack, my heart still pounding like a timpani in my ears.

"Lookin' for yer *boyfriend*, I bet," he laughed. "Wait'll I tell --"

I scooped up the backpack as fast as I could, wanting to escape sooner than immediately, but the strap caught on the canvas over the old crates next to me. I tugged, and the canvas slid sideways. A very non-dusty six pack of Coors glinted up at me.

Ah, so *that's* what Tobias the hick was doing up on the jogging track balcony. If he'd had an IQ above room temperature, he could've framed me for stashing the beer under the canvas. Fortunately, he instead had the IQ of a sheep. Okay, a mighty big sheep, but still a sheep. So I had something on him.

I smiled into his scowling, freckled face. "Tell you what," I said with friendliness I didn't feel, "why don't we both just forget all about meeting up here tonight? I won't say anything; you don't say anything. Okay?"

Before he could reason out that complicated deal, I was halfway down the stairs. All I wanted was to put as much space as possible between the cowboy and me so he could forget about what had just happened. Of course, it'd take him a few minutes to find a new hiding spot for his beer, so -- Holy crap!

At the bottom of the stairs was a young man in a white lab jacket, casually transferring clear plastic bags of human blood from a small cooler to a larger one on a rolling cart.

"Hi," he said, smiling up at me with teeth so white they looked fake against his brown skin, "Want to help transfer the bags?" He pulled a pair of white plastic gloves out of his pocket with his right hand.

But in his left hand he held a bag. A bag sloshing with warm, *human* life, sweet over the tongue, like I hadn't tasted in more than two years. And this time I wasn't dreaming.

I couldn't blink. I couldn't move. But warm vampire saliva was now sloshing up the inside of my cheeks. All it would take was one swift grab to get it out of his hand. Then I could run outside, rip open the bag, and drink. It wouldn't hurt anyone. The blood was already out of the body, but so fresh it must still be warm. Just one second would be enough to get that bag.

"Hey, are you all right? Sorry. I was only joking, you know," he spluttered at me.

I could feel the spit oozing out of the corners of my mouth as I shifted my gaze from his hand to the brown eyes behind the gold-rimmed glasses on his nose. Self-consciously, I moved my hand to cover my mouth.

"Nausea?" he asked.

I nodded a lie to this and then I ran. But not to a bathroom to barf. I ran for the horse corral behind Monty's Gas 'N' Go. Less-tasty but safer blood was waiting for me there. Horses can't talk.

Final assessment of the evening: Near-death experiences with stupid cowboys = one. Vampire sightings = zero. My chances of becoming a phlebotomist in the future = slightly less than zero.

I figured my chances of getting up the guts to ask a cute girl to the Valentine's Dance weren't much higher than zero, either. But then Kacey solved that problem for me the next evening. With a text.

Eric,
Me N a bunch of others --Alexis, Britni, Mallory, N Dani -- R dyin 2 no who UR takin 2 the dance. If u don't Dcide soon, we won't have NE time 2 get ReD!
KC

"'Won't have time to get ready'?! The dance is still two weeks away!" I said to the phone in my hand, but Mom overheard me and came into my room, holding a copy of *The Historian*.

"Kacey just means they all have to plan what to wear," Mom explained, leaning over me to read the tiny screen. Fortunately, Mom could read both text-speak and girl-speak.

"It doesn't take *you* two weeks to decide what to wear," I told her.

She laughed. "*I'm* not fourteen anymore," she said, standing upright again and straightening a couple of the dusty action figures from my old *Star Wars* collection on the shelves above my desk with her free hand. "But I think you should go to the dance," she added.

"Yeah, I want to," I said, twisting up to look at her. "It might make me seem, you know...."

"More like the other kids and less like a partially home-schooled vampire?" she asked, raising both eyebrows and cocking her head sideways.

"That's about it."

"Well," she said, pointing to my phone, "it appears that Kacey has just volunteered to be your date for the evening, so all you have to do is confirm it with her."

"I guess," I said, looking back at the list of possibilities, "but Britni's cuter than Kacey. There's no way I'd go with Dani; she's such a freakin' snob! But Alexis might --"

"Eric, my dear," Mom interrupted me, "if you don't want Kacey to hate you forever, you'd better take her to the dance or not go at all. It's obvious she's dying to go out with you, and the other girls probably had no clue she was going to send this text."

I raised one eyebrow and continued staring at my phone. "That's not what she said," I told Mom.

"But that's what she meant."

"How the heck do you know?"

"Because I was once a fourteen-year-old girl," she said, cuddling her huge book up to her chest and laughing a little.

"Then why didn't she just ask me?"

"Because she wanted you to ask her, but you weren't doing it fast enough, so she's put it right in your path."

"Oh." Well, that was kind of sneaky. But whatever. It did make things easy for me -- no stressing out over whether or not a girl might reject a date with me. And Kacey was pretty cute.

KC,
QL. Let's go2the dance 2gther.
E

"You are the soul of romance," Mom said, reading over my shoulder again and laughing.

I shrugged. What did she expect me to say to Kacey? It was a frickin' *dance*, not an engagement. Geez.

I hit send.

"So, the dance is Friday after next?" Mom asked.

"Yeah."

"I have this weekend off, and *Cats* is playing at the Pioneer Memorial Theater in Salt Lake. Would you like to go see it? We could stay overnight and hit the Old Navy store before we come home."

"Hey! Great!" I said, turning to smile at her.

"Then it's a date," she said and left the room with her book.

Since I only got to have one parent, I thought it was really cool of God to give me a mom like mine. She trusted me more than most parents trust their kids and occasionally spoiled me rotten with trips or music stuff I really liked. It was hard to complain about her, really. Even though she wasn't a vampire.

I hit the bookmark on my computer to go to my online physiology reading for this week when a total newsblurb ran across the lower screen of my mind: Salt Lake is lots bigger than Emma City. There could be vampires there.

Yes! Agent 707 is back on the trail again!

I did a websearch for vampires in that area and got over 500,000 results. That looked pretty impressive until I started checking the sites.

A YouTube video. Something on eBay. A job opportunity for cross-dressers. A newspaper story about someone claiming to have found a vampire tooth. A costume shop. A Halloween party from two years ago. Another news article about drug users. Vampire bats at Hogle Zoo. A lame-looking webpage for a book I'd never heard of before. Weird personal ads. A rock band.

Then finally something that just might be what I needed: a two-line ad on meetups.slc for a club called SLCVamp. It listed group meetings as every other Friday -- including this Friday when I'd be in town! My heart started beating just a little faster.

I found a map website and typed in the address given. Whoa! It wasn't too far from the Pioneer Theater!

"Hey, Mom?" I called. "Are we going to stay in the same motel as when we went to see *Camelot* before Christmas?"

"I was thinking we would. It's cheap, and it's close to the theater. Why?"

"Just wondering," I said, as I typed in the address of the Mountain View Motel. Yes! It was close enough for me to walk to the meetup at midnight! I'd be able to slip out once Mom was asleep. Perfect. In three more days, I would be able to talk to another vampire. Life was looking pretty dang good.

Mom, of course, wasn't even worried that I didn't climb into the bed opposite hers in the motel room when we got back from the play. She's used to my weird sleep habits, and, in Emma, she doesn't even care that I go out roaming around at night. I can see in the dark, and Emma's not exactly the crime capital of the West anyway.

But I wasn't so sure she'd like my idea of going out to meet a group of people I didn't even know so late at night, so I hadn't mentioned it. I'd just put in my earphones, found the *Cats* playlist on my iPod, and sat in the armchair, playing sudoku in the dark (hey, I could see the pages just fine!) until she was breathing very regularly and it was a little past midnight. Then I stuck the motel key in my pocket, put on my coat, and slipped out the door very quietly.

It was super-cold, and snow chunks crunched loudly whenever I stepped on one, so I hurried to the intersection I'd memorized from the online map and went west a couple of blocks to a gas station, now closed except for the all-night pumps. But next door was the address I wanted.

It was a long-ish, one-story building wedged in between the gas station and a barbershop. It had big windows like a supermarket -- blocked two-thirds of the way up with white boards on the inside -- but I could still see that the lights were on. The sign over the door looked much newer than the building. It read: Desert Bodies.

Uh, that sounded kind of... well, *kinky,* actually. Especially for a place that obviously didn't want people looking in the windows. Maybe it was a bar with dancers. Or a porn shop. Ugh.

I stopped dead on the sidewalk. Maybe I didn't want to meet another vampire that badly.

But wait. There were houses just down the street. Nice looking houses with clean yards. Like the people who lived there wouldn't tolerate living so close to a bar -- or worse. So maybe Desert Bodies wasn't anything I shouldn't see.

I had to do something because my feet were freezing inside my sneakers, so I walked up to the door and opened it just a little bit. Warm air rushed out at me from a vent over a white counter where a computer stood next to a fat, potted cactus. I could hear men laughing, but I couldn't see past what was obviously a reception area. A restaurant? Nyah. I couldn't smell food. Except coconuts. I could smell coconuts. Weird.

I slipped inside and breathed the warm air. Another burst of laughter came from behind the flimsy-looking wall near the counter.

So, what was I going to say to these people, anyway? Hi, I'm Eric and I'm a half-vampire? What's your favorite blood type? Do you make your friends wear turtlenecks when they hang out with you?

I moved quietly past the cactus and looked around the corner. There were four twenty-something guys looking over a couple of small booklets on a card table. Three of them had their backs to me, including a chubby dude wearing a black, ankle-length cape. The fourth man was tall, with long brown hair hanging to the elbows of his leather jacket, and several silver rings through his eyebrows.

So... Bela Lugosi and a Hell's Angel? Was this a costume party?

Behind them was a shiny metal thing that looked way too much like a coffin. Or maybe a space coffin. There were posters of people in bathing suits on the wall behind them. The coconut smell was even stronger now.

I squinted in the bright lights of the place. Capes, coffins, and tropical fruit? What the crap was this anyway? But if these guys really were vampires, I was willing to deal with their weirdness.

Suddenly, the tall man looked over at me and smiled. "Hello," he said quietly with an accent that would've made any Spanish teacher proud, "did you wish to join us this evening?" As he turned toward me, a nose ring also became visible on his face.

The others moved to have a look at me when he spoke. The Lugosi dude in the cape was wearing a tux and had his hair slicked back off his face.

I stared at him. "Uh, yeah. This is the vampire meeting, isn't it?" I said.

"Yes, it is," said the tall guy. "You are most welcome."

I smiled a little and took one step toward the group.

"Hey, great! Fresh blood!" said the Lugosi wannabe. Then he laughed.

"What level are you on?" said a third guy, who had short brown hair and glasses. He looked pretty normal in jeans and a black hoodie. No cape. No piercings.

"Level?" I asked. What the heck did he mean? There were *levels* of being a vampire? What kind of levels?

"Jerry, he's confused," said the other man, who was short and had a black goatee. He looked back at me and asked, "Is this your first time?"

"Uh, I've never been to a vampire meeting before," I said, staring behind him at that space-capsule coffin thing.

"No problem," he said cheerfully, handing me a card. "We're always glad to have neophytes."

Neophyte. I'd have to look that one up later. But just then I looked at the card.

Venue Virtue: Faith
Venue Vice: Wrath
Description: The Promised Land hides within itself a dark secret.
Will the Sundancer bloodline maintain its dominance in the city?
Play Style: Action
Combat: 4
Death/Corruption: 2
Pace: Varies from 2-4

I'd read geometry proofs that made more sense.

I looked up from the card and scanned the room for clues.
"What is this place?" I asked the pierced guy.

He smiled. "It is the only place we can meet where we do
not bother our girlfriends or families. It is the tanning business
of Jerry's sister."

"Vampires in a *tanning salon*?" burst out of my mouth in a
gush of sarcasm before I could stop myself. But at least I knew
what the space coffin was now. And that the coconut smell was
tanning lotion.

"Yes, it is rather incongruous, I think," the pierced guy said,
shrugging.

"Yeah, but like he said," Jerry told me, motioning his thumb
toward his buddy, "we haven't got anyplace else to play."

"'Play'?" I was lost here.

"Play 'Unrighteous Minions.' This is the Requiem Venue."

Oh. Reality splatted onto my brain like a bug on a windshield.

A role-playing game. They weren't *real* vampires. They
probably didn't even believe in real vampires.

I could feel a blush burning up my neck and onto my face.
How stupid was I to think that vampires -- true ones -- would
advertise where they were so people could come after them?!
I'd had neighbors and friends treat me like a fiend often enough
to know not to do that.

"Uh, I guess I'm in the wrong place then," I stammered,
handing the card back to the goateed man. "I didn't understand
what it said on the website. Sorry."

"Hey, stick around, why don't you? We can teach you!" the
Lugosi wannabe offered.

I was already backing away. "No," I said, "my mom
doesn't even know I'm here." Ah, the classic kid excuse.

"Here," the pierced guy said, setting down the booklet he'd been holding and gesturing to the entranceway, "I will walk out with you, even though we wish you to stay."

He sounded genuinely nice, so I smiled at him and turned around. Right into a plastic palm tree. Which I knocked over.

"Sorry," I said, making a dive for it. But there was an odd silence behind me. It wasn't until I actually got the tree upright again that I realized why. Behind the fake palm tree was a full-length mirror. And my red eyes and semi-translucent skin were very visible in the bright, reflected light. The pierced guy's surprised face was even more visible above that.

Panic started up in me. They'd *seen* my evil reflection! They'd *know*! Gah!!

"Gotta go before my mom gets mad!" I lied. Then I ran like an escaping convict, the icy air outside cooling my flaming cheeks fast.

It wasn't until I got to the motel I began to breathe properly again. None of those people had even moved when I ran off. For sure they hadn't tried to come after me. And maybe they'd all convince themselves they hadn't really seen a vampire in the mirror. Trick of the light or something. I hoped. But I'd be gone from the neighborhood tomorrow, and they wouldn't know where to find me. That was comforting.

I sighed quietly as I tossed my coat onto the TV and slipped into the hotel bed. Things learned: real vampires don't risk blood drives, and only freaks and geeks advertise online. So much for Agent 707 and his quest for a vampire mentor. It was time to lay off it for awhile and concentrate on appearing extra-normal to everyone else. It was time to think about the Valentine's dance.

Chapter Four

"Now, Eric, don't complain," Mom told me a week later. "I'm not trying to baby you."

I knew she didn't mean to -- after all, she leaves me alone for several days at a time at least once a month when she's gone on business -- but I felt like a little kid when she insisted that I practice with the corsage.

"But, Mom," I whined, looking at the red, pink, and white carnations in the plastic box, "I don't need to practice! How hard can it be to pin flowers on Kacey's dress?"

Mom's voice dropped in pitch. "She might slap you pretty hard if you get your hands in the wrong place, young man," she said with a chuckle.

I rolled my eyes. Get real.

"Seriously, Eric," she said, more normally now, "a corsage can be awkward. What if you poke her with the pin?" She tilted her head sideways so that her soft, blondish-brown hair brushed down the side of her arm.

"She'll get over it," I retorted. Honestly, Kacey just wasn't the type to get upset about a pinprick. And she'd apparently forgotten all about my drooling-in-first-period episode. We were just going to be a guy and a girl going to a dance. Perfectly normal. Nothing freaky. No vampire stuff.

"Eric, what if the pin draws blood? Will you be able to control yourself?"

Oh, yeah.

I sighed and got the corsage out of the box. Maybe it would be a good idea to practice pinning it on Mom's blouse a couple of times.

Mom dropped Kacey and me off at the church at 9:00 or so. Anyone over age twelve could come to the dance, so a lot of parents were there, but my mom wasn't going. She said something about never being in town long enough to find anyone to date, but then she winked at me.

"So, does that mean she's got a hot date somewhere else tonight?" Kacey asked me as we walked up the wet sidewalk to the church. Someone had obviously put out a lot of rock salt earlier in the day to melt the ice. Little chunks of salt and stubborn ice crunched under my Sunday oxfords as we walked.

I laughed. "That was just her getting out of the way so she wouldn't be hovering over us tonight. Mom doesn't ever date. She goes places alone or with her friends. Or with me, if it's a movie or something."

But Kacey wouldn't let it drop. "Do you think that's because your father didn't stay with her? Do you think she just doesn't trust men?" she asked, opening the door. "I don't think I would, if something like that happened to me."

Actually, I'd always suspected that Mom just didn't want to explain to men that her son was a half-vampire. That could be a real problem in a relationship. But telling Kacey this could create a real problem in *our* relationship, so I just shrugged and said, "Maybe she dates when she's on business trips. Sometimes she goes back to the same city three or four times." I doubted this was true, but it sounded good.

I took Kacey's coat and hung it up for her, like Mom had warned me to do. The corsage -- which I had pinned on Kacey's dress at her house without incident -- looked a little flattened now.

"Look, there's Joseph," Kacey said suddenly, "and he's with *Britni!*" She took my hand and pulled me toward the gym to talk to them.

I guess I should've felt nervous or something. I mean, this was my first time holding hands with a girl. But I was too happy to be nervous. Kacey wasn't scared of me. She didn't think I was a freak. She wanted to hold my hand. I hadn't thought about this side of Kacey's being sneaky and getting me to ask her. Cool.

I was grinning stupidly by the time we reached Joseph and Britni.

"Well, you made *him* happy!" Joseph told Kacey while punching me in the ribcage.

Kacey looked a little embarrassed, but she didn't let go of my hand.

"You didn't tell me you were going to the dance with Joseph!" she told Britni.

44

"That's 'cause he didn't ask me until *two hours ago*," Britni teased back.

Joseph shrugged. "Hey," he said, "I like to keep things spontaneous. Let's go dance; we're blocking traffic in this doorway."

"Maybe you could claim it as a handicapped parking spot," I said as Joseph spun around to go into the gym. I was careful not to let his wheels get near my toes.

"Oh," he said sarcastically, "you know I'm just too lazy to walk!" But he laughed and sped off onto the dance floor so fast that we all had to run to catch up. Actually, even though Joseph uses a wheelchair most of the time, he's really about the *least* handicapped person I know.

The decorating committee had really put some work into the place. There were heart-shaped helium balloons with their streamer tails taped to the ground to form a sort of festive fence around the dance floor area. On the sides were tables with punch and cookies. The D.J.'s table was nearly hidden behind what looked like mounds of pink and red flowers. And in the corners of the gym were large sheets of crinkly plastic with lights behind them and electric fans blowing on them to make them ripple in the breeze. It was really impressive -- kind of a liquid effect. The silver ones looked like some kind of glass waterfall. And the red ones looked like streams of fresh --

Oh, no. I swallowed hard. I was salivating way too much here. I mean, nobody else would think like that.

"I don't know if I like those decorations," Kacey said, pointing at the corner. "That red plastic stuff looks like blood."

Please, God, don't let me start drooling now.

I closed my eyes so I wouldn't have to look at the decorations, but my stomach started growling anyway. I'd been too excited to eat much at dinner, and now my body was interested in only one kind of food.

"Yeah," I heard Britni say, "maybe they should use this stuff for Halloween instead of Valentine's. What do you think?"

With a great deal of effort, I opened my eyes and looked at my friends instead of at the bloody streamers. "I think we should dance," I said weakly.

Since there were a lot of parents and grandparents at the dance, the D.J. played a lot of older music. Some of it was old, like the Beatles and Queen, and some of it was really old, like Glenn Miller and the Andrews Sisters. The only reason I even know who those people are is because my mom has a lot of weird playlists. And not just Glenn Miller weird, either. Bulgarian women's choir weird and Chinese opera weird. Maybe that's why Mom doesn't date.

But we all danced to the old stuff anyway. Sometimes we could dance normally, and sometimes not. We did the hokey pokey at one point; Joseph hoisted himself out of his wheelchair and danced on the floor. Since Joseph's arms are normal length even though his legs have been amputated right below his butt, he has this amazing trick of crunching his torso upward and walking on his hands -- or in this case, dancing on his hands. It looked bizarre, but we had fun. Later, we all bounced around when they played a polka. Kacey and Britni each took one of Joseph's hands, I took the girls' hands, and we got that wheelchair spinning. And, since Mom had made me learn to fox trot in about the fourth grade, I showed Kacey how so we didn't have to shuffle around in a circle on slow dances like the other kids did.

Well, Joseph didn't shuffle either.

Look, just because he doesn't have legs doesn't mean girls are turned off by him. No way. For one thing, he looks kind of like Daniel Radcliffe in the early *Harry Potter* movies; slightly messy dark brown hair, eyes the color of rootbeer, and wire-rimmed glasses -- all of which seem to be girl-pleasing. Plus, he danced *in* the wheelchair, too, which didn't look quite so strange as when he danced on the floor. On the slow numbers, Mr. Romeo-on-Wheels pulled Britni into the chair with him, swung her legs over the side, put one arm around her to snuggle up, and slowly pushed the two of them around in a circle with his other arm. Britni put her cheek right against his and her arms around his neck. I seriously doubt she cared about his lack of legs.

"That is so cute," Kacey said, looking over my shoulder at them as we fox trotted.

I looked back at them, careful not to glance at the bloody streamers in the corners, and grinned. "I can tell Joseph's having a great time," I told her.

Kacey pulled a little closer to me, and my stomach went into a knot that wasn't about being hungry. With her face right by my ear, she said "I wonder --"

But I never got to find out what she was wondering because suddenly a girl's voice said, "Hey, you two," and then there was giggling. Had to be Becca.

Kacey and I stepped apart from each other, and there was Becca, holding Rudy's hand. He towered above her like he was her dad or something. I gave a the room a quick scan just to make sure her brother wasn't here, too. I didn't want him to remember our last little chat. But Becca was the only Clyde sibling in the vicinity.

"Hey," I said lamely to Becca and Rudy. "Having fun?"

Rudy rolled his eyes, and Kacey coughed into her hand and kept her mouth covered for a few seconds.

"I saw you guys doing the hokey pokey," Becca said, oblivious to what'd just happened and to Rudy's opinion of their date.

Kacey smiled and her eyes widened. "It was fun," she said. "You should've tried it."

I tried to imagine Rudy shaking various limbs and turning himself around, but I had to stop. It was a rather gruesome image, like the Jolly Green Giant shaking off dozens of attacking sprouts.

"Well, I don't like to dance too much," Becca said. "It makes me sweat, and I don't want to ruin my dress."

"The hokey pokey makes you *sweat*?" I asked incredulously. Kacey coughed into her hand again.

Rudy was trying to inch his way toward the refreshment table, but Becca still had hold of him. He looked like a doberman on a short leash.

Becca used her free hand to finger the filmy material of her dress. "Well, Daddy just bought me this for Christmas, and I don't want to take any chances," she said sweetly. "Kacey must not have to worry about such things, though. Her dresses seem to last a *very* long time." She smiled again and dragged Rudy -- who was still looking longingly at the trays of brownies and oatmeal cookies -- toward another pair of dancers.

I was just about to ask Kacey if girls normally talked about stuff like sweaty dresses when she said, "Oh, how rude can you get?!" Her eyes definitely had too much water in them.

I was confused. "But what was Becca talk ---?" I couldn't finish because Kacey was walking away -- really fast.

Shoot. That wasn't supposed to happen. Now, should I follow her or not?

Wait a second. Kacey's dress was okay, white and kind of swingy so she could dance. And she definitely didn't smell like sweat -- and I'd been close enough to know that. So... Ah! Elementary, my dear Watson! Becca had a new dress and Kacey didn't!

I didn't care, but Kacey obviously did. And having my date upset could ruin my first big chance to look normal.

I stared after where Kacey had disappeared out into the classroom hallway of the church and bit my lip.

Now, this is not a wise thing to do if you're a half-vampire. My cuspids aren't any longer than ordinary, but they're way sharp, and I had blood seeping into my mouth within a second. Yuck. It wasn't very much because my blood doesn't flow as fast as regular human blood, but it was enough to taste -- nasty and bitter.

Sometimes I wondered if all vampires have bad blood so we don't drink from each other. It's probably some weird kind of vampire evolution. But since I hadn't found any other vampires to ask yet, this was just my own theory.

Fortunately, my saliva seems to have healing properties in it -- like a dog's, only it works a lot faster, as long as I get saliva on the cut before the blood starts to coagulate -- so all I had to do was slosh some spit against the wound to stop the bleeding.

I wiped the blood off my mouth and looked at Joseph. The song hadn't ended, so he was still cuddled up with Britni, stroking her smooth brown hair with one hand. Britni's eyes were closed, but Joseph was looking at me. He mouthed the word "GO" and nodded toward the door where Kacey had left. That was good enough for me; I followed her.

The lights were off in that part of the building, but I could see even the woodgrain of each classroom door, thanks to the old vampire vision. All the doors were closed, but I opened three or four until I found Kacey sitting on a metal folding chair and staring out the window in the darkened interior of Sunday School classroom 12.

I closed the door behind me, unfolded another chair, and sat down next to her. I didn't say anything. Mostly because I had no clue what to say.

After a couple of seconds, Kacey sniffed. "I'm sorry I ran out," she told me. "I didn't want you to see me cry. It's just that -- well, Becca knows we can't afford all the new clothes she gets, and...." She gulped.

Now, I could see quite well that Kacey had tear-streaks down her face and that some of the streaks were darkened by the mascara she'd cried off. I could also see that her eyelids were swelling up from tears. In fact, she didn't look all that great, but I didn't think I should mention any of this.

"It's okay," I said instead. "I could tell you weren't upset with *me*. No hard feelings."

She sniffed again but didn't say anything. Okay, well, obviously I was supposed to say something else. I'd never comforted a crying girl before. And I hadn't really thought Kacey would be the crying type, not with all those brothers she's got. Maybe it was just other girls she couldn't deal with.

I looked over at her. She was shivering a little. How was I supposed to get her to calm down and forget about Becca so we could go back to the dance and act *normal*?

Well, I decided on the only thing I had practice doing: I pretended she was a nervous barnyard animal.

I put my arm around her and started rubbing her shoulder gently. "Don't let Becca bug you," I said softly, in the same voice I used on cows. "Maybe she cares about your dress, but I don't. I don't really care what you wear because I don't know anything about girl stuff. But you look nice tonight, so just ignore Becca's stupid remarks."

You have to talk a lot in smooth tones to get a cow to breathe calmly and relax. You have to sound assured and confident but gentle at the same time. I know. I've done it. A lot.

But I'd never tried it on a person before. Maybe it didn't work on higher IQs the way the Jedi mind tricks don't in the *Star Wars* movies. And Kacey had a high IQ, for Pete's sake! Crud. Everyone at Patrick Henry Junior High School knew that Kacey was the only ninth-grader taking Algebra II over at Central High this year!

Nyah. This barnyard calm-the-sheep trick would probably just get her ticked off at me. I stopped rubbing her shoulder and sneaked a look at her. And that was a bad idea. A *really* bad idea.

See, that whole Pavlov conditioned response thing was going on. For a couple of minutes, I'd been doing what I always do before I drink animal blood, so my body was now expecting blood. I was salivating and I heard my stomach gurgle.

But Kacey didn't hear it. Her head had fallen sideways onto my right shoulder. Apparently, I could outdo a Jedi with mind tricks.

I shifted myself forward gently to get a better look at her. Her eyes were shut and she was breathing deeply and regularly.

Holy cow! I had hypnotized so much she was asleep! I'd *never* done that before. Maybe it was because I'd been concentrating on it so hard. Or maybe it's because she wasn't a cow.

It later occurred to me that another guy in my situation might have been tempted to kiss the girl. Or more. But all I could think about right then was her neck.

We'd already done the circulatory system in my online physiology course. I'd done diagrams and virtual cadaver dissections, and I knew where the carotid artery goes. Right up under the jaw bone.

A lot of people think it's the jugular vein because the jugular is so big. But a vein doesn't pulse with each heartbeat. Only an artery beats in time with the heart. And only an artery carries oxygenated blood through the neck. And oxygenated blood tastes sweeter than deoxygenated blood. And human blood tastes better than blood from animals -- animals that eat only grass and hay. Humans eat proteins, carbohydrates, sugars, and fats -- human blood is sweet. They don't teach that in physiology, but I know it.

True, I'd only tasted human blood a few times, but I remembered the taste. And the memory of that sweetness was in every droplet of saliva gushing into my mouth right then.

Kacey's head was sideways on my upper arm now, leaving her neck at a severe angle that showed her carotid throbbing evenly with life.

Her breathing was slow, but mine grew faster as I watched, almost hypnotizing myself with the pulsing. I didn't worry that she'd wake up; I knew she wouldn't now until I woke her. And the tiny incisions I'd make wouldn't hurt her or show because my wonder-saliva would both numb and heal them. She'd be a little weak tomorrow, but she'd just think she'd stayed out too late and gotten tired.

It'd been so long since I'd had human blood. More than two years.

I put my mouth against the skin over the pulsing carotid and let it beat against my lips once or twice. Kacey's skin smelled slightly flowery, like roses maybe. Much better than the skin of the girl I'd bitten at the Halloween party in Denver -- she'd smelled mainly of the make up she'd used to create the fake wound on her neck, the wound that had given me the idea of biting her in the first place.

I opened my mouth against Kacey's skin. In another setting, it might have been seductive or something, but hunger was far more powerful than hormones for me just then, so I shifted my jaw down and gave one quick jab. My cuspid teeth worked like a paper punch instantly, and I pulled them out.

Blood was oozing into my mouth like a warm, sweet syrup, but I wanted more than oozing. I wanted to drink in this sweetness in gulps. So I did something I'd never done before: I began to suck in rhythm with the pulsing of her artery.

It's really funny how fast guilt works. Seriously, it took about a minute for me to bite her neck and drink several big gulps of blood -- about eight ounces, my weekly blood allowance. Then it dawned on me that I was doing all of this without her permission. I mean, it was like I was lying to her.

Suddenly, I wasn't hungry anymore. I licked over my teethmarks on her neck to let my vampire spit coagulate her blood, and then I leaned away from her.

I couldn't tell her about this so I couldn't fully apologize. I'd just been super dishonest with a girl I liked. To someone who didn't think I was a freak. To a *friend*, for crying out loud!

Crap.

I really hated myself right then. Why had I let myself lose control? What had I been thinking?! I wanted to hit something, but I decided I'd better wake Kacey up before I did any more damage.

Feeling like a total slimeball, I shook her a little. "Kacey?" I asked tentatively. "You awake?"

She looked kind of groggy, and I was already deceiving her anyway, so I lied again and told her she'd dozed off while we'd been sitting in the dark room. Hey, at this point, that was a pretty small lie compared to everything else.

She disappeared into a bathroom down the dark hall to wash her face, so I sat and fidgeted with my guilt for a few minutes. Would I ever be able to look her in the face again?

Mom tells me all the time that a guy who treats a woman like an object isn't even worth his own testosterone. Object? Heck, I'd just treated a girl like *food*! I guess I wasn't even worth my own gastric acid. Even though that gastric acid was sloshing around dangerously right now.

Nerves and a full stomach are a nauseating combination. How much worse could I possibly feel?

"Oh my gosh!" Kacey's voice was not a happy one as she marched into the classroom. "Eric, what did you *do* to me?!"

I felt worse.

She must've figured out I'd bitten her. Now there'd be trouble. I saw flashbacks of Mom and me packing up to leave San Francisco, Seattle, Denver ---

Then I couldn't see anything at all because Kacey found the lightswitch.

"What -- what do you mean?" I stammered out, squinting and putting my arms up to ward off the light. Talk about a Freudian slip. I was acting just like Christopher Lee in *The Horror of Dracula*, cowering before the crucifix-bearing hero.

But suddenly it seemed like a fair question. How the heck *did* she know I'd bitten her? My teeth don't leave marks if I lick over the wounds. I was guilty, of course, but how could *she* know that?

"My neck!" she said, jabbing her finger toward where my lips had recently been. "Look at this!"

I blinked back the tears and tried to focus in the strong, sterile classroom light. And that was when I found out what happens when I get greedy and don't let the blood flow out naturally; on Kacey's neck, exactly halfway between her jawbone and her collarbone, was a reddish-purple mark that was quickly darkening into a bruise about the size of a quarter.

That really sucked. And it definitely proved that I had.

I felt my face starting to turn the same color as the bruise, but I forced eyes open really wide and blinked hard again to be sure. No, absolutely no trace of teethmarks. But the bruise was still --

"Don't look so innocent!" she snapped at me. "I know what you did while I was asleep!"

I blinked at her again. What was I going to say? I'd just drunk her blood, and there was no hiding it. Not the bruise, anyway. Might as well admit it now.

I stared at my hands in my lap, took a deep breath, and said, "I shouldn't have done that. I'm sorry." And I was, too.

I looked up as Kacey clapped a hand over her neck. "What am I gonna tell my mom?" she moaned. "I've never even *kissed* a guy before, and now I'm coming home with a hickey!"

My eyes went wide open without force now. A hickey?! She thought I'd -- No way!

The relief was so intense for a second that I could've danced a jig, but that was really more for leprechauns, not vampires.

But then I realized what this meant: she thought I was the kind of guy who'd do that to a girl whether she wanted it or not. Sick. I'd *never* do -- but then, I'd just drunk her blood without her permission. So it wasn't hormone lust; it was blood lust. Which one was worse? And wasn't I a jerk either way?

I looked at my hands again. "I -- I did it while you were asleep," I said. But at least I could confess something to her now. That made me feel slightly less like dirt.

"Well, duh," she said, "if you'd done it while I was awake I *think* I'd remember it!"

I looked up and watched her roll her eyes, then drop into a chair, her arms folded across her chest. She scowled, but her eyes had tears in them again.

I made myself look at her face while I said, "I know it was wrong. I never meant to hurt you; I just lost control."

"Did you do *anything else*?" She was glaring at me now.

I felt myself blushing because I knew she wasn't referring to sinking my teeth into her skin.

"No," I said, "I swear I only... *touched* your neck."

She sighed and stopped glaring. "Okay," she said, "I believe your story. But my brothers won't." She smiled at me weakly.

Ouch. Four older brothers. Maybe I'd be better off confessing to being a vampire. A stake through the heart might be a quicker way to die.

Kacey chewed her lip for what seemed like a couple of minutes, then looked up at me with a smirk on her face. "Nope," she said, "your story won't work. We'll have to change it."

I had no clue what she was talking about. "To what?" I asked her.

"Well," she told me, standing up, "we'll say that you came back into this dark classroom to comfort me, and we ended up kissing, and ... well, we got carried away." She giggled, then added, "Then it's like it was *my* choice, see? So my brothers won't kill you."

I wasn't too sure about adding more lies to what I'd already told. "Okay," I said, hesitantly. "But, really, I just.... uh, went for your neck. I never kissed you."

Kacey smiled. "Oh, we can fix *that* part," she said. And she reached over and flicked off the light.

Chapter Five

Mom laughed. She tried not to at first, right after she'd gotten the telephone call from Kacey's mom and I'd confessed the real story to her. And she did tell me she was disappointed in me for losing control. And even more disappointed for my thinking of Kacey as less than a person (read: object/snack). But then she laughed.

"Oh, honey," she said, putting her arms around me in one of those great mom-hugs that I'd never admit to anyone how much I liked, "I never, *ever* thought I'd hear that you'd been *necking*, of all things! That's hilarious!" Then she laughed until she cried.

I laughed too -- even though she grounded me for losing control. I was just glad that it hadn't turned out worse.

And I was actually kind of relieved to get punished. I knew I deserved it. And it was only for a week anyway -- no phone, no Joseph over to hang out in the evenings, no social websites, and *no* talking to Kacey except at school.

Kacey told me (at school, of course) that her brothers were mainly just annoyed because her mom had decided that one of them had to escort her on all future dates until she turned sixteen -- especially if she went anywhere with me. But I wasn't planning on asking her or any other girl on a date for a while, just to be safe. Apparently, I wasn't quite ready to fake being normal in that way yet.

So things were okay. Sort of.

"Hey, it's lover-lips Eric!" Scott announced loudly, slapping me on the back as I walked into English. He'd done this every day since the dance. "It's the man with the magic vacuum tongue!"

Pathetic. And embarrassing. Especially since -- besides the blood -- all I'd really gotten was one kiss. But I wasn't about to let Scott know that.

"You'd just better hope I stay away from *your* girlfriends, Scott," I said, putting my books down on my desk. "Oh wait --" I added, "my bad. I forgot; you don't have any." I grinned.

"Oh! What a burn!" Joseph taunted. "Did it hurt, Scott? Need some ice?"

Becca giggled. And Britni smiled at Joseph. She'd been doing that a lot lately.

Kacey was sinking lower into her seat, but she was coughing into her hand again.

"Hey, listen up, Hoover-mouth," Scott threatened, but he wasn't really serious, "you'd better watch it 'cause -- 'cause --"

"Because someday," interjected Keith in a bored tone, "he might just trip over a good come-back line, and then you two'll be forced to fight it out."

"But until then," I said, smiling, "I refuse to have a battle of wits with an unarmed person."

Even Scott laughed then, shaking his hair back away from his glasses. Becca giggled and looked over at Rudy, who rolled his eyes and turned away.

I was just opening my notebook to the vocabulary section when the bell rang and Ms. Nielson walked in with a folded paper in her hand.

"This is for you, Eric," she said, dropping it onto my desk as she passed. "Ms. Cook asked me to give it to you."

I opened the note, but all it said was, "Eric, please meet with me after second period today."

That didn't tell me much. Who the heck was Ms. Cook, anyway? Sometimes being in school for only two classes a day made me feel left out of things. But halfway through the vocabulary review, Kacey passed me a note that said, "I told Ms. Cook you could play the piano, and I think she wants you to be the accompanist of one of our dance concert numbers. We rehearse before school every day."

Playing the piano for a dance concert? I could handle that. A dark auditorium. Lots of girls and no other guys. Yup. I could definitely handle that. As long as they weren't doing "Night on Bald Mountain" or anything from *Phantom of the Opera*. No creepy stuff for the old vampire man here. I didn't want anyone to associate me with anything spooky. Bad for the reputation.

But Cook didn't want me to do anything spooky. She wanted me to learn a piece by Billy Joel called "Rootbeer Rag."

Ha! Ragtime! I could deal with that just fine. After all, being the dance club's accompanist was such a perfectly *ordinary* thing to do.

By the first week in March, I had the piece learned and showed up at the practice session.

This was way cool. Me, lots of girls, a piano, a little fame coming my way for being the only student accompanist -- and no vampire stuff. Life was good.

Except that nobody told me what girls wear -- or more like, *don't* wear -- to dance practices.

I'd just assumed they'd show up in t-shirts and shorts like for gym class, but they were all in these skintight leotard things that showed -- well, they showed a lot that a t-shirt would hide.

In fact, some of them showed too much. Really, some of the girls really should've stuck with sweatpants. I mean, who wants to show off bouncing fat rolls?

But a lot of the girls looked really good. Britni, for instance. I hadn't known she had such long legs. She moved kind of like a deer on stage. And Maria, a girl I knew from church. She normally wore big, baggy shirts all the time, but she didn't have one on now. And, well -- wow!

"Oh, good, Eric, you're here!" Ms. Cook said, smiling and pushing me toward the piano. "Let's run this number from the top and see how well the girls do with live music."

Huh? Oh, yeah. I was supposed to do something besides stare at girls.

I put the sheet music on the slightly battered baby grand, sat down, and rubbed my fingers along my thighs to warm them up. (My fingers, that is, not my thighs.)

And I played. I forgot about the girls; I just watched my fingers on the keyboard and the notes on the page, getting lost in the runs and jumps of the music. But I guess my fingers could move faster than the girls' feet because Ms. Cook had to ask me to slow down at least twice.

But when I finished, she acted pleased. "That's really going to make this number special," she said, tucking a piece of her short, blonde hair behind one ear. "We've never had live music for a dance concert number before, but Central High often does. I didn't know we had anyone here at Patrick Henry who could play well enough, but you'll do just fine."

She turned back to the girls while I sat there grinning in the dark. I hadn't bothered to use the little lamp over the piano so I knew the others couldn't see me. They'd all be blinded by the stage lights.

Ms. Cook was making them work on a part of the dance where they'd messed up. Even though the dance was comical one where the girls were supposed to act like the bumbling Keystone cops in those old Charlie Chaplin movies, they still had to bump into each other the right way, apparently. I thought that was kind of funny -- you know, having to *practice* falling down -- but it was fun to watch.

I decided I'd better not watch Britni anymore. She and Joseph had been together a lot since the Valentine's dance, and it didn't seem too cool to be checking out my best friend's main interest. Besides, Britni's a cheerleader. And since I'd just watched the old movie version of *Buffy, the Vampire Slayer* the week before, cheerleaders were spooking me out a little.

And Maria -- actually, I didn't know her all that well. She might be offended if she found out I'd been staring at her.

Well, Kacey, then. She obviously liked my attention well enough, and she wasn't hard to find. Tall with dark, curly hair -- and definitely no bouncing fat rolls. I could deal with that.

Like the others, Kacey was wearing a leotard, but it was a tank-top one, with really skinny straps like ribbons over her shoulders. And it was a deep red-purple color over her pale skin. Like juice spilled on cream-colored carpet. Like a popsicle melting over a chin in little trickles. Like deoxygenated blood oozing from a vein.

The leotard was cut low in the front and back. I could see her scapula clearly when her back was to me, and, when she turned forward, her neck.

The bruise mark had faded now, but I knew very well where it had been. And I knew where that artery was and what it felt like pounding against my mouth. I knew her skin smelled of flowers and her blood was the sweetest I'd ever tasted.

My mouth was full of saliva, dripping, and ready to mix with her warm blood. But just as I went to swallow, I heard, "Hey, Eric, I'm gonna get a close up of you when you start playing, so don't let it distract you, okay?"

It is not wise to inhale suddenly in surprise when you have more than two tablespoons of spit circulating around your tongue.

58

I coughed so hard that my eyes watered and my contact lenses floated precariously.

"What -- what did you say?" I asked, wiping slobber off the keyboard with the sleeve of my sweater.

"Gosh, I'm sorry," she said, giggling a little.

I turned around to look at her. It was Mallory from my English class. And she was holding a *camera*. I stared at her in horror. The remaining spit in my mouth dried up almost instantly.

"I've just been getting some shots for the school newspaper," she said, talking thickly around all the orthodontic appliances that littered her mouth, "and I wanted to get a close-up of you playing." She smiled at me, which looked like it might have been painful with all that metal.

Camera. Not good.

I'd look normal through the camera's viewfinder, but the image on any computer screen would show my glowing retinas and a good portion of my circulatory system. Anyone who looked at a photo of me playing would see the piano and what looked like a head-shaped blob of reddish-purple lace above my navy blue crewneck sweater. A preppy zombie playing ragtime. Not good at all.

"No, not me," I told Mallory. "I'm way camera-shy. Take pictures of the girls." I waved a hand toward the stage.

"Oh, c'mon, Eric," she begged. "What's it gonna hurt?"

Now, Mallory's kind of cute, in spite of all that metal in her mouth, and a guy hates to tell a cute girl "no," but this was serious.

"Nope," I said. "I never do pictures. They might be dangerous. The flash alone could send me into an instant coma, you know." I tried to look sly, and she laughed.

"Party pooper," she said, and stuck out her tongue. "Fine. I got a couple of you from a distance, but I won't take a close-up, since you won't let me." And she walked over to a row of seats and sat down, her eyes focused on the stage.

Crap. She'd already taken some photos in which my clothes, but not my body, would be normal. I'd managed to avoid every yearbook, every cell phone camera, every single Kodak moment in this town for the entire two years we'd lived here. Until now. And now what? How could I lie my way out of being Mr. Artery Boy? A hopeful candidate for *Gray's Anatomy*? Not even.

"Eric, could you run it from the top, please?" Ms. Cook called to me, and I began to play, but kind of automatically, like a wind-up doll on a music box. I had to figure out how to get that camera and delete any pictures of myself.

Glancing over the top of the piano, I saw Tim, who's also on the newspaper staff, come in and sit next to Mallory. He had a pen and notepad, so I figured he was doing an article to go with Mallory's pictures.

If I could just steal that camera -- well, not really steal, just *borrow* it long enough to delete any pictures of me....

Hey! Maybe I could hypnotize Mallory!

"Eric?!"

Huh? I looked up at Ms. Cook in her black tights -- and about forty girls who were all staring at me, squinting in the bright stage lights.

"You got a little carried away there," Ms. Cook said. "There's no repeat in that section."

It's a good thing they couldn't see in the dark like I can because I knew I was blushing.

"Uh, sorry," I said. "I wasn't thinking about what I was doing."

"Obviously not," said Cook. "Honestly, you can't put a boy in a roomful of girls and expect him to concentrate." There was a lot of giggling from the girls, but at least Ms. Cook didn't seem mad.

"It's okay," she continued. "I need to work with them on these jumps here anyway."

Her attention went back to the stage and mine went back to Mallory.

Mallory had put the camera down on the arm of the seat and was telling Tim something. He was busy taking notes, his long hair trailing onto the notepad.

The camera was just sitting there. I stared at it. It was small and metallic black. If I could just get near it.... I pictured myself slipping it into my backpack and -- the camera jiggled on the wooden arm of the chair!

Had I done that?! Nyah. Mallory must've bumped it. But....

I stared at the camera and focused all my attention on it. In my mind, I began to talk to the camera like I was trying to hypnotize it.

C'mon, baby, come to me. Just slip off the chair and glide over. Easy now. No sudden moves.

And there were no sudden moves. Just like I had it on a string to pull it across a table, the camera slid toward me in the air. I didn't dare blink. I just kept talking to the camera. Come to me. That's right. Right into my hand.

And there it was, in my hand. I slipped it into my backpack and sat there stunned.

That was *telekinesis*! I had just moved an object with my mind! Dude! How cool was that?! Yoda would've been so proud.

Hey! Maybe I could clean my room that way! But no, I was sweaty and shaking from the effort. I felt tired, like I'd just done a hundred push-ups or something.

Still, if I could see in the dark, hypnotize animals and people, and use telekinesis -- even though it was hard work -- then, hey, this vampire thing wasn't *totally* bad. There were definitely a few perks to the job.

But how come I hadn't noticed the hypnosis and telekinesis until the last few weeks? Maybe it was because I was growing up. A vampire puberty thing, like growing facial hair -- which I, incidentally, didn't seem to be doing very much of. Maybe vampires don't grow beards. I didn't know. I *still* didn't know any other vampires.

I played the song three more times for the dancers and watched Mallory look around for the camera before the bell rang to go to first period. She even asked me if I'd taken it.

"Yeah, sure, Mallory," I said, shouldering my backpack and trying to look innocent, "I was sitting at the piano and I moved the camera by telekinesis. Schoop! Right into my hand. Magic." I imitated catching a flying object and clutching it to my chest.

Tim laughed, but Mallory shook her head and started looking under the seats again.

I felt a little guilty. This was the second time in a month that I'd lied to a girl. Okay, well, I hadn't actually lied this time, but I had taken the camera without her permission. Still, this was self-preservation, and I'd give the camera back -- as soon as I could figure out how.

Actually, it didn't take me too long -- thanks to Mr. Papinikolas.

Mr. Papinikolas, or Papsi, as we like to call him, is a big guy who kind of looks like a younger version of Santa Claus: semi-gray hair, short beard, big stomach. I hear his wife makes great baklava, which might account for the big stomach.

He's also kind of jolly; he laughs a lot. He teaches geometry, which is serious stuff, but he's always messing around with computers and showing us what he's produced. Today it was how he'd turned a photo of the long-haired history teacher down the hall into Cousin It.

"See?" he told us before the bell rang for second period to start, as Joseph, Rudy, Alexis, Tim, and I all crowded around his desk, peering at the monitor, "I just stuck the little derby hat on top and pasted on some dark glasses."

It was kind of like what my mom had done to get a photograph for my passport. She'd tinkered with the skin color on iPhoto and used the anti-red eye option at its strongest level until the customs officials we met the time I went with her to Tokyo never even realized there was anything funny about me.

"Does Ms. Hunter know about this?" Joseph asked Papsi. He didn't sound too worried.

"Sure," said Papsi, chuckling. "She *gave* me the picture to use!"

"Can you do it to Tim, too?" Alexis asked, twisting a piece of his long hair around her finger. Tim shrugged her off.

"Hey, Papsi," I said, an idea practically bursting in my head, "will you let me use this program after class?"

"Sure," he replied. "What d'ya wanna do, paste yourself next to some hot Hollywood starlet or something?"

I felt myself blushing again as everyone else laughed, but I grinned anyway. "Nyah," I said, pulling Mallory's camera out of my backpack, "I want to delete myself out of a few photos that were taken without my permission."

"Hey!" said Tim. "How'd you get that?"

"Like I told you and Mallory," I said sarcastically, "telekinesis."

Alexis snorted. "Yeah, right," she said. "And so we, like, need a written consent form signed by you to take your picture, or what?"

"That," added Rudy, straightening up so he loomed over the rest of us like an articulate Lurch, "and about five bucks. Eric's charging now."

Alexis was undaunted. "So, who d'you think you are?" she asked Rudy. "His manager?"

Before he could answer, I stuck in, "Yeah, but he only gets five percent."

"Oh, cheap!" said Rudy. But then the bell rang, so we dropped the subject pronto. Papsi starts class ten seconds after the bell -- exactly. He's not too jolly about that.

But Papsi doesn't have a third period, so he left me alone with the computer while he changed the posters on his bulletin board in the back of the room. I had to work fast because the sun was getting pretty bright outside for so early in the spring, and I still had to walk nearly a mile to get home. Preferably without fainting.

I opted for the easiest way out. I downloaded all the pics into a file which I marked "Mallory" and stuck it on the school's server. That took me fifteen minutes, and I was getting nervous about the sunshine -- it was nearly 10:00 AM. As fast as I could, I went through the file and deleted every picture I could find with the piano in it. It was too slow checking for my see-through epidermis.

Whew. It was done. I put the camera back in my backpack, said goodbye to Papsi, grabbed my hat and sunglasses, and ran outside.

It was only about sixty degrees, but the sun was blazing from a cloudless sky. It was the kind of spring weather that makes everyone happy -- except me. I hadn't even put on sunscreen that morning because it was still March. Crap.

I ran past the gas station and cut into the halls of the high school. Junior high kids aren't supposed to go inside the building during school hours, but I was desperate to stay out of the sun. There are big, old trees in front of the Assembly Hall and the library, but their leafless spring branches didn't do me much good, so by the time I got to the church on the corner of 300 South, I was dizzy and panting. I had to rest in the shade of the porch there for about ten minutes before I dared to run the three blocks home. I didn't faint, but my skin had turned pink by the time I unlatched the screen door, and I was so dizzy I could hardly pull down the kitchen blind. I felt like a cat trapped in a clothes dryer.

After gulping down about three glasses of water, I went to the bathroom to put Noxema on my face and hands. Great. Sunburn because I walked home too late because I was trying to keep people from finding out that I don't look human in photos. Because I'm freakin' *not* all the way human.

Telekinesis or not, sometimes this vampire thing really bites.

Chapter Six

"You got a sunburn yesterday? How?" Kacey confronted me the next day after the dance rehearsal was over. "It wasn't even all that warm out there." She jabbed a finger toward the auditorium door.

I sighed. "Look, I have porphyria," I explained -- again. "It makes me sensitive to light. You know I only have two classes every day so I can get home before it gets too bright outside. Well, yesterday I didn't make it home early enough."

I actually don't have porphyria, but since the disease causes light sensitivity, my mom and I have been telling that lie for so long that I don't feel guilty about it anymore. Besides, what am I supposed to do? Tell people I can't be out in the sun because I'm a vampire? Like that'd solve my problems.

The auditorium was dark where we were standing by the piano, but, of course, I could see Kacey very clearly. And I wished she'd put a shirt on over that tank-top leotard; my stomach was starting to growl.

"So, does porphyria make you have any weird restrictions on food?" she asked.

Crap. Had she heard my stomach?

"Uh, like what?" I asked.

"Like limiting sugar or stuff?"

Or like having to drink eight ounces of blood or more every week? Nyah. Better not mention that.

"I think it's just diabetics who have to limit sugar," I told her. "And I'm not allergic to milk or nuts or anything like that."

She smiled. "Good," she said, looping one bare arm around my sweater-covered one. "Then you can help me do research for my science project on nutrition."

She was way too close to me for a girl who wasn't wearing a turtleneck. Saliva was streaming from the glands under my tongue. I swallowed hard, trying not to think about how I'd skipped breakfast.

"What do you want me to do?" I asked nervously.

65

She brought her other hand up to my bicep and started kind of stroking it. I swallowed again.

"Just follow a special diet for two weeks and record the results about how much energy you have," she said, sweetly. "Joseph, Britni, Mallory, Alexis, and Rudy are already helping me. You will, too, won't you? Please?" She smiled at me and then put her head on my shoulder, but I could still see the arched curve of her neck out of my peripheral vision.

Augh! This was *not* fair! Did she have any clue what this was doing to me?! I prayed she didn't.

My stomach gurgled loudly and Kacey laughed and pulled away from me. "See, I'm making you hungry just talking about it," she said.

I decided I'd better not even comment on that. I swallowed hard this time.

"So, will you help me?" she asked.

Don't think blood. Don't hypnotize. Don't bite. Stay in control. I rubbed my eyes for an excuse to stop looking at her. Better just agree with her fast and then get the heck out of here before I did anything stupid.

"Sure, I guess," I told her, staring at the carpet. "What do I have to eat?"

"Oh, good!" she exclaimed and started to run up the stairs to the stage. "I'll give you the full set of instructions after I change clothes, but you basically just have to be a vegetarian for two weeks."

"A vegetarian?!" I half-shouted.

"Sure, that won't kill you," she called and disappeared behind the curtain.

Yeah, right. I didn't know a whole lot about the different forms of vegetarianism, but I was willing to bet that mammal blood wasn't exactly in their food pyramid.

I reached down and grabbed my backpack from under the piano bench. How was I going to get around this commitment?

"Hey, Eric!" I looked up and saw Mallory walking down the darkened aisle.

"Hey, Mallory," I said. "I guess you want your camera back." I began shuffling in my backpack to find it.

"Tim told me you were going to delete photos of yourself," she said, getting close enough to speak without yelling, "and Papsi opened the file you'd made for me. You left about ten pictures alone, but I love that one you made of yourself!" She laughed.

I didn't laugh. "The one I made of myself?" I repeated mindlessly.

"Yeah, where you like zombified your skin and made it all Halloweeny and stuff!" she said, laughing again. "It's fabulous!"

My heart was pounding way too fast. I must've overlooked one picture. But she thought I'd done it on purpose. I decided to fake it.

"You like that?" I asked, forcing a sickly grin. "Papsi showed me how to do it." Okay, so I lied. Again. This was becoming a really bad habit.

"I love it," she said. "It's like when Dracula doesn't show up in the mirror, you know? Is that where you got the idea?"

I couldn't even force a grin now. "Yeah, kind of," I muttered, trying to sound like I wasn't nervous -- and failing miserably. I handed her the camera, staring at it so I couldn't look at the way her hair curled over her neck. I wished she had a scarf on. I was so hungry.

"Yeah," she said, taking the camera and starting back toward the door, "it's like Eric-the-zombie-vampire or something. Just like Ms. Nielson said that one time."

I felt sick. "Well, you'd better get out where it's light, then," I joked lamely. "I just might attack you here in the dark." She was nearly to the back door by then, so I knew she couldn't hear my stomach growling. And she wouldn't know how much I'd had to struggle not to bite her.

"Ooh, I'm scared," she called down to me. "But next time, leave my camera alone!"

"Next time, don't take pictures of me!" I yelled back at her.

She was gone, but I had to stand breathing deeply in the dark for a couple of minutes before I could go to class. And I made sure I didn't even look at Michael with his puncture-on-the-dotted-line neck during English.

Mom was out of town that week -- in Tennessee, determining where a new Max Tux Menswear franchise could make the most money -- or she would've told me not to be a vegetarian. I used to get sick all the time when I was a baby, before she discovered my "special dietary needs."

But I didn't really remember what that felt like. Or maybe I just wanted to be honest with Kacey about this after being dishonest about biting her at the dance. Or maybe I was just being an idiot.

The stuff I was supposed to eat wasn't a problem: pasta, salads, fruit. I eat all that stuff anyway. But after about one day, I was missing the meat. Okay, well, specifically raw red meat, that is. It's -- well, *bloody*, and it keeps me from having to make daily trips over to the Jacksons' corrals. What else is there to say?

But that week I was determined to be honest with Kacey, so I didn't eat any meat, and I skipped my visit to the Barnyard Bloodbank next door. Sure, Kacey hadn't exactly said "no blood" on her list of instructions, but then she didn't know that one of her volunteers for the experiment didn't live off pizza and soda like a normal teenager.

By the weekend I was weak and achy, and I got dizzy when I stood up too fast.

Mom came home late Sunday night, but I hardly saw her. Then Monday morning, I had to be at school by 6:30 to play for one of the last dance practices before the concert on Wednesday, and Mom wasn't about to get up at 5:30 when she had the day off and knew I'd be home before 10:00 AM anyway.

When I did manage to drag myself home, she gave me one glance and got that worried look on her face.

"Oh, honey," she said, smoothing her hand down my cheek as I put my backpack on the kitchen counter, "you're so pale! Are you getting enough sleep? Have you been skipping your naps?"

I can't help being rather nocturnal with the whole vampire DNA thing, so I usually sleep a few hours at night and a couple more in the afternoon.

"No, but I'm still playing piano for those early dance practices," I told her.

Part of me wanted to tell her the real reason I was pale. But part of me wanted to please Kacey -- and I knew Mom would make me stop being a vegetarian as soon as she found out about it. And, like I said, I was being an idiot.

She put her hand under my chin and pulled my face upward, her eyebrows scrunched down over her blue-gray eyes. "Have you been eating right while I've been gone this week?" she asked. "Have you had too much junk food?"

Whew. At least I could answer the junk food part truthfully. "No, I haven't had any," I said.

"Hmmm...." Mom said, not looking satisfied. "Well, I'll be working from home this week, young man, so I'll be keeping close tabs on your meals and sleep." She smiled and kissed me on the forehead. "Now, go get your online homework done and then take a nap," she told me.

I was too exhausted right then to worry about how to keep her from finding out about the vegetarian business. "Maybe I'll do the nap first," I said and went downstairs.

I didn't wake up until about 2:00 PM, but I felt a little better in my dark basement room with only the blueish light from my computer screen. I read some online articles on genetics for my physiology class and then did my Spanish homework, so it was nearly another hour before I went upstairs again.

"Oh, good, you're awake," Mom said almost as soon as my foot was on the top stair.

"Sophie Jackson just called. She's been babysitting her grandson, but Hank's cut himself on some barbed wire, and she needs to take him to Doctor Miller. Can you run over and watch the little boy for a couple of hours? Are you feeling well enough?"

I grabbed a roll from a package on the counter and shoved it in my mouth. "I'm okay," I said. "How old's the kid?" I don't like babies much; that whole diaper-changing bit is gross. But I think little kids -- the ones old enough to use the bathroom by themselves -- are pretty funny.

"Please don't talk with your mouth full, Eric."

"Sorry," I said and swallowed. "I'm pretty hungry."

She handed me a banana and another roll. "He's four," she said. "Eat those and I'll feed you dinner as soon as you come back from the Jacksons'."

I grabbed my jacket and sunglasses, took the food, and ran over to the Jacksons' house; it was a little strange going to their front door while it was still daytime, but then, the Jacksons didn't know that my normal visits to their house were to their animals at night.

The little boy was named Brendan. He was a cute kid with messy red hair and big eyes. He liked toy trucks, so I spent half an hour with him crawling around on the living room floor making engine revving sounds and pushing Tonkas and Hot Wheels under furniture.

When he got tired of that, we watched an alphabet DVD and then played superheroes. It had been a long time since I'd had an excuse to pin a towel around my neck and jump off a sofa, so I had a great time, but by 5:30, I was beginning to wonder when the Jacksons' daughter would be there to pick up her kid. And I was really hungry. All I'd had since breakfast at 5:45 AM was two rolls and a banana.

"Wead me a stowy," Brendan demanded.

I unpinned my towel and took it off.

"Do you want your cape off now?" I asked Brendan as I sat down and put him on my lap.

"Nnuh-uh," he said, shaking his head. "I'm a supewhewo!" He dug a *Jimmy, The Super Cat* book out of the backpack.

I read that story and two more before he zonked out on my lap. I was pretty tired, too; being a kid-chaser is hard work.

The clock on the wall said 6:00, and my stomach growled loudly. I sighed and started to unfasten the safety pin on Brendan's towel-cape before he choked. This was harder than it looked because he was totally dead weight on my left arm, so I had to work with the pin one-handed. And I didn't do too well.

The pin snapped open much too fast, and Brendan jerked violently, then slept on as if nothing had happened. But when I pulled the pin away and loosened the towel, there was a dot of blood the size of a ladybug just above the collar of his shirt.

NO.

I couldn't stop staring at that little, shiny dot of blood. It was like a bead. A cinnamon candy. A miniature cherry. It was more than all those: it was a drop of life itself. And I wanted it.

My saliva glands were working way too well again. I swallowed hard. My heart was pounding very fast, and my breathing was quick and shallow. I was so hungry.

I leaned over and licked the drop off his neck. It was sweet-salty and warm.

I put my mouth against Brendan's chubby neck to sense where the artery was, where my teeth could puncture most easily, where the blood would flow over my lips to soothe the --

The Jacksons' phone rang.

I jerked my head up and wiped saliva off my mouth with my free hand.

The phone rang again.

Had I really been going to bite a little kid? How sick was that?

A third ring.

Still breathing way too hard, I put Brendan down on the floor, ran into the kitchen, and grabbed the phone. It was an old one, and the caller ID screen was dead and blank.

"Hello? Jackson residence. Babysitter speaking."

"Eric, it's Mom. I'm worried; your cell phone's turned off again, and you've been over there so long. Have the Jacksons called? Are you okay?"

No, I'm not okay. My eyes began to water almost as much as my mouth had been a minute earlier. Stop it! I told myself. You're too old to cry.

But that didn't help much. I sniffed into the phone.

"Eric? What's wrong?"

I wiped my nose on my sleeve. Gross, I know, but it was either that or let it drip down my face.

"Mom," I said into the receiver, "can you come over here and help me?"

"What's wrong, honey?" she asked, sounding worried. "Are you sick?"

Yeah, I'm sick. I'm totally sick and wrong. No wonder people have hated vampires for centuries. I *deserve* a stake through my heart.

I took a deep, slow breath and said, "If you hadn't called right when you did, Mom, I would've bitten Brendan."

There was silence for a good ten seconds before I heard my mom say, "Don't go near the boy, Eric. I'll be there in two minutes."

I hung up the receiver and leaned against the kitchen wall in the dark.

Chapter Seven

I felt like a Hollywood vampire the next morning. I had to be evil to keep wanting to attack people like this. And what if it got worse? What if I couldn't be around people at all? Would I have to move into the forest and live like a hermit?

But there *had* to be a way to control this hunger, this blood-lust. My mom hadn't ever seen my dad drink blood. He must've controlled himself. If I could only just *talk* to ---

Whoa.

The school hallways were usually pretty deserted when I arrived to play for the dance rehearsals, but there was Keith Sanderson, resident first period English chick magnet and wise-crack king, standing at an open locker. He had a small, black box in one hand, and from it he was removing a syringe. The syringe was smaller than the one I used to draw blood from animals, but still....

My brain made the jump into hyperspace.

Could Keith be a vampire? I'd never really tried to look at his eyes to see if he had overly-large irises. But maybe he was coming to school early to avoid daylight. Awesome! The coolest guy in ninth grade with the same weird medical condition as mine. And then at least one of his parents would have to be a vampire. Which means I could maybe talk to them about stuff. Sweet.

All of this passed through my surging brain in one nano second, during which time Keith looked up at me.

"Hey," he said, sounding a little bored.

I stared at the syringe, my brain still racing on a one-way track to a conclusion. "So, you're *one*?" I asked him, nodding toward the syringe.

He looked down at it, then back at me, raising one eyebrow. "Yeah," he said, drawing out the word, almost into a question instead of an answer.

"I didn't know that." I said, shifting my backpack a little and taking a step forward. "What about your parents?"

"Nope. Just me," he said, bored again.

I was confused. "But, isn't it hereditary? I thought -- I thought one of your parents had to be a --"

"Sometimes, but not always."

Silence exploded like a car airbag to take up all breathing space for a few seconds.

Keith nodded toward the syringe. "Look, it's not gross or anything. You can watch me inject it if you really want to. My little brothers like to watch."

Huh? Why would he inject blood? Why not drink it?

"Inject?" I asked him.

"My insulin."

Oh. Insulin. He's a *diabetic*. Not a *vampire*.

Flaming hot blood rushed up my neck to make a neon sign of the words "Eric Wright is the world's biggest idiot" across my forehead. Or at least that's what it felt like.

I read somewhere once that psychologists think people suppress bad memories. I guess that's why I have no clue how I got from Keith's locker to the front of the auditorium. I hope I didn't run.

Great. So I was not only a mutant human who attacked my friends and occasionally small children; I was also a total moron for asking a diabetic incredibly stupid questions. Self-pity was now fighting a major war against embarrassment for my mood of the morning. I wanted to be somewhere else. Anywhere else. And preferably *someone* else, too.

Suddenly, I heard a noise behind me. I whipped around.

Kacey was scowling at me and almost clenching the paperwork from my one week as a vegetarian, which I'd stuck in her mailbox after I'd left the Jacksons' last night. "I thought you were just sensitive to light," she said.

Swell. I was *not* in the mood to explain anything right now.

I put my backpack down beside the piano and set up my sheet music. "Look," I told her, trying not to grit my teeth, "porphyria does weird things to a person's body. I was getting weak, so when Mom got back from Tennessee and noticed it, she made me go back to eating red meat."

Really red. And not the meat part. Mom had made me go drink twice as much blood as normal as soon as she'd gotten to the Jacksons' the night before. I didn't think the cow I'd chosen would be feeling too well this morning, but I felt less like swallowing human blood. Especially since drinking so much blood at once had made my stomach a little queasy.

74

Kacey popped her gum. "So, is that why you're acting weird?" she asked, still not moving.

I froze with my back to her. "What do you mean, 'weird'?" Had she figured out it wasn't really porphyria?

"You won't look at me."

Oh. Just that.

I sighed and turned around. She had a right to be mad at me, but she didn't know any of the real reasons why. She didn't know I'd bitten her. Or that I'd been lying to everyone. She didn't know that I had to fight to keep myself from biting her and Michael and anyone else who drew my attention to their necks. She didn't know I'd nearly sucked blood out of a four-year-old the night before. She didn't know what scum I really was.

"Okay, I'm sorry, Kacey," I told her honestly, although it came out kind of hoarse and gruff-sounding. "I really didn't mean to screw up your science project."

"You didn't screw it up," she said, still chewing her gum hard. "You just didn't get the results I expected. But it's not that. It's just --"

"Kacey, get that gum out of your mouth and join us on stage, please!" Ms. Cook's voice was loud and clear.

But I was curious about what Kacey meant. "It's just *what*?" I asked her, grabbing her arm so she wouldn't leave.

"I don't know," she said. "But something about you is really different. Kind of *off*, you know? And it's started being, like, really noticeable lately."

"I have a disease, okay?" I was getting irritated again, even though I knew she was right. Obviously, my being the accompanist for the dance concert wasn't normal enough to fool her.

"It's not just the medical stuff; Joseph doesn't have legs, but he still *acts* normal," she said. "But you just don't seem like everybody else."

"How?" I sounded mad. I *was* mad. Mad at myself for being a vampire and mad at her for noticing I wasn't like all the regular humans she knew.

"You act like there's something wrong with having a disease, all defensive, like --"

"Kacey, NOW!" Ms. Cook wasn't too happy, either.

"Oh, I don't know!" Kacey snapped, jerking away from my hand. "I can't explain it!" She turned and left, putting the papers near the curtain.

75

Great. Now she was really mad at me, and I had one more reason to hate myself. And what had she meant by "defensive"? Geez.

I played the song perfectly every time that morning, and Ms. Cook praised me and said the concert Wednesday night would be even better because of me. Most days this would've made me feel pretty cool, but right then I didn't care.

"What is *with* you today?" Joseph asked me later, as we left English, where I'd been very careful not to get anywhere near Keith in hopes that he'd forget about my stupidity earlier.

"What do you mean?" I asked him cautiously. Had someone told him about my argument with Kacey?

"You're ragging at everyone," he said, swerving around a seventh-grader who was digging into her locker. "So who spit in your Cheerios this morning?"

I felt like I wanted to hit something again. Joseph was the coolest friend I'd ever had, and I was dying to tell him what was really bothering me, but I couldn't. He either wouldn't believe me and think I was an idiot, or else he'd get scared and I'd lose him like I'd lost every other friend I'd ever made.

I sighed. I'd have to be less direct. "Do you ever get sick of being different?" I asked him. "Does it ever just bug the crap out of you that you don't have legs?"

"Yeah," said Joseph, "I wouldn't recommend it. Stay away from tractors." He grinned.

"Hey, I'm serious," I said, but I couldn't look him in the eye. I knew I wasn't telling him the real problem. The real problem was that I was tired of hiding and tired of losing control, tired of being afraid of what people would do if they knew about me and tired of not having any answers.

We were at the door to Papsi's room now, but Joseph stopped so Tim, Mallory, and Scott could go in ahead of us.

"It could be worse, you know," Joseph said, his eyes following the kids going in the door.

"How?" I muttered.

"You could be like Scott," Joseph said, grinning wickedly this time.

"Shut up, Joseph!" Scott called back at him. But he didn't sound too mad. Besides, Scott had no clue what we were talking about.

Joseph rolled up against some lockers that had stickers all over them and looked up at me.

"It's like this," he told me. "Yeah, I'm in a wheelchair. But I don't have time to worry about what I *can't* do because I'm too busy with what I *can* do. I'll probably never be able to sing opera, but I'm okay with that. I don't look good in a viking helmet anyway."

I smiled a little. Everyone knew Joseph had trouble singing anything more challenging than "Happy Birthday." And sometimes he had trouble with that.

"I like me the way I am," he said. "So, you're never going to be a sunbathing champion. Big, fat, hairy deal." He paused a second or two and then added, "Do you like yourself?"

"Not all the way," I admitted.

"Then maybe you're making some of your own problems," he said, pulling his chair back so he was balanced on the back wheels and leaning against the decorated lockers.

Ouch. Making my own problems? I opened my mouth to protest, but the bell rang, making us late to Papsi's class. Then we both had a real problem.

And the problem got worse the next day when an office aide came with a note to Ms. Nielson's class: I had to go see the principal.

I was completely mystified. What had I done? The whole camera incident had been weeks ago, and I was pretty dang sure that not finishing the research I was supposed to do for Kacey's project on vegetarianism wasn't enough to earn me an interview with Mr. Wendall. I hadn't bitten anyone since the dance, and one tardy slip for Papsi's class wasn't *that* big of a deal. What, then?

All this bounced through my mind as I walked down the main hall with its green tile and yellow cinderblock walls interspersed with rows of dull gray lockers. My heart was pounding way too fast, but it had nothing to do with wanting to bite anyone.

I was ushered into Wendall's office, which was lined with the same green tile as the hallway, except that it had motivational posters that said things like "Teamwork!" up on the walls instead of the student-made masks and collages that decorated the hallways.

I'd only seen Mr. Wendall a couple of times before, and he always made me think of the Pillsbury Doughboy on yeast steroids -- like bread dough left way too long to rise until it spills over the edge of the pan. Wendall was so completely round that he had no neck -- kind of like a snowman. He just wrapped his tie between the smaller round ball of his head and the larger round ball of his body. He was also nearly colorless: hair somewhere between blond and white; light gray eyes behind thin-framed glasses; pale, freckled skin -- and he was wearing a beige-colored sport jacket over a white shirt and yellow tie. If he'd been any paler he could've passed for a beached Moby Dick.

I wanted to smirk at the sight of the albino bowling ball with legs -- but I was too dang scared. What *was* I in trouble for?

"Sit down, Eric," he told me. "It's interesting to see what you really look like."

What was he getting at?

"I'm sure you know why you're paying this little visit, but I'm required to tell you the terms of your suspension, so --"

Suspension? What the --?!

"Excuse me, Mr. Wendall," I interrupted him, "but I really don't have a clue why you wanted to see me."

The artery on his right temple started to bulge and his face went from pale to pink. "Now, don't play innocent with me, young man! I've seen the video footage, and we learned from that girl on the newspaper staff that you know how to modify images on the school computers!"

Did he mean Mallory?

"I don't know what video you mean," I told him, trying not to look at that artery. "I did change some pictures that Mallory took of me without my permission, but I haven't touched any video cameras."

"Oh, we know you didn't take the video, so don't try that tactic!" he half-shouted. Wendall was a dark pink now, so the blond-white hair over his pink face made him look like a mutant toy Easter bunny. "We know you modified the security video, removing the skin from your face and hands in it -- as well as your friend's legs -- and making your eyes shine red, but it wasn't very difficult identifying the two of you anyway."

Security video? What security video? Of course my skin and eyes would go all funky in a video, but was he talking about Joseph's missing legs? Surely the man would've noticed the *wheelchair....*

I needed to say something, to defend myself, to lie again if I had to. But that artery was bulging like a tube on the side of his face now.

"... looking for the culprits who vandalized the lockers, of course, but what we found was much more incriminating! The audacity of your actions, young man! How could you sneak into the assistant principal's office?! How could you tamper with the school's security video system?! What kind of delinquent tendencies do you ....?"

It had to be the superficial temporal branch of the carotid artery. Yeah, that was it. But none of the virtual dissections of cadavers had ever shown it as large as this one. Maybe all the fat cells underneath it were pushing it outward, closer to the skin.

"... If we here at Patrick Henry were to allow this kind of deceit to go unpunished, then we would be giving free rein to all types of criminal activity and...."

It would hardly take anything to pierce the skin. Then all that blood would spurt out, warm and wonderful.

My saliva was flowing heavily now. It would take some effort to calm him down with the frenzy he'd worked himself into, but I could do it. I knew I could -- if I used the right kind of tones in my voice.

"Mr. Wendall," I said, softly, "try to calm down a little. There's no need to get angry."

He stopped sputtering and looked at me, stunned, a total Bambi in the headlights.

"You need to take some deep breaths and relax a little. Don't get so upset over this. You're just angry at whoever put stickers all over those lockers. But it's not worth all this."

His eyes had the same glazed-over look that the sheep get when I do this trick to them. In fact, it had required about the same amount of talking to get him to that state, which wasn't saying much for his IQ level.

I had stood up and was leaning toward him over his desk. The blood was still pounding firmly through that artery. One quick bite and --

"What is going on in here? Mr. Wendall! Are you all right?" The sharp, bony hands of Mrs. Engles, the assistant principal, jerked me away from the desk and sat me back into the chair.

A long string of spit was dangling from my mouth onto my polo shirt. I wiped it off and stared at my hand. Had I really just tried to attack the *principal*? In his own office? Without even thinking of the consequences? Without even *trying* to control the impulse?

I felt sick. There was no doubt about it; I was a monster.

"Young man, what's been going on in here?" Mrs. Engles had her hands on her skinny hips. Her dark eyebrows looked like furry caterpillars crunched together on her forehead.

"I -- I -- was trying to calm him down," I stammered out. "He was turning so red; I thought he might have a heart attack or something."

Another lie. And it was obvious that Engles had no intention of falling for it. Fortunately, Mr. Wendall backed me up, saying that he had been pretty angry and I'd been trying to calm him. His eyes still had that not-quite-all-here look as he spoke, but Engles had no choice but to accept what he said.

Not that that stopped her from suspending me, though. For insubordination. Because I kept insisting that I hadn't done anything to any security videos. I wouldn't explain why I looked so strange in the footage she showed me (like she would've believed me anyway!), so she wrote me up for being uncooperative and for refusing to comply with a reasonable request -- and gave me a three-day suspension.

When I pointed out that I was supposed to play the piano for the dance concert that night, she told me that Ms. Cook would have to use the recorded music and that Billy Joel could play his own piece just fine.

The whole thing just sucked.

I walked home very slowly in the rain, so I got soaked. But I didn't care. I really hated being a vampire. Why couldn't I control myself?

And since I couldn't find any other vampires to talk to about it, maybe it was time to contact my dad. I'd never doubted that he was a jerk like my mom had always said, but at least he'd know what it was like to grow up as a vampire. At least he'd be able to tell me what to expect: what was normal and what wasn't.

That's what I told Mom, too. And she didn't say anything for about three minutes as we sat at the kitchen table. She just kept drinking her cocoa and staring at the placemat.

Finally, when I was starting to wonder if I'd touched on a sore nerve by mentioning that I wished I could meet the man who'd deserted her as soon as she was pregnant with me, she looked at me instead of the table and said, "I'd really rather not track down your father at this point, Eric, but I realize it could be really tough on you not knowing anyone else who's been through what you're dealing with. How would you feel about talking to another vampire besides your father?"

She'd thought of that, too?! Did she actually know someone?!

"How -- How many of them -- of us -- are there?" I asked her.

She chuckled a little. "I have no idea," she said, not looking at me, "but there must be quite a few. Your father told me -- even though I didn't believe him at the time -- that being a vampire was genetic, so there must be family lines of vampires. Your father certainly wasn't Romanian, so he wasn't related to the Count Vlad that Stoker used as a basis for his story. Therefore, I can only assume that there's a smattering of vampires in various countries."

Oh, so she didn't already have someone in mind.

"But, Mom, I've tried finding them before," I told her. "I mean, you can't just do an internet search for one. You get freaks and geeks." Maybe I'd tell her the specifics of my search attempts later.

Mom laughed again and traced her finger around the rim of her mug. "I bet you do," she said. "But there is this..." she paused and looked at me funny.

"What's wrong?" I asked her.

"I, uh -- I just had an idea," she said, standing up quickly. "Let me check something really fast." And she disappeared into her office.

Weird. But I felt relieved that I'd told someone my problems. I should've trusted her earlier.

I finished my own cocoa, went downstairs to my bedroom, and started my geometry homework, but I still had two proofs left to do when Mom came downstairs, grinning like a Cheshire cat.

She plopped down on my bed and said, "I have great news. I had a ton of frequent flyer miles, and because someone else just canceled their ticket, I was able to book you a seat on the flight with me for Saturday. What you really need is a change of mind after all that's been happening, and I want to make sure you're eating right while I'm gone this time, so I'm taking you with me!"

Hey. Good idea. And fun, too. Mom had last been in Tennessee, so this could mean Nashville. I'm not too big on country music, but seeing the Grand Ol' Oprey and that stuff might be all right. I was starting to feel a lot less lousy.

I grinned at her. "Cool, Mom. Thanks. How long'll we be gone?"

"Almost a week," she said. "Do you know where your passport is? I know you haven't used it since we made that three-day trip to Tokyo when you were eleven."

I dug into my bottom desk drawer to find the box where I keep stuff I don't want to lose but don't use all that often: two screwdrivers, a padlock, some firecrackers we'd gotten in Wyoming, my social security card, a spare key chain, and my passport. I dumped them all on the bed.

"Here," I said, handing the blue booklet to my mom, "and here's hoping this trip is more interesting than the Tokyo one. I didn't even get to leave the hotel."

"Well, that was a convention; this is finalizing a franchise deal," she explained. "Besides, you're older now, so, as long as you have a map, I won't be too worried about letting you roam around. I could hardly have turned an eleven-year-old loose at night in Tokyo."

"I guess not," I said, "but -- hey, wait a sec! Why do I need a passport to go to Tennessee?"

Mom laughed. "You don't," she said, curling her knees up and wrapping her arms around them. "I finished the Max Tux contract; now I've got to finalize the deal in Scotland."

Scotland?!

"Do I have to wear a kilt?" I asked her. But I wasn't really all that worried. They couldn't *make* me wear one, and at least I'd have a whole week in which to forget about almost biting people and lying to my friends and getting suspended. And maybe I could even look for another vampire.

"They're only worn by men in the tourist industry or for special occasions, like weddings," she said, laughing again.

I frowned. Where would I find blood while we were there?

"Are we staying near sheep?" I asked her.

"Not exactly. Edinburgh's a sizable city, but we'll be there less than a week, so if you visit the Jacksons' the night before we leave you should be okay," she said. "And if you need more blood while we're there, we could always look for stray dogs." She winked at me.

I picked up my geometry book again. "So, do you think we *might* find any vampires there?" I asked.

Mom hesitated for a second, picked at some fluff on my bedspread, and then said, "Maybe so. Anything's possible," in an overly cheerful voice. "But at least you'll be away from your problems for awhile." She reached over and patted my hand before leaving the room.

So I was going to Scotland instead of sitting at home feeling sorry for myself. I could handle that.

Unfortunately, I kept doing internet searches about golf, bagpipes, and other Scottish stuff when I was supposed to be finishing my proofs for Papsi's class. I think those last two proofs were the worst I'd produced all year.

Chapter Eight

It's about a one-hour flight from Salt Lake City to Los Angeles, and it's pretty interesting. You get soda and pretzels. You can try out all the pre-recorded music stations with the cheap plastic-tube earphones they give you. You can stare out the window when you take off and see just how huge the Bingham Copper Pit Mine is and how the weird red algae makes the Great Salt Lake look brown in places instead of blue. And when you approach L.A., you can watch the smog rise up and swallow the plane as you go down -- kind of like when Luke Skywalker lands in Yoda's swamp in the Degoba system.

But the flight from L.A. to Paris is eleven hours long. On a good day.

Nothing is fun after eleven hours of it. And being strapped into a padded chair with twelve inches of legroom while a baby across the aisle from you screams for eleven hours is enough to make you relate to lunatics in straightjackets.

I tried watching the in-flight movies on the six-inch screen ahead of me, but there were only two choices: *Haunted High School*, which I'd seen about four times, and some chick flick called *Sarah's Darling*. I tried reading the Anne Rice book I'd brought with me, but it was full of violence and killing. None of her vampires seemed like me at all. I sincerely hoped her stuff was truly fiction, but wondering whether or not I might turn out like that made me start feeling guilty -- again -- about everything I'd done lately.

The guilt, the screaming kid, and the roar of the plane's engines made my brain want to explode. I tried to sleep, but my legs kept twitching because I couldn't stretch them.

My only excuse to move around was to use the bathroom. I tried to pick times when there was a line so I'd be "forced" to stand and wait. Not that standing in an eighteen-inch-wide aisle was a whole lot of fun, but it was a picnic compared to being seat-belted in that chair.

Using the bathroom in an airplane is like trying to use a port-a-john while it's on a trailer being delivered to the next construction site. And I've seen broom closets with more walking room.

The freakiest things are flushing the toilet -- which changes the air pressure in the whole little compartment and makes your ears pop -- and draining the water out of the sink -- which sucks. Literally, that is. I hoped no small children were ever allowed to use an airplane bathroom unsupervised. I could just picture some little kid like Brendan flushing the toilet while he was still sitting on it and getting sucked out into a parallel universe.

After about the fifth hour of the flight, I had decided that I could never have my mom's job and travel all the time. She seemed unperturbed by being trapped in the seat. She either worked on her laptop, read a biography of Theodore Roosevelt, or put the earphones on and slept.

It was during one of her naps that I found something to do: telekinesis.

It started as revenge on the screaming toddler across the aisle from me. The baby's mom was asleep with the kid in her arms, and the little girl was fussing because she'd dropped her plastic frog.

I could see the frog by the mom's feet, so I started to concentrate on the frog like I had with Mallory's camera.

C'mon, frog. Up. Up.

And it *was* up, hovering about two inches above the mom's ankle.

I realized that if I looked just a little bit above or to the right or left of the frog and then willed it to be there, it would move into that place. This made the whole business a lot easier, and I didn't have to break a sweat to move a three-ounce toy.

I got the frog up to where the baby could see it. She smiled, dropping her pacifier out of her mouth, and reached for the frog. But I moved it. She reached again. And I moved it again.

The baby was waving her arms all over the place now, trying to get the frog, which I kept low enough behind the seats that other people wouldn't notice it. The kid thought it was a great game. So did I. I guess five hours on an airplane had reduced my entertainment level to hers, but I didn't care. It was getting easier and easier to move the frog. I could move it pretty fast now, and I had just gotten it to circle the confused child's head, when I heard a hoarse whisper, "Eric, what in heaven's name are you doing?!"

"Huh?" I turned to look at my mom. There was a sharp whack of plastic hitting a skull in the seat across the aisle, and the baby let out a shriek that probably woke up everybody on the plane.

"How did you *do* that?" Mom asked again, staring at the frog, which had rolled into the aisle by the time I glanced back at it.

I looked back at Mom and grinned. "Telekinesis," I said, softly. "Cool, huh?"

"I didn't know you could do that," she said, still looking a little stunned, like I'd just hit her with a snowball or something.

"I didn't know either until a couple of weeks ago," I told her. "So far, this and having the super night vision are the only good things about being a vampire."

Mom stared past me at the frog on the floor. "I don't think that's something all vampires can do," she muttered. "I don't know if Pa--" she broke off and looked at me, then away, then at me again. "I mean, I don't think your father could move things with his mind," she said, almost too fast. Then she slowed down to regular speed and said, "At least, he never did it when I was around."

"You mean, this is, like, unusual -- even for vampires?" I whispered, even though the engine noise was loud enough that I would've had to shout for anyone else to have heard me.

"It could be; I'm not sure."

"Whoa!" I said. "That is *so* awesome!" I didn't bother to whisper this time.

Mom smiled at me and put her hand on my arm. "But don't practice anymore where people might see you," she said.

"Sorry," I told her. "I was bored."

Mom smiled wickedly. "I have the answer to that," she said. And she pointed to my backpack under the seat. "Geometry homework," she told me.

Thanks to Mom and the fact that I didn't want to think about my friends for awhile -- especially since Kacey hadn't even called or texted me since I got suspended and had to miss the dance concert on Wednesday -- I'd finished off the next week's worth of geometry assignments before we reached Paris.

The Charles DeGaulle Airport is actually pretty far outside of Paris. And it's huge. You have to take a bus to get from one terminal to another. I figured it'd be really easy to get lost in that airport.

Apparently, my duffle bag thought so, too, because it stayed an extra day there. At least that's what the City Jet people told my mom and me when we got to Edinburgh and my bag didn't. They also said they'd deliver the bag to our hotel room when it arrived in Scotland.

I was worried about the bag until we got into the taxi to go to the hotel. Then I was too busy wondering whether or not being a half-vampire would make me close enough to immortal to survive the crash that had to be inevitable in a place where everybody drove on the wrong side of the road. Right-hand turns were the worst. The cabdriver would swing clear out into the intersection into oncoming traffic before turning. I gripped the seat cushions really hard every time, but Mom didn't seem to notice; she just kept staring out the window and smiling.

Our hotel was on Holyrood Road in what Mom called Old Town. A lot of the buildings we passed did look pretty old -- all made out of the same gray stone.

Our cab driver, a sixty-something guy wearing one of those cool-looking, flat driving caps, hadn't said anything during the whole drive into town, but once we were in front of the hotel and he was pulling Mom's suitcase out of the cab for her, he said, "That's thierrteen pound thierrty, please."

"Huh?" I said, scowling behind my dark glasses, even though it was early evening and very cloudy. I turned to Mom and half-whispered, "I thought people in Scotland spoke English."

The cabdriver chuckled and Mom gave him two bills and said, "Keep the change," to him and then, "I think he's Glaswegian, dear," to me.

"Aye, lassie," he said. "That A am. An ye'll ken the wirds soon eneuch, lad." He tipped his hat to both of us and got in the cab.

I was still confused. "What's with calling you 'lassie'?" I asked her. "And where's Glasway? Is it by Norway?"

Now Mom laughed. "I guess to him I look young enough to be called a 'lassie,'" she said, motioning for me to pick up her suitcase. "And it's 'Glasgow,' not 'Glasway.' It's a city west of here, and they have quite a distinctive accent."

Mom's suitcase was pretty light so I didn't mind carrying it. "'Distinctive'?" I said, "It's more like 'incomprehensible.'"

Mom laughed again. "Like the man said," she told me, "you'll get used to it soon enough."

"Oh, *that's* what he said!" I muttered, following her inside.

At about 5:00 the next morning, I went for a walk to decide what I wanted to see in the late afternoon. Mom had said it probably wouldn't be sunny enough for me to worry about fainting then. Scotland isn't exactly a desert like Utah.

The morning was cold and misty, but I didn't mind. The city was still pretty empty, so I didn't have to worry too much about crossing crowded streets when the cars were coming from the wrong directions.

Mom had told me to go up one of the "closes" -- either Bull's Close, with about a million steps, or Crichton Close, with just a steep incline -- near our hotel to get to a street called Cannongate and then walk up the main hill. And not to get freaked out if the street name changed a few times. "There's one I've noticed that was called Clerk Street," she'd told me the night before, "but it changed to Nicholson in a few blocks, then South Bridge, then North Bridge."

"So, what you're telling me is that nobody in Edinburgh went by the Brigham Young method of logically numbered streets, like every town in Utah did?" I'd asked her.

She'd smiled, looking a little tired. "I think the Scots like to tease foreigners," she'd replied.

But she hadn't warned me enough about those "close" things. They were basically alleys, but "claustrophobias" would've been a better name for them. Bull's Close looked like somebody's back staircase; it was so narrow. And Crichton Close wasn't much better. Neither were most of the others I looked down. Sure, they'd been made before cars existed, but I doubted if someone could've ridden a horse down most of them without skinning both knees simultaneously on opposite walls.

Cannongate was an actual street, though, and I emerged onto it just across from a church with a graveyard straight out of Alfred Hitchcock's imagination. That was my first mental note of something to check out later in the day when the gates were unlocked, but for now I continued my tourist reconnaissance mission.

I climbed up the hill, passing the Museum of Childhood, which looked kind of interesting, and a museum about John

Knox, which didn't. And shops. Lots of shops. I could tell this had to be a main tourist drag.

I didn't stop to look in many of the windows. I mean, why would I want to shop for a kilt, anyway? I'm always trying to *fit into*, not *stand out from*, the crowd. And I was sure there were more guys in Emma City who owned Wranglers and cowboy hats than there were who owned kilts. Personally, I preferred to avoid both of those fashion statements.

The air got wetter as I walked up the hill until it felt like I was inside a cloud or something.

I crossed the street that was called South Bridge on one side of the intersection and North Bridge on the other, but neither side looked much like a bridge to me. And the name of the street I was on changed to High Street for no apparent reason.

"Crazy Scots," I muttered, but then I stopped to look at the building I was in front of. It was made of stone, like all the others, but it was black and moldy-looking in the dim, early morning light, like Casper the Ghost's dream home. It looked like a horror movie waiting to happen.

"Tron Kirk" the sign read, but all that made me think of was early computer animation movies. I couldn't see the connection, so I tried looking at the five or six painted signs standing all around the entrance, but those just advertised ghostwalks and tours of underground tunnels and stuff like that. Nothing explained what this strange building was.

I was still staring at the signs when I suddenly had this weird feeling I was being watched.

Normally, I don't worry much about being out alone when it's not light. My night vision's better than my day vision, so I can usually see trouble coming before it happens -- and get the heck out of there. Even my mom's not too concerned about it. Vampire-boy is safer than most teenagers when it comes to avoiding weirdos in the dark.

So I looked quickly to my left. There was a man, just standing there and staring at me. It was pretty strange, but he looked too much like something out of a Charles Dickens novel to be creepy. Seriously, the guy was about my mom's age, with cheeks that were pink from the cold air. He had short brown hair and was clean-shaven. All this gave him a wholesome look. He was wearing a blue jacket, a red plaid scarf, and dark glasses. If he'd ditched the glasses and added a top hat, he could've been Bob Cratchit off to find Tiny Tim.

He smiled at me. "'Kirk' means 'church' in Scots," he explained, as if he'd known what I was thinking. His accent was odd, but I could understand him fine, so I figured he wasn't one of those Glaswegian types.

"It used to be a church," he continued, "but it isn't needed as one now, so the floor was torn up to reveal the remains of the old closes below, and it was turned into a tourist information center."

I stared back at him. He was talking to me like he'd been my neighbor for years and we'd just bumped into each other at a local 7-Eleven, not like a total stranger in a foreign city at dawn.

"Uh, thanks," I said.

"You'll want to have a look inside when you come back this afternoon, then," he informed me. "It's quite brilliant what they've done with it."

"Uh, yeah. Sure," I said. How'd he know I was coming back in the afternoon? This was getting kind of freaky.

He nodded up the hill and said, "Be sure you notice where Mary King's Close is on your way to the castle."

Castle?! This place had a castle? I must've been way too busy being traffic-paranoid the day before if I'd missed something like that!

I looked up the hill, but even to my vampire eyes, the city just looked like a jumble of buildings all shoved too close together in the fog.

I was still trying to find the castle in the mist when the Cratchit-wannabe said, "I must be off now to pick up a few things at Tesco's before it gets too light. Cheers."

I waved my hand at him without turning around. If there was a castle up that hill, I just had to see it. After reading *Dracula*, I really wanted to go and --

Wait a second. What was that about "before it gets too light"?

I turned around and watched the man walk briskly around the corner and onto the street called South Bridge. He had a kind of bounce in his step, like he was really happy about something.

Why had he wanted to go someplace before it was *too light*? And why had he known I'd have to come back in the afternoon, when it wasn't so bright? *Could he possibly be a vampire*? But if he was, how'd he know that I was one? Did he check out my reflection in a hand mirror, the way I'd tried to do with people at the blood drive? Or did he just make a lucky guess about me?

I took a step toward South Bridge and then stopped.

What the heck was I doing?! Some guy waltzes out of *A Christmas Carol* and talks to me on the street, and I'm thinking of *following* him? He could be Jeffrey Dahmer's brother, for all I knew! Or worse, what if he was just an ordinary person and I made a fool of myself like I had with Keith? What kind of an idiot was I?

I shook my head over my own stupidity and hurried up the hill.

I did pass a place with a sign about an underground tour of Mary King's Close, but I didn't stop. I also passed another big, really cool-looking church, but I didn't stop there either. The sky was light gray now, and I wanted to make it to the top of the hill to see the castle before the sun came out for real.

The hill got steep and and the street got narrower. All I could see were the shops that lined the road, which had stones set in it, like cobblestones, only flat. Then, just at the top of the hill, everything opened up into this big parking lot kind of place -- and there was the castle, looking like something from way before the last couple of centuries.

It was awesome! It was all stone, perched up on top of this solid rock hill. There was this bridge over what I figured had once been the moat and little guard houses and towers and turrets and battlements -- all way above the rest of the city.

There was a dirt pathway that led down the steep hill next to the parking lot. I could see a big garden at its base and then another section of the city beyond that. Well, I could see a little bit of it, anyway; it was still pretty misty.

The whole place had to be about the coolest thing I'd ever seen in my life. Maybe it was because I was part vampire, but I was sure I could've handled living in a castle just fine.

Well, that was it: I knew where I was going to spend my afternoon once the sunny part of the day was over. And the morning was starting off nice and cloudy. This was a good omen; maybe I'd be able to leave the hotel earlier than I'd thought.

I half-ran down the long hill until I got past Tron Kirk, and then I realized I couldn't remember the names of the two closes that'd get me back to the hotel. I remembered one started with a "B" and one with a "C," so I thought I'd found the right place when I got to Blackfriar's Street, but when I got to the bottom, it didn't look right at all, so I went back up. I tried a couple of other random closes, but they didn't go anywhere except into courtyards. Finally, I turned down St. Mary's Street and found Holyrood Road at the bottom, so I knew I just had to follow it until I saw the hotel.

I was pretty sticky and sweaty from running around by the time I got back into the hotel room, but it was only a little after 7:00, and the sun wasn't very bright yet with so much mist, so it was all good.

Chapter Nine

Mom was brushing lint off of her navy blue blazer when I came in.

"Hi, honey," she said. "Your luggage was delivered from the airport." She nodded to where my green duffle bag now sat in the corner.

"Oh, good!" I said and went over to dig out a clean shirt. Mom's an experienced traveler, and she'd warned me to take extra underwear and socks in my backpack just in case something like this happened, so I was okay in that department, but I'd been wearing the same yellow polo shirt for about forty-eight hours now, and I wanted something different.

"I've got a meeting in the newer part of town at 9:00," Mom said, "but it'll take me forty minutes to get there by bus. Plus, I've got to stop for food someplace, so I'll need to leave by 7:30. I'll be back to the hotel by 6:00 PM or so, and I've got a surprise for you this evening."

I stopped digging in the bag. "Like what?" I asked.

She winked at me. "If I told you, then it wouldn't be a surprise," she said.

"Oh, sure. Tell me just enough to make me wonder about it. That's evil!" I grabbed a white Old Navy sweatshirt in my bag and pulled it out.

Mom laughed. "You can use my laptop to do your online homework this morning," she said. "I won't need to take it with me today because we'll be out touring the three possible sites for this new Paco's Taco Palace."

I took my polo shirt off and shoved it into the laundry sack Mom had put on the chest of drawers. "They have Mexican food here?" I asked.

"Not the fast food kind," she answered. "That's why the Paco people want to open a place in Edinburgh. They want to be the first ones."

She put her jacket on and fluffed her hair. I tried to look only at my pants sitting on the bed behind her in the mirror. That was all of me that looked normal, since I didn't have a shirt on and my whole chest looked like a diagram on an anatomy website.

"Can I go to the castle this afternoon?" I asked, watching how Mom's eyes never looked directly at my reflection.

Mom came over and sat down by me. "Sure," she said, putting one arm around me and ruffling up my hair with the other hand. "You'll like the castle. It has a military museum and bookstores. Oh, and be sure you see the tower they excavated by the restrooms. That part seems so old; I guess because it's never been restored."

She gave me a kiss on the forehead and continued, "I'll leave you some money for the castle and food -- enough for some souvenirs, too."

I leaned my head on her shoulder for a second or two. I had questions I wanted to ask her, but I didn't want to hurt her feelings by talking too much about my dad. I didn't want her to think she hadn't done a good enough job as a parent so I wanted to find him. And to be honest, I didn't really want to find *him*; I just wanted to know more about the vampire part of me.

Finally, I took a deep breath and asked, "Mom, was my dad, like, *Scottish* or anything? I really like that castle, and I was -- well, I just wanted to know if there were maybe any Scottish vampire castles in my ancestry somewhere."

Mom kissed me again, then said, "No, dear. You father was actually Irish -- not just Irish-American, but really from Northern Ireland. He was working in California on a green card when I met him. If I'd put his last name on your birth certificate instead of mine, you would've been Eric Kelly instead of Eric Wright. But your father wanted nothing to do with you, so I couldn't see the point in giving you his name."

"Aren't there castles in Ireland, though?" I asked, ignoring the name bit for right now, even though I'd never heard my dad's name before.

"Yes, quite a few," she said. "Maybe that's why you like castles, although, just so you know, my third great-grandpa was a Scot."

"Cool! So there *are* some Scottish castles in my history!" I said, pulling away and looking at her.

Mom laughed again. "Yes, but only in the background as scenery," she said. "The family line was made up of merchants. They lived in this city, not in the castle. And they weren't vampires."

"Maybe they knew some," I said, teasing her.

Mom stopped smiling. "Their descendants don't even know one," she said, shaking her head. "You know your grandparents disowned me when they found out I was pregnant. They've never even seen you."

She sounded close to crying. It's been about fifteen years, but she still gets upset. Not that I blame her. Losing your whole family would be pretty tough.

Anyway, I didn't want her to cry, so I said, "I know; let's send them a photo of me!"

"Terrific," she said, sniffing but smiling, "that would explain everything, I'm sure."

She took some money out of her purse -- strange bills of different sizes and colors with pictures of famous Scottish people on them. Then she blew her nose, gave me a hug, and started out the door.

"Get your homework done before you leave, and be back by 7:00 tonight, please," she said on her way out.

"Gotcha," I said, flipping open the laptop.

I had three e-mails from Kacey, all of which were basically complaining about why I wasn't returning her phone calls today. So she'd finally started calling me again? Huh. Go figure.

Hey,
I've gone to Scotland with my mom for the week.
My phone doesn't work here. Catchya later.
Eric

That'd take care of her. But Joseph's e-mail wasn't so easy.

Dude, where are you?
What's up with running away someplace just cuz you got suspended?
You could've at least taken me with you. lol.

Running away? Sure, Joseph was joking, but the words were like a punch in the jaw. Mom and I always left places when things got too hot under the old vampire collar for us. It was survival, wasn't it? How else could we keep ourselves out of trouble when people found out about me?

Feeling a little nauseous, I didn't answer Joseph's e-mail. I didn't want to think about it anymore. Instead, I did some reading on the nervous system and then worked on my paper about the terracotta warriors in Xi'an.

Just before I got suspended, Ms. Nielson had assigned our English class our first research paper, and everybody had been whining about it. Everybody but me, that is. I'd been taking classes online from the community college all year, and my mom had taught me how to write papers for them, so Nielson's paper on the author of our choice -- with only three sources -- didn't sound very hard compared to the other papers I'd written. I didn't even plan on starting it for a day or two yet.

I was pretty hungry by the time I finished my homework -- probably because I hadn't eaten anything since we'd gotten off the plane the night before -- but I also felt too lazy to go looking for food, so I just lay on the bed and listened to the rain on the windows. Well, I did for about five minutes, anyway. Then I was out cold for about three hours.

It was almost 2:00 PM when I woke up. At home, I wouldn't dare go outside so early, but the sky here was so thick with rain clouds that it looked like the sun was already going down. Still, I put sunscreen on just to be safe before I grabbed the money Mom had left for me, put on my jacket and dark glasses, and left the hotel. I went straight up the nearest close -- the one with all the steps -- to the street called Cannongate and then up the long hill to the castle. I wanted to spend all the time there I could.

And the castle totally rocked! It was more awesome than anything I'd ever read about or seen in a movie. It was built of grayish-brown stones right onto the rock of the hill. Parts of some of the walls were made of the natural rock -- from an old volcano, I read on a plaque. And some of the outer walls still had cannons pointing out of narrow openings. They don't use the cannons anymore, of course, but it was really cool to climb on top of them and look out over the city -- well, through the mist, anyway.

The absolute best thing in the castle was hands-off stuff, though. They called it the "Honors of Scotland," but it was really a sword and a crown that were used for the kings of Scotland before the country kind of merged with England back in Shakespeare's time.

Joseph would've loved the sword. That thing was wicked! But I didn't think the tower where they kept it was wheelchair accessible; I couldn't see elevators or ramps anywhere, and there were tons of stairs. Not that that would've stopped Joseph, though. He would've left his wheelchair at the bottom and walked up on his hands, like he'd done at school the time he wanted to see the balcony seats in the auditorium.

Okay, so I could skip answering the question about running away in his e-mail and just tell him about the Honors of Scotland instead. Yeah, that'd be good.

After I left the room-sized safe that held that stuff, I remembered to check out the tower by the restrooms (or "toilets," as they called them) that Mom had told me about. It was dark and damp inside with half-crumbled walls, and it smelled like dirt after a rainstorm.

It looked exactly like the crypt in Bela Lugosi's version of *Dracula* -- minus the coffins. And why everyone assumes vampires sleep in coffins is beyond me. I certainly don't sleep in one. Too crunched up. And too hard. Besides, the last time I checked, I wasn't dead.

The castle closed at 5:30, so I didn't have time to buy a souvenir book, but I figured some of the tourist shops on the main street would have stuff like that. The real problem was that I was hungry -- really hungry. And my head was starting to hurt a little, too.

I started looking for food and book shops as soon as I got back on the street. Right outside the castle parking lot, there was a store that sold kilts and sweaters. I looked at their displays on the history of the kilt, but I couldn't find any books about the castle.

Not very far away was a restaurant, but it was way too expensive. Then I found a tiny sandwich shop, but the sign said it only opened for lunch, which I thought was weird.

It was starting to get dark now, and it looked like it might rain soon, too. I took off my sunglasses and looked at my travel watch; it was almost 6:30. I'd been walking around for about four and a half hours this afternoon and I hadn't eaten since the night before. Duh. No wonder I was tired and had a headache.

I kept walking down the steep hill called Lawnmarket -- which was a pretty dumb name because there weren't any lawns anywhere, just sidewalks and buildings -- until it changed into High Street. I was on autopilot, looking for a fast food place or a grocery store. Preferably the grocery store. I wanted something raw and juicy. Okay, well, raw and *bloody*, really. I wasn't exactly craving oranges.

But there wasn't anything like a food store on this street, just shops and offices. And then there was that really big church.

I stood there in the plaza next to the street and just stared at the cathedral I'd passed this morning. Emma City certainly didn't have anything that big. I'd seen a couple of big cathedrals and temples in Seattle, San Francisco, Denver, and Salt Lake City, but this thing was so *old*. And I'd never seen so many pigeons in my whole life.

I was standing there wondering if Mary Poppins and Burt the chimney sweep would show up to give a tuppence to the bird woman, when I heard someone behind me say, "You look lost, mate. Can I help you find someplace?"

I turned around, and there was this guy -- he couldn't have been more than twenty-two or so -- in a dress shirt, suit coat, knee socks, and a plaid skirt. Okay, it was a kilt. But he was just standing there, holding a folded-up umbrella in one hand, and acting like it was perfectly normal to be dressed like that!

I almost laughed, but then I decided he might be able to help me out.

"Uh, yeah," I said, digging my hands deeper into my jacket pockets. "Do you know where I can find a grocery store or something around here?"

He twisted the left side of his face upward, raising the eyebrow and half-smiling, then said, "If you go down South Bridge and follow it about fifteen minutes, you'll find a Tesco's." He pointed directions with his umbrella.

I didn't feel like walking that far. "Is there anything closer?" I asked. "McDonald's? Pizza Hut?"

He smiled. "Fancy some American junk food, then? There's a Pizza Hut on Co'burn Street, but I think it's closed for remodeling. Still, there's a Mexican restaurant a wee bit farther down."

My stomach growled. Too bad Paco's Taco Palace wasn't open yet, but at least I could probably get an appetizer pretty fast in a restaurant. Mmm. Guacamole. I could definitely go for that. True, there's not much blood in an avocado, but a vampire does not live by blood alone, you know. Plus, I love Mexican food.

"How far away is the Mexican place?" I asked the kilted guy.

"Oh, just a minute or two," he said, then started pointing directions with the umbrella again. "Turn left before you reach Tron Kirk and go down Co'burn Street."

That didn't sound too hard. "Thanks," I said, took one step, then stopped and asked, "Uh, are you, like, here to help lost tourists or something?"

He laughed really loud, and I felt kind of stupid until he said, "No, mate, I'm just a nice kind of lad. I help wee grannies across the street and that sort of thing." Then I could tell he was laughing at himself and not at me. I grinned.

"Do you always dress like that?" I asked him.

He smiled again. "No, it's too posh for everyday. This is only for weddings and ceilidhs," he said, nodding up the hill. "Tonight's a ceilidh. I'm meeting my mates first in a flat off Lawnmarket at half six." He glanced at his phone and added, "And I'm late! Cheers." He waved the umbrella at me and hurried off.

It took me a few seconds to translate what he'd just said. Let's see, "mate" is friend, "flat" is apartment, "half-six" had to be the time. But what the heck was a "ceilidh"? Some kind of party, I figured.

I shook my head. "Gotta tell Joseph about this guy," I muttered. Men in kilts. Too bizarre.

I was a little more alert after that conversation, so I found a street with a plaque that read "Cockburn" pretty fast and headed down toward that guacamole.

Chapter Ten

Cockburn Street twists downhill like a rattlesnake. I doubt there are very many rattlesnakes in Scotland, but I got messed up with some fangs about halfway down the hill anyway.

It was starting to get pretty dark with all those clouds, and there was a misty rain falling as I walked down the right-hand side of the street, past the closed-for-remodeling Pizza Hut, and toward the sign with a sombrero on it, which was sticking out at an odd angle from a stone doorway. My mind was on that guacamole.

There were a lot of people out on the sidewalk, looking in store windows, and I started to notice that most of these people were wearing black. All black, or black with red heavy metal band logos printed on their shirts. It could only mean one thing: goths. I smiled.

We don't really have any goths in Emma City. They apparently don't hang out where rodeo is considered a sport and where the "nightlife" consists of one all-night truck stop café. Of course, my dad had been into that sort of thing; Mom had told me once that he used to wear all black, all the time. But that had been in California, not in a small town in Utah.

I started past a gothic clothing store with lots of *Rocky Horror Picture Show* t-shirts in the window, but the last t-shirt caught my eye, so I stopped to stare. It had a picture of red lips with two white fangs poking out in what was probably supposed to be a sexy way. Underneath the lips it said, "Be a blood donor."

Fangs! Real vampires don't have fangs. At least I don't. My cuspid teeth are super-sharp, sharp enough that I cut up my own mouth a lot when I chew too fast, so it's a good thing my saliva heals up wounds almost immediately. But my teeth aren't extra long and pointy.

I smirked at the shirt.

"What's so funny?" The voice came from the side of me, so I turned to face it.

Or face *them*, really. There were four goths -- two guys, two girls, all about eighteen or so -- standing there and scowling at me. And one of the girls was wearing the same t-shirt that I'd been laughing at. I could see it in spite of her half-zipped, black leather jacket.

She and the other girl were also wearing black miniskirts and combat boots. I thought they looked pretty stupid, actually.

"I just thought the t-shirt was kind of funny," I told her. She didn't scare me, although it was obvious she thought she should.

The guy next to Ms. T-shirt took a step forward. He turned down the collar of his trench coat (black, of course), revealing a white, frilly-collared shirt that looked like something Thomas Jefferson might have worn to a party. I sincerely hoped that my father had never worn anything like that in his goth days.

"It's not a joke," the Thomas Jefferson guy said, shaking back his straggly rasta hair and pushing his high, fancy collar down on his neck. "She needs donors now that the Master has initiated her."

There was a purple blotch on his neck and two clear puncture marks just over the carotid artery.

My eyes widened and my saliva glands started to work -- really hard.

I didn't say anything for a few seconds; I had too many thoughts to sort through all of them.

She'd *drunk* his blood? She was a *vampire*? My dad had hung out with goths, so maybe she was doing the same thing. Was she full-blooded or half? Would she talk to me and answer my questions?

This was so cool! I'd actually found another vampire!

Her eyes, though. Her irises were normal-sized, while mine resembled Lady GaGa's in the "Bad Romance" video. But maybe not all vampires had the freaky eyes.

And that purple spot on the guy's neck. Blood. Maybe one of these people would let me have some, too. I was so hungry I could almost feel the warmth of his blood running down my --

Wait a second. How come there were marks?

My face started to burn as I realized I'd almost sucked this up like a sponge. Crap. These people weren't for real! My emotions went for a spin-dive and anger was my best defense to cover the mess of crashed hopes.

I scowled at the guy's neck, then looked at Ms. T-shirt and sneered a little, even though I had to wipe saliva from my mouth as I asked, "Did *you* bite him?"

She ran a hand up the back of his thigh and he smiled at her. "I did," she told me.

"So, are you *pretending* to be a vampire or what?" I asked her, letting my skepticism sound in my tone of voice.

She slunk a little closer to me. I didn't know it was possible for any girl to walk sexy in combat boots, but she was trying. I wiped my mouth again and she smiled at me. I guess she thought I was drooling over her.

"That's what makes a vampire, love," she crooned at me. "You're not frightened of blood-drinkers, are you?"

A short laugh burst out of my mouth. As if!

I shook my head at her and rolled my eyes. "Not even," I told her, then added, "But, *if* you're a vampire, why are there teethmarks on his neck?"

All of them laughed as if I'd said something stupid. "Only the Master can drink without leaving marks," Ms. T-shirt told me.

I rolled my eyes again. So she thinks she has connections with Dracula or something. What a wannabe. "Look," I said, "I'm glad I made you laugh, but I need to get some food; I'm hungry."

She stopped laughing and grabbed my arm. "I'm hungry, too," she said, in a fake-seductive voice, "and I'd like to invite *you* for dinner."

Whoa. She wanted to drink *my* blood? Ha! That'd be a laugh! Like she'd be able to get it out of my arteries. It coagulates so fast that only big gashes bleed much for me.

"Sorry," I said. "No dice." I hadn't meant to say anything else, but somehow I found myself staring at the wound on the Jefferson-dude's neck and adding, "Not unless I get to do the drinking." Dang, I was hungry.

They all looked at me for a second or two -- stunned, kind of like a bunch of dogs who've just smacked into a sliding glass door they'd thought was open. Apparently these people weren't used to preppy American teenagers offering to drink blood with them.

In a second or two, the light-haired guy -- the one who didn't look like Thomas Jefferson with dreadlocks -- said, "He's serious."

And suddenly, I was serious -- and seriously stupid. I'd managed to forget how awful I'd been feeling about biting Kacey and almost biting Brendan and Mr. Wendall. I also didn't care if these dweebs knew I was a real vampire or not. All I could think about was not looking like a dumb kid who believed them. And about blood. And it seemed like I could combine those two things right then.

"Of course I'm serious," I said. "I told you I was hungry."

The girl in the fang t-shirt did about the most bizarre thing I'd ever seen: she opened her mouth wide, curling her upper lip into a snarl so that her filed-to-a-point cuspids were visible, and she *hissed*. I swear it; she really did.

Okay, this chick had seen one too many episodes of *Dark Shadows*.

I laughed again, but she was too caught up in her own little melodrama to pay attention to my mocking. She motioned me into the nearby Fleshmarket Close, and her groupies came along.

We went down a few stairs, past a fish-and-chips shop on the first landing, then down another short flight of stairs to a sloping alleyway that seemed to cower between the four-story buildings on either side. As soon as we'd stopped, five or six more goths in black lace, Megadeath t-shirts, or trench coats showed up so fast it was like they'd crawled out of the brick. All we needed now was a little of Bach's "Cantata and Fugue in D Minor," and then Gomez Addams would've felt right at home.

Ms. T-shirt spread her arms out wide and said to this circle of "Thriller"-extra wannabes, "This boy wishes to become a child of the night. Shall he feed? Yea? Or nay?"

"Yea," came a chorus of voices.

Unbelievable. I looked around to see if I could spot a camera somewhere. Someone had to be filming this for YouTube, right? But all I could see was that the clouds were breaking up a little, way above the narrow close I was in. It had stopped raining, but it was pretty dark -- too dark for filming, so this had to be for real. I wiped the slobber from my mouth again.

"Look," I said, "we can skip the ceremony bit here. I'm already a --"

"Who shall feed him and initiate him into the cult of blood?" she continued, putting her arms above her head and turning slowly in a circle. I wondered if this was what she did every time she wanted to drink blood. I certainly didn't plan on trying this with Hank Jackson's sheep any time soon.

Suddenly, someone stepped out of the circle toward me. He was wearing all black, without any color at all. And he was way older than the others. His light brown hair was uncombed, but I could still see that his hairline was receding from the corners of his forehead. His skin was an unhealthy whitish-color, except around his eyes, where it was kind of red and sunken, and around his chin, where it looked dirty from the razor stubble growing there.

He swayed a little as he moved, like he might fall over, but his voice was clear enough when he pointed at the blond guy from the original foursome I'd met and announced, "The Phantom shall feed the initiate." Then he kind of stared off into the crowd like he'd lost interest in the whole situation.

I figured he might be drunk, but I'd never really seen a drunk before, so I wasn't completely certain. All I knew for sure was that I didn't want this guy anywhere near me.

The blond guy immediately bowed his head like he was praying or something. Maybe he was asking a blessing on the food. But he *was* the food. Weird. Seriously weird.

But Ms. T-shirt wasn't through yet. "The will of the Night Children has been voiced by the Master: the Phantom will provide the food!" she said, rather too loudly for someone who was about to be part of feeding blood to a minor.

This was too much. When she finally shut up, I folded my arms across my chest and said, "So, can I eat now, or should I go find a Burger King?" Cocky, I know, but she was getting on my nerves. Which is probably why I totally forgot about common sense at this point. I wanted food, and I wanted to show her she wasn't a real vampire. Hunger and irritation: bad mix. The result is pure stupidity.

"Wait," she said, holding out one palm toward me, "You have not prepared your teeth. You will have need of this." With her free hand, she pulled a knife with a three-inch blade out of a sheath attached to that leather mini-skirt of hers.

I should've been scared at this point. I mean, hanging out with people who carry large knives is not normally my kind of thing. But I was in idiot mode, so I just said, "I won't need it, thanks." And I took hold of the blond guy's bare, outstretched arm. I'd show her how sharp a *real* vampire's teeth were!

Blood. I started fingering the soft skin of the inner elbow where the arteries are near the surface. I could feel the throb of the liquid -- too fast; he was nervous.

I looked up at him, not paying enough attention to how quiet the others had gotten, thinking only of the blood. After swallowing as much spit as I could, I said quietly, "Relax. You won't feel it; I promise. My saliva will numb your skin and heal the wounds. Really, it's okay. Just breathe deeply now."

He wasn't as upset as Mr. Wendall had been when I hypnotized him, and I didn't want to put him to sleep like I'd done with Kacey, so I kept it short. And the low, soft tones worked, as always. His breathing got deeper and his pulse slowed. Just like a sheep.

I smiled.

"You must take the knife. All initiates must use the knife."

Not with my teeth, girl. I ignored her, closing my eyes to shut out my eerie audience, and licked my tongue over the blond goth guy's inner elbow to numb it like I'd promised. Then I bit quickly, puncturing the skin. I never even thought about using my trusty vampire night vision to check his arm for other puncture marks. Like other teethmarks. Or *needle* marks. No, I was too busy being stupid.

Gulps. I was so hungry I drank in gulps, not worrying about whether or not I'd leave a bruise. Not worrying about anything. So, it was only after six or seven gulps that I realized there was an odd taste in the sweetness in my mouth. It was *too* sweet -- then bitter as it slid to the back of my tongue. I'd never tasted blood like that. It wasn't even like my own blood, which is completely gross and bitter-tasting -- never sweet.

Something was wrong here.

I licked over the wound to coagulate his strange blood and close the openings, then wiped the saliva and blood off my own chin. The blond guy had gone very, very pale -- almost as pale as the older guy who'd volunteered him to be my dinner.

"Uh, thanks," I said, timidly. Then I glanced around at the others.

I don't know what I was expecting at that point -- like they were merely going to wish me a pleasant evening and leave after I'd just swallowed their friend's blood and proved I didn't need a knife to get it -- but I know I wasn't expecting what happened when their stunned silence was broken.

"Master?" Ms. T-shirt asked tentatively, turning wide-eyed toward the older guy in all black. She looked dazed.

But the pale man didn't look at her; he was staring straight at me out of those creepy, darkened eye sockets. Even with my great night vision, he looked wrong -- unhealthy, almost un-earthly. And his eyes, they looked totally black, his pupils dilated until his large irises disappeared completely. Really large irises. Too large for an ordinary human being.

Oh my gosh! Was he a *real* vampire?!

After about two seconds, the guy reached toward me and grabbed my arm. His fingernails, I noticed, were ringed with dirt. Ugh. I cringed backward, but there was no place to go, no break in the human wall that encircled me, this pale man, and the t-shirt queen.

He looked at me through narrowed eyes. "Where do you live, boy?" he asked me, scowling. A puff of his breath hit me in the face. It reeked of tobacco smoke.

I pulled my arm away from him, glad my jacket had kept him from touching my skin. "Uh, I'm, uh, not from around here," I said, glancing around for a way to escape. But for about five seconds, he just kept glaring at me. None of the others said anything, either. Even Ms. T-shirt had shut up.

Fear was bubbling up inside of me. Was he going to follow me to the hotel? He might be a vampire, but what if he was some kind of pervert? Or a murderer? Holy crap. What had I gotten myself into?! This was *not* how I'd wanted to have a conversation with another vampire.

About right then it would've been nice to have had Dracula's powers. Hey, I could've turned into a bat and flapped off. Like a bat out of -- well, like a bat.

But it turned out my own powers were enough. Just at the moment when the pale man seemed ready to speak again, the blond guy they called the Phantom decided to prove he shouldn't be first in line to donate to the Red Cross any time soon. He'd lost about a cup of blood to be my dinner, and... he fainted. Plop. Right onto the steps going back up to Cockburn Street.

My whole cocky attitude had been sucked right out of me when the Master-guy grabbed my arm. This was frickin' scary! Before anyone else reacted, I stepped over their unconscious friend and ran up the two flights of stairs as fast as I could.

Chapter Eleven

I went up Cockburn Street rather than down it. I no longer wanted the guacamole; all I wanted was to get back to the safety of the hotel, even if I had to run like a terrorized rabbit, dodging around people instead of expecting them to get out of my way.

I paused for a second and looked back when I got to the top of the street, but the Jefferson-Dreadlocks guy and the scary maybe-vampire had emerged from Fleshmarket Close and were running toward me, so I took off down toward Cannongate as fast as I could.

Because I stay inside most days, I don't normally do much running. I'm fast enough, but when my body heats up, I usually feel kind of sick to my stomach. And just then I had a stomach full of warm blood that was sloshing around. And it was funny-tasting blood at that.

I felt like I had a gut full of mop water. Blech.

But I kept running. The cars were stopped in all four directions at the intersection to let pedestrians cross, so I ran across it diagonally. My heart and head were both pounding.

I began to check the metal plates that identified each close, looking for the ones that started with either "B" or "C" -- because one of those would lead me to the hotel. But how far down were they? Cannongate was the right street, but where were those two closes?

Blackfriar's? No, that's a street; it's too wide.

I kept running. South Gray's, Hyndford's, Fountain, World's End. World's End? That didn't sound very promising.

Another intersection -- a busy one: St. Mary's Street. Was this where I'd been this morning? I couldn't remember.

I stopped and looked back up the way I'd come, heaving in breaths and trying not to heave up anything else, but the first thing I saw was the scary guy, pushing a lady out of his way as he came rushing down the hill, only half a block away from me, with Mr. Jefferson-Dreadlocks right behind him.

Yikes!

I ran into the intersection, dodged a car, and ignored the honking horns. I had to get back to the hotel!

More closes, a big gate that I didn't remember seeing before. Was I still going the right way? Sugarhouse Close. Then Bakehouse Close.

Bakehouse? It started with "B." Was that it? It had to be!

I ducked into the alleyway, but there were no steps! Didn't the "B" close have all those steps? Or was that the "C" close?

I weaved around a couple of trash cans and kept going -- but suddenly I was looking at a building. The close wasn't straight, but turned left ninety degrees there. This wasn't it! Wrong close! Shoot!

I wheeled around to retreat, but I saw the two goths starting down toward me. I had no other choice but to follow the close to the left -- and all too soon to another left. I hesitated. The sign said "Cooper's Close." That meant a "B" close next to a "C" close. But neither one led to Holyrood Road and the hotel. Where the heck was I?

Cooper's Close went straight, but there was a left turn that said "Wilson's Close," so I took it. I wasn't even sure where I was heading now, but I was positive that I didn't want my life to end in a deserted back alleyway in Scotland, so I just ran.

Wilson's Close curved around like a fishhook and put me back on Cannongate. I shot out it like I was coming out of a slide at a water park -- and I plowed right into a man.

"Oh, gosh. Sorry!" I half-yelled, pulling away from him and trying not to hit anyone else.

Then I looked at him: clean-shaven, rosy cheeks, plaid scarf. It was the Bob Cratchit guy from this morning! But he wasn't wearing the dark glasses this time.

"Oh, good," he said to me. "I've been looking all over for you!"

What the ---?! Not *another* freak out to get me! And why him? What did he want? Maybe he really was some pervert after teenage boys. Well, I didn't want to find out. I had enough going on right then.

I darted across the street as fast as I could and into the first available opening between buildings. The sign on the archway said "Dunbar Close." I knew it wouldn't take me to the hotel, but it would take me away from the men chasing me. I hoped.

I was expecting more trash cans and darkened doorways, but I got a surprise: a garden.

No joke. It was some kind of ornamental garden with trimmed bushes, neat paths, and big hedges. Not what I'd expected after all those narrow closes.

I turned right down a path and right again. A metal gate. Clear to the top of the archway. Obviously, I wasn't exiting this way. Crud.

I spun around to go back the way I'd come, but the Cratchit guy for sure must've seen me come in, and the others might have noticed as well. I decided to look for an exit at the other end of the garden.

Stomach still churning, I ran as fast as I could to the opposite end of the uneven stone path, turning my ankle. Pain burned up my leg, but I kept moving.

Stairs! I started down, but -- oh, no! There was a brick wall! Stairs going into a wall!! How stupid was that?!

I went back up and turned right, but found only more garden, bordered by a stone wall. I stopped on the little patch of lawn behind the hedge. No one would be able to see me unless they actually entered this area of the garden. I had a few seconds to think.

I leaned over, resting my hands on my knees. I wanted to puke. I felt like my head was going to fall off and roll under a shrub. And I couldn't seem to get enough air.

Still, my eyes were working just fine, so, when I looked up, it took about a second for me to notice that the stone wall nearly covered by the branches of a huge tree in the far corner of the garden was only about five feet high. I could climb a five foot wall -- even with a stinging ankle.

I could hear footsteps slapping hard and fast on the path beyond the hedge, and adrenaline took over my actions. In about three seconds, I was over the garden wall.

I didn't even have to jump the whole way; there was a ledge thing sticking about six inches out of the stone. I stepped onto it and then kind of toppled down about three feet onto my hands and knees on a spongy, mossy surface -- a large rectangle between two other short stone walls.

Where the heck was I *now*? I stared around, trying to make sense of the place, clutching my heaving stomach with one hand.

The next rectangle down from me had a patch of grass. And there were more rectangles of grass in terraces going down a hill to my right and connected by paths. And there were stones: big, cut stones with writing on them, some like pillars, some built right into the walls that bordered the terraces. The stone I'd stepped on was a crumbling part of a similar one.

Tombstones. They were frickin' *tombstones!* I was a vampire in a graveyard. Swell.

Then it dawned on me: the Hitchcock graveyard I'd passed this morning! I must be near the closes that led to the hotel. If I could get back to the street without being caught --

"He climbed over! I saw him!"

I froze. The voice came from over the wall. I didn't dare breathe.

But then a different voice said, "And you'll leave him alone, Sean. I'll not stand by helpless this time."

"You?! And just what the f--?" Was that voice number one or voice number three? I couldn't tell.

"Yeah, bugger off, you -- Hey!"

I heard a smack and a thud, followed by more scuffling and cursing. Uh, oh. Not good.

I stood halfway up in a crouch and staggered to my right, where the ground sloped to a gravel path between the terraced plots of grass. At least there should be some good places to hide in an old cemetery. It wasn't clear to me just who'd hit whom on the other side of that wall, but I wasn't about to wait around to find out who was coming after me and whether they'd climb the wall or go to the graveyard gate.

Actually, a lot of things were no longer clear to me. My brain felt fuzzy with trying to think. Still holding my stomach with one hand, I limped as quickly as I could down the path, which had a few stairs every twenty feet or so to keep it even with the terraced ground. I could see buildings at the bottom of the hill, so I hoped there'd be a gate or something there where I could get out unseen -- unless there was another stupid stairway leading to a wall, like in the garden.

My sore ankle turned again on an uneven step at the bottom of the hill, but I kept moving, turned the corner, and -- ah, ha! An arched doorway! I went through it -- and discovered that I was in a box. There was a gravestone in the wall, but no way to get to the buildings behind it.

I stood there dazed for a second or two, then went back to the path and listened, but my hearing isn't extra-good like my night vision is, so the fact that I couldn't hear anything didn't really make me feel better. I still didn't know if anyone had followed me into the cemetery.

Maybe I could climb one of these walls and.... My stomach lurched. No, I couldn't. These were too high. I was going to have to hide and wait until I felt better.

I was standing in front of a short stone tower with only bars for a roof. I stumbled in because I couldn't think of a better plan. The walls were blotched with moss and the corners were filled with broken beer bottles and used syringes. So, this was a place where drug users came to stay hidden. Maybe it'd keep me out of sight, too -- at least from anyone who hadn't seen me go into it.

I leaned against the wall in the corner to the left of the doorway and tried not to retch. I'd never been this sick from running before. But then I'd never been so freakin' scared in my whole life, either.

What if whoever had won the fight found me? I'd either have to fight him or run. I hoped I could still run without falling over.

I looked at my watch. Crap. It was almost 7:30! Mom'd kill me when I got back to the hotel! That is, if someone else didn't do it for her first.

Pity that vampires aren't really immortal. I bet Dracula never felt this close to barfing when he was being chased.

I had to lean my head back against the wall to keep any sense of balance. I could breathe better now that I wasn't running, but I felt so sick! Why? Running shouldn't make me feel this awful, should it? Even if I was scared?

Mindlessly, I stared at the plaque on the back wall. It was engraved with:

Robert Suttie
third son of
Sir George Suttie, Baronet of Balcone
Born April 1776
Died February 1843

So I was standing in the tomb of a rich guy who'd been dead for way over a hundred years. I hoped he didn't mind sharing the place for awhile. Hey, a scared half-vampire had to be better than a drug user, right?

Suddenly my thoughts were interrupted by the sound of crunching gravel. Someone was walking on the path toward my hiding place. I tensed up.

The crunching stopped. Whoever it was must be right outside. My heart was racing, but I held my breath. Please, God, don't let me die this young.

"Eric?" It was a male voice.

As far as I knew, the only person (besides me) in Scotland who knew my name was my mother. And unless Mom'd had intensive testosterone injections this afternoon, this voice was not hers.

So how the -- oh, shoot. I could see a shadow on Robert Suttie's plaque. Well, at least it was only *one* shadow. Maybe I'd have a chance.

As the owner of the shadow stepped inside the tower, I threw my entire body weight -- a massive 120 pounds or so -- into him, hoping to knock him off balance so I could run for it.

And it worked. Well, the first part did, anyway. I did knock him over. But I knocked myself over, too. Right on top of him. Temporarily.

By then I was so dizzy that I couldn't figure out which way was up for about ten seconds, and when I got my senses back, I realized that "up" was above my face.

He'd pinned me flat on my back, his hands on my shoulders, his knee in my stomach. And that last part was a mistake.

I wish I could say I threw him off with brute force. But what I did was throw up. That made him move fast, though, and I managed to roll over before things got really gross.

Actually, that's when I finally realized I was safe. He -- whoever he was, Jefferson gothic or Dickens dude -- could've hurt me pretty easily at that point, but he just waited while I retched up what seemed like a gallon of blood mixed with gastric fluids.

I could hardly move when I finished, but he took hold of my shoulders and pulled me away from the steaming, revolting, sticky puddle now disgracing the weeds of Mr. Suttie's tomb. And he handed me a little package of tissues.

I wiped my mouth and hands, then wrapped the used tissues in a couple of clean ones and shoved the wad into my jacket pocket.

I turned to thank the guy, but the effort made my head feel like it was going to explode.

Still, I recognized him. It was Bob Cratchit. With a cell phone to his ear. Now that was something you didn't see every day.

He smiled at me as he took the unused tissues back, but he was talking into the phone.

"Kim?" he said. "I've got him, but he's been sick, so I -- What? No, he's *vomited*. No, no -- he's fine now. Where are you? Right. Take a taxi to Cannongate Kirk and walk to the north side of the kirkyard, then. I'll watch for you. Cheers, love."

I vaguely wondered how Bob Cratchit knew my mother's name and whether or not Tiny Tim would be coming along in the taxi. Then I passed out.

Chapter Twelve

Weak afternoon sunlight was sneaking in around the closed curtains in the hotel room when I opened my eyes.

I had a headache and I was incredibly hungry, but otherwise I felt okay. Well -- kind of grimy, actually. I was still in the same sweatshirt and pants from the day before, although Mom had obviously taken off my shoes and jacket for me.

Mom. Was she at work? Maybe she'd left a note. I turned and half sat up to face the other bed.

Mom's bed was neatly made, and Bob Cratchit -- fully clothed, but obviously dozing -- was lying on top of it.

I sat up all the way and threw back the covers. I needed to figure this one out.

Okay, the clock said 3:06 PM. Mom must be at work since I obviously hadn't been sick enough to go to the hospital. And she'd told me yesterday that she had a surprise for me that evening. Had to be this guy. He'd known my name in the cemetery. He'd called Mom on his cell phone. He obviously worked nights since he'd been on his way *home* yesterday morning when I saw him at that Tron Kirk place.

So, Mom must've been a little worried about leaving me all alone and sick while she went with the Taco Palace people, so she'd asked him to come to the hotel when he got off work this morning and stay with me, just in case.

Yeah. Cool. It all fit. Except for one thing: who was he? Someone she worked with? Her new boyfriend? And how do you wake up a total stranger who's asleep in your hotel room? "Excuse me. Do you know Ebenezer Scrooge?" Nyah. Skip it.

As it turned out, I didn't have to wake him up. The noise of my taking a shower did it for me. So, by the time I was dry, coming out of the bathroom with brushed teeth and clean clothes, he was sitting up and looking at a magazine.

He stood up as I walked in, sticking out his hand for me to shake. "It's about time I properly introduced myself," he said, tossing the magazine on the bed. "I'm Patrick, and I met your mother about two months ago through her job. I do maintenance and updates on computer systems, and we -- by fate or accident -- were in the same office at the same time very early one morning last January." He smiled.

He seemed likable enough. And his handshake wasn't the kind you get from a salesman working on commission, either.

I decided to skip all the subtle stuff and go for the throat. Uh, figuratively speaking that is -- even though I was way hungry.

"So, are you my mom's friend or her boyfriend?" I asked. But I tried not to look angry so he wouldn't think I resented him or anything. Because I didn't. In fact, he seemed cool enough that I was kind of hoping Mom *was* dating him.

"I hope to be the latter," he said. "But it's a bit early in the relationship. We've had only four dates."

"Well," I said, turning to grab the dirty clothes bag off the chest of drawers, "if I'd known that last night, I wouldn't have -- Holy crap!!"

I'd forgotten the mirror was right there, reflecting my weird alien skin and veins very clearly. But the fact that Patrick would be able to see all that was not what had startled me.

Next to my green polo shirt in the mirror was a blue sweater and beige chinos -- and THE SAME TRANSLUCENT SKIN AS MINE.

Patrick grinned, then deliberately pulled off his tinted glasses and turned to face the mirror. My gaze followed his motions, and I ended up staring at the two of us, side by side, with demon-red retinas glowing through the nearly-clear, overly-large, inhuman irises of our eyes.

Coolest. Thing. Ever.

When I remembered that my mouth could move, I stammered out, "You're -- you're a *vampire*!" to the mirror. Even though I'd suspected it earlier, it was still hard to believe.

"That I am indeed," Patrick said. He was grinning like he was pretty pleased with himself.

"Dude!" I yelled, throwing my dirty clothes onto the bed and sitting down. "That rocks!"

He laughed. "There's quite a bit to explain," he told me. "I would've told you more last night if you hadn't been under the influence of a controlled substance."

"Huh?" I said. "Look, if you think I do drugs --"

He laughed again. "Not you -- directly," he said and sat down on the opposite bed. "Whose blood did you drink?" he asked.

"I drank drugged blood?!" Holy Hannah! No wonder I'd puked and been so dizzy!

"Very probably," he said. "Now, why don't you tell me your side of the events of last night? And then I'll share my version of the tale."

Well, if Mom trusted this guy -- this *vampire*, who would understand more than just being careful around mirrors, who'd understand what it was like to crave blood so much that you couldn't think straight -- then that was good enough for me. I spilled everything that'd been crammed up inside me. I talked on and on about how I couldn't seem to control myself lately. How I'd bitten Kacey. How I'd wanted to bite Michael. How close I'd come to biting Brendan and Mr. Wendall. How I'd bitten the goth without even trying to control myself.

And Patrick listened -- really listened, asking questions about the vegetarianism, about when I'd eaten and what I'd eaten each time I'd wanted to bite, about how much and what kind of blood I drank. He seemed surprised about the telekinesis, but he asked me all kinds of details about the pale man who'd been with the goth teenagers.

Then Patrick told me about how he'd recognized me yesterday morning from my mom's descriptions and how he and my mom had been out looking for me -- in different areas -- last night when I'd smacked right into him. He'd run after me, only to find himself also chasing the Jefferson gothic and the pale man into the garden.

"I'm sure those two were high on something -- probably heroin," he said, "so it's likely that their blond friend whose blood you drank was in a similar state."

"I drank heroin-laced blood?" I said. "Gross! No wonder it tasted funny!"

"And we vampires tend to be extra-sensitive to any mind-altering substance, which would explain how ill you were. That's why it is very important to avoid drinking blood unless you're certain it's safe," he said.

"That's the first and the last time; I swear," I said. "Uh, as long as I can control myself, that is. And I'm not very good at that." I paused for a second and then asked him the question I was dying to know the answer to, "Can you teach me how? I mean, what do *you* do?"

He smiled, looked at his watch, then walked over to the window and peered around the curtains at the now-dim light. When he turned back to me, he looked very pleased again.

"It's dark enough now," he said, picking up my jacket from a chair and tossing it to me. "I'll do more than just tell you; I'll take you to do something about your self-control."

I put my jacket on while he got his own from a hook behind the door. "Okay," I said. "Where are we going?"

"Do you realize," he asked me, "that, by what you've told me, every time lately you've had problems controlling your urges to bite a person, you've been overly hungry?"

I just stood there. Michael. Kacey. Brendan. Wendall. The phantom goth. Yep, Patrick was right; it all tallied up.

"You're not eating enough or regularly enough, for one thing," he said, putting a hand on my shoulder. "You get too hungry, and then the bloodlust kicks in. It still happens to me when I'm not careful. That's why we're going to get food. *Now.* You need it."

It had happened to him. He understood. Really understood -- not just empathy, like Mom. Patrick really *knew* what it felt like to crave blood and lose control and be ashamed of it.

I grinned.

"And I think you ought to get more animal blood every week, too," he continued. "That will help a great deal. I try to get some three or four times a week. Every day, if possible."

I didn't know quite how to feel. Or what to say. Or do. It was like I suddenly had a dad. I kind of wanted to hug him, but that seemed a little creepy with a guy I'd just met. So I just stood there and felt stupid for a second or two.

Finally, I worked up the guts to say, "Geez, this is like having an uncle or a brother or something."

It was a lame thing to say, but Patrick didn't seem to notice. He opened the door and ushered me through it, handing me the hotel room key at the same time. "First cousin once removed, actually," he said.

"What?"

Patrick stepped out into the hall with me and closed the door. "My full name is Patrick Michael Kelly," he said, "and I am the first cousin of Sean Kelly. We're both from Belfast, originally. I moved here to Edinburgh when I heard he had. The family had hoped I could find him again."

Kelly. I'd heard that name recently. But where?

"Who's Sean Kelly?" I asked.

"Your father," Patrick said.

I stared at him. What the --? Suddenly, I pictured Darth Vader saying, "Luke, I am your father." Except that Patrick wasn't evil. Still, how many bombs could get dropped on a kid in one day?

"We have much to discuss," Patrick continued, motioning to me to follow him, "but there's a brilliant pizza restaurant just at the base of Crichton Close where we can eat and talk at the same time."

But I wasn't about to go anywhere just yet. "You -- you know my dad?" I stammered, clutching the hotel room key like it was attempting to escape.

Patrick sighed slightly. "Unfortunately, yes," he said. "Your father is the sort that gives vampires a bad reputation. I've been hoping that he might change, but after --"

"What do you mean?"

Patrick answered carefully, like he was afraid he might tell me something I shouldn't know. "Well, he used to kill animals -- often the neighbors' pets -- unnecessarily, and then leave their bodies for people to find," he said.

"That's *sick!*"

"And once he attacked a girl coming home from the cinema," he said, scowling as if he could see it in front of him there in the dusty hotel hallway. "She was walking alone. He pulled her into an alley and drank her blood violently, without hypnotizing her, and she fainted. It wasn't enough blood to do her any real harm, of course, because no vampire could possibly drink that much at one time, but I have no doubt she was deeply traumatized by the experience."

My mouth was so dry it felt sticky when I spoke. "Who told you he did that?" I asked.

Patrick shook his head. "No one told me," he said quietly, starting down the hallway toward the stairs, "I was there with him, but I was younger -- only about your age -- and smaller, so I couldn't stop him. I did, however, go back to the cinema and tell the manager I'd found a girl in the alley. I was too afraid of Sean to report him to the police." He paused at the top step and stared at the flowered carpet for a few seconds. "I've always been ashamed of that," he added.

Dang. My dad was messed. I'd always assumed that he was a jerk because he'd dumped my mom rather than face the responsibilities of getting married and being a parent, but now it was obvious I'd had it backwards: he'd dumped my mom *because* he was a jerk, not the other way around.

"My dad must be total scum!" I said, kind of too loud. "How could my mom have even dated him?!"

Patrick had started down the stairs, but he talked as he went. "Sean can be very charming -- and manipulative," he said. "Perhaps she was fooled because she was quite young at the time, but from what she's told me, I gather that he used his vampiric hypnosis powers on her at least once, which resulted in your birth." I could see the tops of his ears turning red as he explained, and he seemed to be forcing himself not to look back up at me.

My head felt like it was filled with helium as I followed Patrick down the steps in silence. Good thing my dad hadn't stuck around. It was bad enough being a vampire without having a psycho-vamp dad around, slashing the neighbors' poodles and giving every Halloween trick-or-treater much more than they'd bargained for. I *never* would've had any friends if my dad had lived with us. Really, I mean, like, who'd let their kid come over to hang out if my dad wanted to lap up some of their O-positive? So all this meant I had the genes of some sick, perverted man who had tricked my mother and then --

Patrick stopped at the door and put his hand on my shoulder again. "Are you all right, Eric?" he asked.

"Huh? Oh, sorry. Yeah, I'm okay."

He just looked at me for a second or two, then said, "You're not at all like your father, you know. Not even physically."

It was like his words hurt. My eyes started to water. "But I've attacked people before," I kind of whispered. My voice had gone all raspy-sounding. "There was Andy at the sleepover when I was ten and Carla at the Halloween party when I was twelve. Oh, and that girl in Seattle when I was nine. And now Kacey and almost Michael and---"

Patrick's grip on my shoulder was tighter now.

"Listen, Eric," he said, shaking me a little, "losing control isn't the same thing as a pre-meditated attack or something done just to be vicious. You have never intended to frighten or harm anyone as your father often did."

Oh, yeah. That was true. Something that was wound up inside me started to loosen a little.

Patrick steered me through the door. "A person who accidentally hits the neighbor's dog with his car needs to learn to be a better driver, but he doesn't need to be fined for cruelty to animals, right?"

I nodded and swallowed hard. "Yeah, you're right," I said, as we left the hotel and began walking up the street in the cloudy evening dimness.

"Well," Patrick said, "you're like the careless driver; you've harmed people *accidentally*. It doesn't make you a bad person, but we do need to teach you how to avoid doing it again."

I sighed. "That'd be good," I said. A few raindrops were starting to splatter onto the cement patio area by the glassed-in front of the Pizza Express as we walked up to the door.

The hostess at the restaurant tried to seat us right by a window, and it was way cool not to have to lie to Patrick about why I didn't want to sit there. He didn't want anyone to notice his strange reflection when it got dark outside either.

Once we were at a table farther back, I suddenly thought of something. "Patrick," I asked while he was checking the number on his buzzing cell phone, "where's my dad now? Do you know?"

"It's your mum," he said, glancing up from the phone. "Shall I invite her to join us?"

"Sure."

He pushed the "talk" button, asked my mom to hold for a second, and then told me, "When I last saw him, your father was running away from Dunbar Close Garden. Until last night, I hadn't seen him since he attacked the girl outside the cinema more than twenty years ago. I'm not normally the violent type, and I had hoped to put him back in touch with our family, but when he seemed so intent on harming you, I lost control and punched him in the face. He'd hurt your mother and was trying to hurt you, though, so I believe I did owe it him. I suppose my reaction surprised him, however." He smiled and began talking to my mom.

But I didn't listen to a word of the conversation.

The pale guy who looked like he might be a vampire. He was my *dad*? He was *here*? Teaching goths to bite people and shooting heroin? I'd been right there with him, and he hadn't known I was his son. Heck, *I* hadn't known I was his son! But he must've known I was a real vampire after watching me bite without needing the knife!! Was that why he'd grabbed my arm like that? Had it dawned on him that I looked like his old girl-friend? Or was he just curious because I was a vampire he'd never met before?

I shuddered, remembering the revulsion I'd felt when he touched me. I was glad that Patrick had scared him off before he could get to me.

But if my dad was high last night, maybe he wouldn't re-member any of it, or else it'd be all confused in his mind today. I hoped. I really didn't want him to come looking for me. He'd never been a part of my life, and I sure didn't want him in it now. Especially now that I knew what he was really like.

But I found myself hoping Patrick would be around for a while.

"Brilliant," Patrick said, breaking into my thoughts, "your mother's on her way, and I just had an idea, if you'll excuse me while I make another quick call. Would you like it if my friends Sharon and Alasdair joined us tonight?" He leaned over the ta-ble and added quietly, "Sharon's a vampire, too."

My eyes went wide involuntarily while I nodded speech-lessly and Patrick began punching numbers on the phone.

Another vampire? For almost fifteen years I'd never met even one other vampire, and then I meet three in two days. Whoa. This trip to Scotland was turning out to be more educa-tional than I'd ever thought.

Chapter Thirteen

By the time Mom, Patrick, and I had finished off our pizza, Patrick had explained that he'd met Sharon and Alasdair one night at a pub where Alasdair was playing keyboard for a jazz band. Sharon had known Patrick was a vampire immediately.

"All vampires have the night vision," Patrick said, "but some -- like Sharon -- have other keen senses as well. Sharon can smell differences in blood and sweat on people with almost canine sensitivity. She could *smell* that I had vampire blood -- even through my skin."

"That seems a little eerie," Mom said, fiddling with her paper napkin.

"No," Patrick reassured her, "Sharon's very open and friendly. You'll like her."

I was trying to balance the pepper shaker on top of the salt shaker. "Does she have telekinesis?" I asked, wishing I could use it then to make the shakers stay put, but I didn't dare to with so many people around to notice.

"No, that's quite a rare talent," Patrick said, putting his arm around my mom's shoulders, "but Sharon has what the Scots call 'second sight,' which is also rare."

"How rare is telekinesis?" I asked, but, at the same time, my mom asked, "What's 'second sight'?"

Patrick laughed and gave my mom a small hug. She didn't pull away from him. It was kind of weird to watch because I'd never seen her with a man before, but they weren't being gross or flirty or anything, so I was okay with it. It seemed almost normal, even though it wasn't. And that was weird, too.

"Well, now, my gran had telekinesis, but other than her and you, I don't know of anyone else," Patrick explained. "And second sight is a sense of the future, of feeling ---"

"An Irishman who disnae ken nothin about it is explainin the second sight?" said a youngish woman who suddenly pulled out the chair next to me and plopped down into it. She was wearing a short black skirt, a shirt the color of a swimming pool, and shoes with multi-colored sparkly things all over them. She had short, dyed-black hair with a yellow-blonde streak right across the front. Had to be Sharon. I liked her already. But I couldn't understand a word she said.

Patrick, with his old-fashioned manners, stood up to greet both her and Alasdair, and Alasdair shook hands with him and then sat down between my mom and Sharon. Alasdair was a lot more ordinary-looking than Sharon, except that he had really high cheekbones and really blue eyes below his sandy-blond hair.

"The second sight is when ye dream a true thing whilst ye're no sleepin," Sharon told me, after all the greetings were overwith, patting my arm on the table. "It's seein the future or the past."

I stared at her for a second or two, wishing I had a babelfish program inside my head so I could understand her instantly, instead of having to process it all.

My mother giggled. "It's a type of prophecy," she said to me, across the table.

"Aye," said Sharon, digging into her purse and pulling out her wallet, "but it disnae work on command, now; ye cannae *make* it work for ye. It only happens when ye dinnae ken it will. Once I saw my flatmate's bicycle stolen afore it really happened, but I couldnae see the thief." She then turned to Alasdair and added, "Let's get some Irn-Bru; I need caffeine."

"What?" I asked.

Mom giggled again. Either she was amused that I couldn't understand Sharon's speech or she was enjoying Patrick's attention -- or both. "It's a soda that tastes like carbonated cough syrup and has more caffeine in it than three pots of coffee," she told me. "It's a bit of an acquired taste, but you ought to try one while you're in the country, honey."

So Alasdair, whose accent was just about as crazy as Sharon's -- only he used more normal words -- ordered a bunch of Irn-Brus for us, while Sharon asked my mom a billion questions about Paco's Taco Palace and how she was liking Scotland. Or at least I think that's what she was talking about. I couldn't be too sure.

And then the grown-up talk about pubs and jazz bands went on while I drank my whole Irn-Bru -- which was pretty much like Mom had said: like a really sweet, really strong orange soda that made me jittery.

Once I got used to their accents, I learned that Alasdair was studying at the university here, getting a PhD and doing research on some Scottish author named James Hogg, which I thought was a pretty funny name. Alasdair had a theory that this Hogg guy, who'd never fit in with the other authors of his time and had gotten made fun of a lot, had really been a vampire, and he'd been working on proving his theory when he'd met Sharon at the pub where he was in the band, gotten to know her a little, and realized she had the same nocturnal habits and characteristics as the vampires he'd been reading about. He'd come right out and asked her if she were a vampire.

"And you weren't scared of her when you figured it out?" I asked him, poking into the conversation.

"No," he answered, laughing a little. "I don't think I need to tell you that vampires are just people with a genetic disorder. There's nothing more to fear from a vampire than from a person with any other medical condition, like cerebral palsy or asthma."

I was stunned. Everyone who'd ever suspected anything about me had been terrified. "But -- but, you didn't think she'd bite you or turn you into a vampire or anything?" I stammered out at him.

"No, of course not," Alasdair said. "I knew the difference between folklore and fact. I wasn't going to pass up on a brilliant girl like Sharon just because of a wee medical problem." He took her hand off the table and squeezed it. She smiled at him warmly.

Patrick leaned forward a little. "Eric," he said, "ignorance breeds prejudice and fear. People who fear us are those who know only those ridiculous stories of the undead."

"But even doctors don't know about our crazy blood!" I protested quietly. "Every time I go in for a check up, they look at me like I'm a freak when they can't figure out what's up with my blood! How are ordinary people supposed to deal with vampirism being a medical thing if doctors don't even know what makes us this way?!" Mom looked worriedly at me.

Sharon patted me gently on the shoulder. "The whole world isnae ready fer us yet, lad," she said, comfortingly. "But a vampire needs tae have a friend or two who know the truth. Otherwise, ye'll be all alone wi yersel. Yer mum's brilliant, Eric, but ye need a friend who accepts ye fer what ye are, too, an the only way tae dae it is by bein honest wi 'em."

"She's right, Eric," Patrick said firmly. But Mom still looked uncomfortable.

It got really quiet for a minute. I stared at my empty soda glass and wondered what Joseph was doing right then. And if he'd believe me if I told him the real reason why I couldn't be out in broad daylight. And if he'd be scared. But it was hard to imagine Joseph scared. Maybe having survived the horrible business of getting his legs chopped off at age seven had been enough to cure him of being scared for the rest of his life. He'd try anything: rock climbing, swimming, doing a comedy skit in the school talent show last year. So maybe he'd be willing to try being friends with a vampire, too. *Maybe.*

"So, would that be all right with you, Eric?" Mom asked me.

"Huh?" Oops. Had they been talking again? What had I missed here?

"Would you be okay with spending the evening with Sharon and Alasdair if I go to the pub with Patrick to hear this band that Alasdair's been telling us about?" she said.

I blinked a couple of times, then it dawned on me, and I grinned at her. "You mean, you'd like me out of the way so you guys can go on a date?" I asked slyly.

Mom blushed and Patrick chuckled. "Yes, actually," he said, smiling. "But don't worry; I'll be a gentleman."

"You'd better be," I said, "Or I won't ever let her go out with you again." I winked at Mom, who'd recovered from her embarrassment and was laughing at me now.

"Watch it, kiddo," she said, pushing back her chair and standing up. "I still control *your* social life, you know."

"So, what would you like to do, now that you have personal tour guides for the city?" Alasdair asked me as we walked out into the wet, windy night.

I shrugged. In spite of all the caffeine in that Irn-Bru, I felt tired, but I didn't want to make Sharon and him feel bad, so I said, "Well, I've already seen the castle. What else is there to do?"

Sharon laughed, "Quite a lot, lad," she said. "We could go on a walkin tour o' the kirkyards or the underground vaults where the resurrection men used tae hide the bodies afore sellin 'em tae the doctors for dissection, if ye fancy somethin a wee bit spooky."

I shook my head. "Sorry," I said, "but maybe Patrick told you how I spent last night getting chased into a kir-- uh, a grave-yard and hiding there. I don't think I'm ready for another one yet. I don't want to run into anymore of those drugged-up goths."

Sharon scrunched her eyebrows together and looked at me hard. "Ye drank some bad blood, then?"

We were wandering into a creepy-looking street now, one with lots of dark doorways and no lighted windows, just a few signs identifying which pub was which. Every time we passed a narrow close I could smell urine, which was pretty sick, and I was starting to feel a little claustrophobic. "Yeah," I said, look-ing up a dark close to my right, hoping not to see my weird, heroin-using father stumbling out of it. But there was nothing to see except trash cans. "Patrick thinks it was probably laced with heroin. It made me puke last night, and I still feel kind of strange."

"Do you have some good blood with you?" Alasdair asked. "Maybe you should drink some; it might make you feel better."

I stared at him. What a crazy idea -- carrying blood *with* me? What was he talking about? But I couldn't see a smile on his face; he was serious.

"'With me'?" I asked, turning to Sharon for some back up on this.

But she was as surprised at me as I was at Alasdair. "Ye dinnae carry any blood wi ye?" she asked, pulling her scarf closer around her neck as a gust of wind rushed at us from under the second bridge we'd passed. "Ever?" Her eyes were wide open, and I could see that her pupils were dilated completely to the edge of her huge irises. No wonder vampires can see so well in the dark and have trouble in the sunlight; our eyes are *de-signed* for the night.

"I'd never carry blood with me," I told her, shaking my head. "How the heck would I explain that if someone got into my backpack at school?"

"But if ye dinnae carry any wi ye," Sharon protested, "then what d'ye do when the cravin hits ye? How d'ye keep from bitin people when ye dinnae hae animal blood tae quieten yer stom-ach?"

Oh. So that's how she controlled herself.

I didn't answer her. I just stared at the sidewalk and noticed how much litter there was on this street. It seemed dirtier than other places I'd seen so far in the city. I hoped we'd get to a nicer part of town again soon.

Alasdair nudged me with his elbow. "Have you ever bitten one of your friends, then, Eric?" he asked.

"Yeah," I mumbled, still looking down. "A couple of times. Sometimes Mom and I have had to move because of it, but the last time I lied my way out of it." Well, Kacey had come up with the lie, but I didn't feel like telling Sharon and Alasdair the whole story. "That's why I don't want to carry blood with me," I added. "It'd just make people suspicious."

"No if ye disguise it," Sharon said, winking at me. She dug into her purse and pulled out a silver flask. "I carry empty wee tins o' tomato juice tae work wi me," she explained. "Then, at break time, I pour the blood intae ma glass and put the juice tin by it. People see the flask an think I've put a nip o' whisky intae ma juice -- but there isnae any juice in the glass!!" She giggled.

I smiled at her and shook my head. "Look," I told her, "I can't do that. I'd get hauled to the cops for underage drinking! And then they'd check what was in my bottle and find the blood, and then I'd really get --"

"But what if you put it in a plastic juice bottle?" Alasdair interrupted me. We'd come to a complicated intersection now, and he motioned to me to turn left up a steep hill. "Does the head allow you to carry a packed lunch to school?"

Packed lunch? Head? Where did these people *get* these words?

"What?" I asked him. This street seemed much friendlier. It wasn't all dark walls, and it didn't smell like the restroom at a truck stop.

"Won't the head teacher allow packed lunches?" he repeated. "If you put the blood in juice bottles in an insulated lunch bag with one of those imitation ice packs to keep it cold, then --"

Suddenly Sharon was excited about this idea. "Dark bottles!" she added. "If ye use dark bottles an say it's tomato juice, then yer friends who dinnae know about yer bein a vampire will --"

"*None* of my friends know I'm a vampire," I stated flatly. We'd reached the top of the hill now, and I stopped to look around. There was a statue of a dog right next to where we were standing. What the heck?! A dog?!

Alasdair, in spite of his ordinary eyesight, noticed I was looking at the thing and laughed. "That's Greyfriar's Bobby," he told me. "He's a famous dog that's buried in that kirkyard." He nodded in the opposite direction. "We can pay him a visit if you fancy it," he added.

"Uh, no thanks," I said, laughing a little. Good thing he'd been joking because I wasn't about to go looking for some dumb dog's grave.

But Sharon hadn't been distracted by the dog. "Ye're only a half-blood, are ye no?" she asked me.

I nodded. "My father was -- is -- Patrick's cousin," I said. Unfortunately, the image of my dad, with his pale face and sunken-looking eyes, flashed into my mind again. I shuddered a little and looked around at the other people on the street. Would he be out looking for me? I took a step closer to Alasdair.

"Then ye'll be able tae go oot when the shops open the morrow, afore it's sunny," she stated. She dug into her purse again and pulled out a pen and some paper. "This is the store," she said, drawing a little map on the paper. "They'll hae the dark plastic bottles ye'll be needin."

Maybe she was right. I could try it, at least. Patrick had said I needed to drink more mammal blood so I didn't get cravings around people. If I had blood with me, then I could just drink it when I needed to. Except it'd be cold blood. Ugh. But still....

But Sharon wasn't finished yet. "An where d'ye get yer blood, then?" she asked me.

Huh? Oh.

"Uh, I sneak into the neighbors' barnyard next door and put a syringe into the neck of a sheep or a cow," I said. But she looked startled, so I quickly added, "It's okay; I always hypnotize the animals first, and I sterilize the needles."

"But d'ye ask the owner, then?"

Ask? Yeah, right. What was I going to tell Hank Jackson? That I needed the blood for medical research on vampires? Not even.

"Look," I told her, "I live in a little farming town. I can't just go telling people this stuff. They'd go ballistic! And we'd have to move. It's happened to me before. I know what it's like. I can't tell my neighbors I drink blood."

"But ye cannae just *take* it, lad; that's stealin!"

I was ready to answer her, but then I didn't. Stealing. She was right. It *was* stealing.

Crap. Now I had something else to feel guilty about.

We all just stood there for a couple of seconds. I stared at the modern-looking building across the street and wondered what it was; it looked so different from all the others around it.

The strange thing was that it was Alasdair, the non-vampire, who came up with the solution.

"Well," he began slowly after several seconds of just blinking in the cold wind, "Sharon gets her blood from the butcher, who thinks she's using it in black pudding recipes. You might get an odd pet that drinks blood. Perhaps a bat?" he said, shrugging his shoulders a little and smiling. "But," he continued, "if you offered to work for the blood -- surely there's something a young lad like you might do on a farm! And if the farmer thought you had a good reason for the blood, and you showed him that you sterilized the needles..... Well, if he's a reasonable man, he'll make the deal, I think."

I stared for a second, then smiled. "I bet I could think of something believable," I said. "And then I wouldn't have to feel guilty about taking the blood."

Sharon put her arm around my shoulders and gave me a hug. "Aye, that's the way," she told me.

We decided to go to Sharon's apartment -- or "flat," as she called it -- because she thought her flatmate had one of those insulated lunchboxes that she didn't use anymore. So we all walked through a big park and down a street with lots of old-fashioned looking apartments on it. I certainly hoped that Alasdair or Sharon would be walking me back to the hotel later because I was now clueless about where I was in the city. All I knew was that we were about half an hour away from Holyrood Road, where the hotel was.

Sharon said her apartment was on the second floor, but then we went up to the third floor before she let us in. She told me Americans count stories differently than the Scots do. I thought it was pretty strange that the Scots wouldn't count to three the same way we do -- I mean, how many ways are there to count to three? -- but the night was just about to get even stranger.

I followed Sharon through a door with a carved wooden frame and into a small hallway with high ceilings and more carved door frames. The place was clean, but it looked old-fashioned. And it smelled like spices. Lots of spices. Maybe Sharon's flatmate was baking something.

Alasdair, coming in behind me, was loosening his scarf. He sniffed the air and said, "It smells good in here."

"Och!" Sharon said, rolling her eyes while she took off her jacket. "Kirstie's been buyin more soap, then!"

"And what are you complaining about?" called a voice from down the hall. "Your old flatmate used to come home drunk all the time and couldn't pay the rent after she'd spent her paycheck on Ecstasy! I buy soap -- you got a problem with that, honey?"

The voice sounded strange and yet familiar at the same time. The way she said her "r's" was so... so... so *American*. Oh, that was it; the voice was an American one! I smiled at myself. It was scary how I'd gotten used to this Scottish stuff in just a couple of days.

Sharon was good-naturedly bantering with her American flatmate, so I hung up my jacket next to Alasdair's on a peg by the door, and then followed him into the kitchen. But the two women were right behind me.

"I told Kirstie about yer wee problem an needin the lunch-box," Sharon said, rummaging in a cupboard under the sink, while Alasdair watched her with an amused expression on his face.

Suddenly, I wondered just how much she'd said. Did this American woman know she lived with a vampire and had another one in her kitchen right now as well?

I turned to look at Kirstie. She wasn't all that old -- maybe twenty-five or something. She had brown hair that went to her waist and big brown eyes that made me want to keep staring at them. She was as thin as Kacey, but she looked kind of... well, kind of sophisticated. She was wearing a black sweater, tight jeans, and a strange necklace with a sword and a star on it.

I swallowed hard, but it wasn't from too much saliva this time. "Uh, hi, Kirstie," I said, my voice squeaking embarrassingly.

She blinked at me with those extra-long eyelashes and smiled as if she knew exactly what kind of effect she was having on me -- and was thoroughly enjoying it.

Then suddenly she was completely casual. She stuck out her hand, shook mine, and said, "You're an American; you can say my name, and it's 'Kristen.' I'm from New York."

My voice was sort of working now. "Then... then why....?"

135

"Because these bloody Scots can't seem to remember 'Kristen,' so I let them call me 'Kirstie'!" she said, elbowing Sharon, who'd just pulled a navy blue nylon lunchbox out of the cupboard.

"Aye, 'Kirstie's' a lovely name, anyway," said Sharon, motioning me over to the counter to have a look at the box.

I was glad to have an excuse not to look at Kristen/Kirstie, so I fiddled with the lunchbox while Sharon filled her flatmate in on a few details of my life. Apparently, Kristen was just fine about living with a vampire.

"I'm a pagan," she explained at one point, playing with the star on her necklace, "so I don't have the bizarre Christian fear of folklore that seems to be getting in the way for a lot of other people."

"So, pagan's, like, a religion or something, right?" I asked her, staring at her necklace instead of her eyes. Oh, the star was a pentagram! Duh. I'd handled one at a jewelry store once when I'd been checking to see if crosses and stuff bothered me.

"It's a nature-based religion, like a lot of Native American tribes have," she answered.

That sounded simple enough to me. Hey, and at least she didn't freak out over vampires. Maybe I ought to get to know more pagans. Except there probably weren't any in Emma City. No pagan cowboys that I knew of, anyway.

Sharon and Kristen gabbed on about Kristen's fancy, good-smelling soap she'd just bought, and I yawned. I'd met two vampires, learned about my freaky dad, and tried to decide how to keep more blood near me and whether or not to tell Joseph the truth -- all in one afternoon. My brain was tired. Maybe it was also because I'd gotten kind of sick from the drugged blood yesterday, too, but I certainly wasn't feeling all that great right now.

I found a chair and sat in it.

Suddenly, Sharon noticed me again. "Are ye no feelin well, then?" she asked. "Are ye hungry?"

I was. Even though I'd had a lot of pizza a couple of hours before, I was hungry again.

"Kind of," I said. "You don't happen to have any of that extra blood around, do you?"

"Och! No!" she said, shaking her head. "I'm sorry. I had the last wee bit fer breakfast. I wish I hadnae used it; o' course ye'll be wantin some after ye didnae get any last night, then."

Kristen looked confused, but Alasdair filled her in on the basics of what had happened with me in Fleshmarket Close and the graveyard. And I didn't expect her reaction.

"Well," she said slowly, drawing out the sound of the word, "if Sharon will let me, I'll donate a little blood."

I stared right at her again. She was no vampire wannabe playing games in dark alleys, for sure! But she was offering blood?! Why?

"I've offered it to Sharon before," Kristen explained, "but she's always turned me down."

Sharon shuddered. "It's no good tae know the taste o' my flatmate's blood," she said, putting her hand over her heart. "Then I'd be cravin human blood again, an wi ye livin right here...." She closed her eyes and grimaced.

Kristen shrugged. But I understood. That would be bad. I'd *never* want to taste my mom's blood, for example. Somehow that just wouldn't be right.

"She's never wanted mine, either," Alasdair offered.

"An fer the same reasons, man!" Sharon said, leaning over the counter now.

"But how often am I going to see this kid again?" asked Kristen, moving toward Sharon and touching her shoulder. "Let me do it. I want to know what it's like to have pain numbed by hypnosis; I keep wondering if that really works in holistic medicine and natural healing."

Sharon shook her head. "All right, but I cannae watch it!" she said. And she left the room.

Alasdair walked over to Kristen. "I'd like to see it done, though," he said. "Sharon always drinks her blood from a bottle or a glass. I've never actually seen a vampire bite."

I just sat there for a second. They'd decided all this without me. Did I want blood? You bet! But Kristen's? Could I stand to get that close to her? She was so... so... well, she was doing things to my hormone levels; that was for sure. And I didn't know if that was okay to mix that with blood drinking or not.

But they were both staring at me, so I got up and walked over. I was scared now. What if I couldn't get my saliva to flow? What if I couldn't hypnotize her? Then it'd hurt her. And I'd feel like an idiot.

Kristen had obviously guessed I was nervous. Of course, I got the feeling she was used to seeing guys get nervous around her. "It's okay," she said. "I give blood all the time for the Red

Cross." She held her hair back with one hand and added, "Which side of my neck will be easier for you?"

I stopped right where I was. Neck? She wanted me to *put my mouth on her neck?* I was sure I couldn't do that. Kacey was one thing, but Kristen? Nyah. I'd probably faint from terror.

"Uh, how about your arm?" I stammered out, pointing at the one still hanging by her side.

Alasdair laughed at me, but he didn't say anything. I figured he understood what I was going through. He didn't have to be a vampire to understand hormones.

Kristen let go of her hair and shrugged. Leaning against the dishwasher, she pulled up one sleeve of her black sweater and held her arm out level to me. "Hey, if it works for the Red Cross, it ought to work for him," she told Alasdair.

Concentrate on the circulatory system. Don't worry about what she looks like. She's offering blood; that's all that matters.

I stepped up beside her and took her arm in my hands, prodding for the brachial artery before it branches into the radial and the ulnar arteries, just as I had with the blond goth guy. Except that Kristen's blood would be heroin-free.

I found the artery and put my thumb on it. Her pulse was hard and steady, but not too fast. She wasn't scared of me. And neither was Alasdair. Heck, for the first time in my life, I was standing with two people who knew I was a vampire and didn't mind. They were curious, not horrified. They thought I was just a person, not a monster. And if I got enough blood often enough, like Patrick said, I'd be able to control my biting urges like he and Sharon did, and then I'd never be like a monster attacking again. I'd never be like my dad, either. Shoot, I wasn't like my dad now.

I smiled and looked up at Kristen. She wasn't all that distracting anymore, now that my mind was on important things.

"You ready?" I asked her. She nodded and looked at her arm.

I looked over at Alasdair and said, "All I'm going to do is numb her arm with my saliva, which has some weird chemical in it. After I do that, she won't feel any pain at all when my teeth break the skin." I was talking to him, but I'd started using the calming tones I always use, and the effect was exactly as I'd expected: they were both relaxing even more. Kristen's hair had dropped over her face, and her chin was nearly on her chest. Alasdair's pupils had dilated slightly and he was just staring at me. I rubbed my thumb over Kristen's inner elbow and continued talking around all the saliva that was seeping under my tongue, "I don't know if she'll feel anything, but I know it won't hurt her. And if I let the blood flow naturally, without sucking it out, there won't be a bruise. When I finish drinking, my saliva will heal the punctures up really fast, so nothing will be visible."

I turned to Kristen. "Do you feel relaxed? Can I go ahead?" I asked, even though I knew what the answer would be.

"Sure," she answered sleepily.

I smiled. She trusted me. Alasdair trusted me. Maybe Joseph would trust me if I told him the truth.

"Great," I told Kristen, and I put my mouth to her arm.

Chapter Fourteen

We'd had two more days in Scotland after my night out with Alasdair and Sharon. Mom had finalized the deal with Paco's Taco Palace, and the two of us'd done sightseeing in the afternoons when it was cloudy and "night-seeing" with Patrick after dark since he'd taken a couple of nights off work to be with us. I hadn't seen those drugged-out goths or my dad again -- I hoped he'd run off to some other place by now -- but we'd done a ton of stuff. I'd even eaten haggis!

But once it was time to head for home, I'd had to make some important decisions: one of them was that I was going to tell Joseph the truth about myself. And Mom wasn't exactly keen on the idea.

"Are you sure you want to tell Joseph?" Mom asked me Sunday night, back in Emma City, as we were putting dishes in the dishwasher. "Every time someone's suspected you were a vampire, they've made life hell for us." She looked worried.

Yeah, I remembered. That minister who'd convinced my friends' parents not to let them associate with me. The grandma at the birthday party in Seattle who'd threatened to call the police.

I sighed. "Mom, I think that's because they found out instead of being told, and because they didn't get *all* the truth," I said, handing her two plates sticky with spaghetti sauce. "They only found out I drink blood and that I look freaky in photos. They never learned that I can't turn anyone else into a vampire or that I'm not some kind of anti-Christ, like in *Dracula*. That's why we had to run aw-- to leave every time. If I tell Joseph the truth and explain it all to him, then maybe he can accept it. I mean, Patrick told you what he is, didn't he?"

Mom set the plates in the sink and began to rinse them off. "But before he told me, Patrick had learned from me the name of the father of my son, a man he knew was his own cousin. Since he realized my son must be a half-vampire, Patrick didn't exactly have to be a psychologist to guess I wouldn't be terrified of a full-blooded vampire," she said. "But your friends don't know any other vampires. All they know is what's in the books and movies, and they're going to judge you by that!" Her voice sounded a little funny, like she was going to cry, but she didn't.

I set down the glasses I'd brought from the table. "But Alasdair and Kristen both accept Sharon and Patrick, and *they* didn't know any other vampires before," I told her.

Mom sighed. "But Alasdair and Kristen are more open-minded than the people of Emma City, Eric," she said.

Well, she was right about that. Most people in Emma even got upset if they found out someone voted for a Democrat. They weren't too big on new ideas. But I still felt I had to try. And Joseph wasn't like the rest the people in Emma.

"Joseph's open-minded, Mom," I said gently. "I think it's because his body isn't like everybody else's, so he understands other people who don't quite fit in."

"You think he's ready for this kind of not fitting in? Something he doesn't even believe in? Can he accept *that* much of a difference?"

I walked around the counter to her and gave her a hug. "I've got to try, Mom. It was so cool in Scotland not to have to hide all the time. I'm really tired of hiding everything from everybody here. Just having even one friend on my side will make a big difference to me," I told her.

But when was I going to tell Joseph? And how? "Hey, I'm back. Did you know I'm a vampire?" Not even.

Patrick had warned me just to let the subject come up naturally, but I wondered if it ever would.

Kacey practically pounced on me when I walked into English on Monday morning.

"Eric! You're finally back!" she half-squealed, dropping her notebook and throwing her arms around my neck.

She moved so fast that I didn't have time to set down my own books and binder, so all of that, plus my arms, got crushed against my chest. It had all the romance of being greeted by a golden retriever, but it was still pretty cool.

"Uh, hi," I half-choked into her hair, secretly glad she wasn't still mad at me.

"Whoa, boy," Scott yelled from across the room, "*some-body's* got a *girlfriend*!" He made a whoop that sounded like something that must've come out of the mouth of a Sioux warrior just before the slaughter of General Custer.

"Well, that certainly rules you out, doesn't it?" I shot back at him, even though Kacey wasn't my *girlfriend*. More like just a cute friend.

"I'm *so* glad you're back!" Kacey whispered and planted a very wet kiss on my cheek before letting go of me and bending down to get her dropped notebook.

"Yeah, uh, me, too," I tried to say, but I seemed to be having a hard time breathing.

Scott whooped again, but I couldn't think of a reply because I was wondering if all the blood rushing to my face would be hot enough to make the wet spot left from the kiss turn to steam. I hoped it wouldn't.

But I didn't have to wonder very long because Joseph had started bumping his wheelchair into my legs.

"Hey, are you people going to stand in the aisle blocking traffic all day or what?" he asked.

I put my stuff on a desk then vaulted over it out of his way.

"What's up?" I asked, leaning over the desk and high-fiving him.

"Been busy with stage crew stuff for the school play," he said, wheeling over to his own desk and hoisting himself out of the wheelchair. "Your princess here," he pointed his thumb toward Kacey, "got herself the lead part and pissed off a couple of other girls who wanted it." Then he added, "So, did you bring me that wicked sword from the castle?"

I started to laugh, but Kacey interrupted me. "That's not true about my part," she said, walking over to us.

"Britni just told me what she's heard; that's all," Joseph said, shrugging. Then he turned to me and added, "Britni's in the chorus for the play."

"Tim and Rudy and Becca are all in the play, too," Kacey said, taking my arm, "and Ms. Cook wants you to help out in the orchestra pit because she knows it wasn't your fault you couldn't play for the dance concert. Will you?"

I blushed again. How much had Cook heard about my suspension? How much had Kacey heard? I couldn't think of an answer for Kacey, but I didn't have to because Joseph was talking again.

"Becca's one of the girls who's pissed off at Kacey," he said.

"Shh! Rudy'll hear you," Kacey said, nodding toward the back of the room and then glaring at Joseph.

"Look, Kacey, I know you're trying not to sink to her level after how much she upset you at the dance, but Rudy doesn't care whether or not Becca wants to stick pins into voodoo dolls that look like you," Joseph told her, almost snorting. "He just wants her 'cause --"

"Shut up!" Kacey growled, as Becca came into the room. But Becca didn't even glance at us. And she didn't giggle, which was probably a sign that Joseph was right about how she felt.

"Anyways," Kacey said, turning back to me after a second or two of silence, "Ms. Cook told Mrs. O'Flannery, the band teacher, how well you could play the piano, and O'Flannery wants you to help out. We're all in the play, and it would be so cool to have you in it, too. Please?"

She'd pulled herself so close to me now that my arm was right up against her chest. It was a good thing the bell rang just then because I was having a really hard time concentrating on what she was saying.

"Sure. Yeah. Whatever," I coughed out as Kacey moved to her seat.

Wait. What had I just promised to do? I couldn't quite re-member. And it was really hard to take vocabulary notes for the first five minutes. But at least I wasn't drooling. This had to be just normal hormone behavior. No bloodlust taking over. Cool.

By five o'clock on Tuesday evening, I had arrived at my first rehearsal for *Once Upon A Mattress*. O'Flannery had given me the piano score to the whole show right after I'd gotten out of Papsi's class on Monday, so I'd had two afternoons to work on it after finishing my online homework -- and, of course, my naps. (I wasn't giving those up even for a seat with the orchestra.)

Even Papsi was involved with the play. He was constantly running back and forth from the stage to the light and sound booths faster than I thought was possible for a man who'd probably eaten way too many gyros in his lifetime. Mallory and Alexis were also on the tech crew, helping him out. Becca's brother, Tobias, wearing his usual boots and Wranglers, had come over from the high school to help with set building. I hoped he'd forgotten all about our meeting at the blood drive, but I made sure I avoided him just in case.

"Hi," I said to Michael, as I squeezed past the folding metal chairs and music stands to get to the piano. I'd never dared to talk to him before because I'd always been worried about his throat. But no worries tonight. I had my backpack with me, and in it was Kristen's old insulated lunchbox with its ice pack and a couple of plastic juice bottles filled with the blood I'd gotten from Hank Jackson's sheep after mucking out two stalls in the barn very early this morning. (I'd already taken care of offering to muck out his two horse stalls three times a week in exchange for blood, which I'd said was to feed carnivorous plants I was growing for a botany class. He'd said we had a deal as long as both the horse stalls and the needles were clean.) If Michael's moles made me want blood, well, I had blood with me. I was so prepared I could've been a Boy Scout, but I doubt they give merit badges for blood storage.

Michael smiled back. "Hey," he said, nodding and picking up a saxophone. "O'Flannery's been telling us you're good. Hope it's true."

"I hope so, too," I told him, putting the backpack on the piano bench and pulling out the music score.

Michael introduced me to his twin brother Jeff (who, fortunately, didn't have any moles over his carotid artery), his older brother Rich, who was over from the high school to help with percussion, and to Rich's girlfriend, Kathy, who played cello for Central High. I knew all the other kids in the orchestra pit already, but I didn't know the three or four adults who'd showed up to play clarinets and oboes. Michael, however, seemed to know everyone, so I figured I could always ask him later if I needed to find out. Now that I wasn't scared of biting him, I could talk to him.

Plus, I had eaten dinner before I came -- just like Patrick had warned me to do. I decided to see if all this would really help.

"Hey, Michael," I said, staring directly at his neck, "how long have you been playing the sax?"

"About a year," he answered, sorting out sheets of music. "I only played the trombone and sousaphone before that."

"Gee, 'only,'" I said and laughed.

Wow. It worked. His throat looked tempting, but I was full. No drooling. No hypnosis. No being afraid. I had stayed in total control of myself. Yes! Life was good.

145

In fact, life continued to run as smoothly as ice cream melting over a cone for about two more hours. Then it changed.

O'Flannery kept us musicians about fifteen minutes extra after the cast had been dismissed so we could go over some of the trickier parts of a song called "The Minstrel, The Jester, And I," which had a lot of rests in it, and we kept screwing them up. So it was almost eight o'clock by the time I started packing up my music, and I was hungry.

But hey, I had stuff with me. Why worry? I took out one of the little juice bottles -- black, just like Sharon had suggested, so nobody could see what was in it -- and started to drink.

Cold blood isn't my favorite. It's just too reptilian for me. I prefer fresh, mammal body-temperature blood. But ninety-eight degree stored blood just wasn't going to happen. I didn't have any spare bodies to store it in, for one thing. And warm blood *smells* like blood. That would mean every stray dog in Emma City following me. Nope. Not good. That, and the risk of E. coli developing, meant I just had to deal with cold snacks.

Maybe this is why some people don't like eating out. Nothing like fresh, home-cooked food. Or, in my case, *uncooked* --

"Hey, Eric, what are you drinking?"

I coughed and had to wipe ewe's blood off my lips. Fortunately, it hadn't gone up my nose, because it was Kacey I turned around to see. No guy wants to face a cute girl when he's got blood running out of his nostrils. That is *definitely* not cool.

"Uh, it's a snack," I told her. Kacey. Should I tell *her* the truth about me? How would she take it? I hadn't thought about telling her, only Joseph. But if I didn't tell her, then I'd have to continue to lie to her.....

"Since when did you start carrying food around with you?" she asked.

Maybe part of the truth. "My mom's got a friend in Scotland who's also -- well, he's got the same medical issues I have," I said honestly, "and he told me I'd -- I'd, uh, feel better if I kept snacks with me all the time."

"Oh," she said, slinging a duffle bag over her shoulder and stepping out of the way for Kathy and Rich to move the cello past her, "is that why you had a hard time being a vegetarian? Not enough food?"

I watched Becca and Rudy walk past Joseph, who was out of his wheelchair, wrapping up an extension cord on stage.

"Well, sort of," I told her, "but it's more like I need certain *kinds* of food."

I was still holding the juice container in my hand. Kacey pointed at it and asked, "So what are you drinking? And can I have some? I'm starving!"

I froze for a second. I had to decide now: tell her or lie again. Could I trust her? I'd never even considered telling Kacey, but maybe I should. I thought of Alasdair's understanding Sharon. And my mom's liking Patrick in spite of her very bad experience with another vampire. Could Kacey accept me for what I really was?

I looked up at Joseph on the stage. He'd put the wrapped cord around one shoulder and was walking in that strange, ape-like way on his hands back to his wheelchair. He appeared to be the last one left in the auditorium besides Kacey, me, and Papsi up in the light booth.

Emotionally, I felt like I was taking a deep breath and plugging my nose before a dive.

Well, here goes.

I put my free hand on Kacey's arm. "I think you'd better not try any of my snacks until I explain about my medical situation, but I'd like to tell Joseph about it, too. Will you wait with him for a second until I get all my stuff?"

She looked a little confused, probably because all she'd wanted was juice and she'd gotten a speech instead, but she nodded and went up the stairs. I could hear her talking softly to Joseph as I put the music into my backpack.

I didn't put away the juice bottle, though. I kept it in my hand as I went up the stairs and over to the side of the stage where Joseph and Kacey had gone, partially hidden by the shabby black curtains along the side. Somehow I felt there should've been ominous music playing in the background; this was such a big deal for me. But there was no music, just the sound of a box dropping off of something on the other side of the stage. Someone must not have stacked stuff very carefully. That kind of thing was happening a lot lately, and the actors were getting yelled at for damaging props.

Kacey and Joseph looked at me expectantly as I put my backpack down near them and put my sunglasses on to protect myself from the bright stage lights that were still on.

"Kacey says you want to explain why you're a lousy vegetarian," Joseph said. He was still holding the orange extension cord on his lap -- or, well, where his lap should've been, anyway.

"Yeah, that's one way of putting it," I said, grinning a little in spite of my nervousness. The cold blood I'd just drunk felt like it was carbonating itself in my stomach. What if this didn't work out right? What if they freaked out? What if --?

"So, does this have anything to do with why you were so mad at yourself and the rest of the world before you got suspended?" Joseph broke into my thoughts. Kacey just stood there looking a little worried.

I took a deep breath. "Yeah, it does," I said. "I was mad at myself because I kept losing control and eating -- well, *drinking* stuff I wasn't supposed to. I've been lying -- or at least not telling the whole truth -- for a long time now, so basically, I was hating myself for all those reasons. I can't tell everyone the whole truth about myself, but Patrick -- that's my mom's friend -- has been helping me with the self-control part. And, Sharon, another, uh, person with the same medical problem as I have, told me I ought to trust some of my friends with all of the truth so I won't feel like a total scumbag anymore."

Whew. That much was out. I felt relieved, but I knew it'd take Kacey and Joseph a few seconds to process everything; I'd said it all like I was on fast forward.

Now Joseph looked worried. He shifted himself over in his chair, leaving his hands by his hips like he was ready to spring out and escape, and he was scowling. "Eric, what the crap are you --?"

But Kacey cut him off, throwing her arms around me and half-shouting, "Oh, Eric! Does this mean you're an alcoholic?!"

I wanted to laugh. Yeah, I could see it now. Bloodaholics Anonymous. I'm Eric, and I'm a bloodaholic. Really, I'd make a lousy alcoholic. I'd taken one swig of a beer at a neighbor's house once, and it'd made me gag. Gross. Nope. Patrick was right about that stuff. No alcohol for the vampire boy. A blood addiction was enough; I didn't need anything else.

Kacey's idea was so funny that I relaxed just a little. I put one hand on her back to reassure her a little. I still had a half-filled juice bottle with now-almost-body-temperature-again blood in the other hand.

"Shh," I told Kacey, patting her back. "I don't want a ton of people to come in and hear what I have to tell you guys."

She let go of me and stepped back a little. She wiped her nose and then said, "Well, *are* you?"

"I'm *not* an alcoholic," I stated, looking back and forth from Kacey to Joseph, "and I can't ever be a vegetarian. And -- and I really don't have porphyria; I just tell people that to cover up the truth." Geez, that sounded dumb.

"Then why can't you be out in the sun?" asked Joseph. He was still scowling, but not so much now.

I took another deep breath, hoping it would force my heart rate down a little. "For the same reason I never have my picture taken or get near a mirror. And why Wendall thought I'd been messing with the security video," I said.

Joseph opened his mouth to ask something, but I was afraid that if I didn't finish now, I never would, so I plunged ahead, telling them, "And for the same reason that I can move things without touching them."

There was a second or two of silence, and then a wicked grin spread across Joseph's face. "Because you're Peter Pan, and Tinkerbell is helping you with her sparkly fairy dust?" he offered.

I smiled a little. "No," I said and looked at Kacey, "because my father was a vampire, and I'm a half-vampire."

They stared at me. Joseph's grin disappeared faster than a pizza in front of the wrestling team. I got the impression he preferred the Tinkerbell explanation.

Kacey raised one eyebrow. "You're joking, right?" she asked timidly.

I shook my head at her and held out my black bottle. "It's sheep's blood," I said. "I have to have mammal blood every few days, and if I don't -- well, I get tempted to bite people. I almost bit a kid I was babysitting a couple of weeks ago, I wanted to bite Michael that day I was drooling in class, and I --" I swallowed hard and forced myself to add, "and I *did* bite you at the dance when you thought I'd just given you a hickey."

"You *bit* her?!" Joseph asked in a loud whisper, his eyes opening really wide. "You, like, *drank* her blood?!"

I nodded at him, then looked at Kacey and admitted, "And I'm really sorry about it. I lost control of myself."

Kacey put a hand to her neck. "Am I -- will I be a vampire, too?" she asked. Her voice didn't sound as confident as it had that morning when she'd told off Scott for stealing her pen in

Nielson's class. And she was staring at the juice bottle like it was radioactive.

"No," I said. "You have to be *born* a vampire. You can't *become* one later. And I only drink about a cupful of blood each time. I don't kill anything -- not even the sheep." I nodded toward the juice bottle again.

"Let me see that," Joseph said, pointing to the bottle.

I handed it to him. He took the lid off, sniffed the contents, then gingerly took a tiny sip. He scrunched his eyes closed and stuck out his tongue. "Sick! It *is* blood!" he said, handing it back to me.

I took it and offered it to Kacey, but she backed away, so I drank the rest of the blood to show them I was for real.

"So," I asked tentatively, "do you guys believe me?"

"Anybody but you," Joseph said, "and I'd think they were out of their frickin' little mind."

I looked at Kacey, but she was staring at the stage floor, so I turned back to Joseph. He had finally relaxed his body down into the chair and was starting to roll up one shirt sleeve. I wanted to laugh with relief. Good old Joseph. At least he wasn't scared of me.

"Okay, let's see if you're for real," he said, stretching out his right arm on top of the wheel of his chair. "What kind of vein do you like best?"

I grinned. "I need an artery, stupid," I said, putting down the bottle and walking over to him.

I ran my fingers up to where I felt a pulse just below his elbow. The brachial artery. Just like on Kristen and the blond goth guy. Joseph's pulse was strong and slow. He wasn't at all nervous.

"That'll be good," I said, and knelt on the ground next to his wheelchair.

"Are you really going to drink his blood?" Kacey whispered. She sounded disgusted and a little scared.

"Well, I've already had yours, and he's offering, so at least I'm being honest this time," I told her. But she just stared at me without blinking.

"I'm going to do some hypnosis on you to make you relax," I told Joseph, using my calmest voice and rubbing two of my fingers over the soft spot on his arm. "My teeth won't hurt because of some chemical in my saliva, which will also heal the wound up quickly afterwards. You won't see teethmarks at all --

and if I let the blood flow out without sucking it, you won't even have a bruise. You won't bleed and you won't die and you won't turn into a vampire. Bram Stoker made all that stuff up. It's not true at all."

I glanced up at him. He was just watching me calmly, but he nodded slightly. I could feel that his pulse had slowed even more under my fingertips.

I looked at Kacey. She seemed less nervous now, but she was still gripping the strap of her bag rather tightly.

"It's okay; I promise," I told her. And I hoped it was. I hoped I didn't end up craving Joseph's blood every time I saw him after this. But it couldn't be any worse than craving Kacey's and Michael's blood all the time. And now that I was keeping "snacks" with me, that was going to be less of a problem.

I turned back to Joseph's arm and put my lips to the skin, feeling the blood beat past for a second or two. His skin smelled faintly of soap.

I wasn't super hungry after all the sheep's blood I'd just drunk, but having my mouth against human skin started my saliva glands working, which was good because I needed the spit.

I licked quickly to numb Joseph's skin, made the puncture with my teeth, then drew them out to let the blood flow into my mouth.

It was good blood, better than from any sheep -- warm and salty-sweet and drug-free. I wouldn't get sick from this blood. And I didn't have to feel guilty about it. Joseph, like Kristen, had offered. He wasn't freaked out by my being a vampire. Maybe he could accept me in spite of it, just like Kristen and Alasdair had done with Sharon and Patrick.

After only two swallows, I licked over the wound, wiped my mouth off, and stood up.

"Thanks," I said.

Kacey stepped over, and she and Joseph both stared at his arm. "I can't even see anything," she said. "It's just wet."

"Weird," said Joseph, still sounding very calm, "I could *feel* you drinking, but it didn't hurt at all. So, is this all it takes to be a vampire?"

"No," I said, "I ran into some druggies in Scotland who *thought* they were vampires because they liked drinking blood. But I *have* to have it. I get sick if I don't get enough." I decided not to mention there'd been one real vampire with the goths. I wasn't up to talking about my psycho dad just yet.

151

"Like when you tried to be a vegetarian?" Joseph asked.

"Yeah," I answered. "But there's more strange stuff that a non-vampire just couldn't fake. Like I told you, my reflection's all scary-looking, and --"

"Wait a sec," Kacey said, then dug around in her bag a little until she pulled out a little blue plastic case, which she handed to me. "I wanna see this for myself," she said.

I opened the case; it was a mirror. Fine. She obviously didn't completely believe I'd drunk Joseph's blood, but I could certainly prove the reflection part was true.

"Watch," I told her. I put my hand so it would show in the mirror. And there it was, the whole network of veins and arteries showing through my skin.

Kacey looked up at the stage lights, then, scowling, she looked at herself in the mirror, then handed it to Joseph. I showed the same thing to him. He shook his head and said, "That's the freakiest thing I've ever seen!"

"There's more," I told her, taking off my sunglasses and putting the mirror where Kacey could see how my retinas glowed right through the tinted contact lenses in the mirror's reflection.

"How do you *do* that?" Kacey said, as I rubbed my eyes and put the comforting glasses back on.

"Do what?" Joseph asked. "What's up with his eyes?"

"I don't 'do' anything," I said, shrugging. "Vampires just have almost-clear irises that are bigger than what normal humans have. Plus, our pupils dilate really far. That makes us see well at night, but we're super-sensitive to bright lights. And mirrors and cameras catch what people's brains automatically 'correct' otherwise. What you see in the mirror is what I really look like."

Her eyes were narrow now. "And just why does this stuff happen?" she asked skeptically.

"I don't know; it's genetic," I said. "I'm thinking about going into science in college to study this kind of thing."

"Wow!" interjected Joseph. "Being a vampire is, like, a *disease*! That's bizarre!"

I smiled at him. "A 'disease.' Gee, thanks, buddy."

Kacey reached over and took her mirror back, but she stopped before putting it in her bag. "Wait a minute!" she said, her eyes widening. "There *aren't* any pictures of you in your house! I remember noticing that. My mom's got tons of family photos everywhere in our house, but there isn't even *one* in yours! Is that why you won't put your own photo on your friendsite profile?"

I nodded at her. "Do you believe me now?" I asked.

Kacey just stared at me, like she couldn't decide. She was fiddling with the shoulder strap on her bag.

"I believe you," Joseph said, "but it's pretty bizarre."

I smiled. "It gets more bizarre," I told him. I pointed at my juice bottle on the floor by his chair. "Watch."

Staring at the bottle, I willed it up. Not too far, just in case Papsi or a custodian walked near the stage. I just made it levitate up into Joseph's chair and land on the coiled extension cord.

"Dude!" Joseph whispered, staring at the bottle with eyes so wide they made mine water in sympathy. A second or two later, he looked at me and said, "That was *awesome!*"

Kacey was more skeptical. "How did you *do* that?" she asked, her eyebrows drawn together.

"I just concentrate on whatever I'm trying to move and tell it what to do in my mind," I told her. "It's kind of a rare talent, even for vampires."

Kacey said nothing, but she kept staring at the plastic bottle in front of Joseph.

"It's not a trick, Kacey," I told her. "This is really what I'm like, and I'm asking you to believe me."

Kacey looked at Joseph, who was poking at his arm where I'd bitten him, probably looking for non-existent holes, then she turned back to me. She'd stopped scowling, but she looked worried. "I don't know, Eric," she said sadly. "This is just -- I mean, it's so --"

I figured I'd better not pressure Kacey too much. Maybe she just couldn't handle this kind of thing all at once. I touched her arm lightly and interrupted her with, "Even if you can't accept all of this, will you at least keep it a secret? Emma City doesn't need a vampire hunt."

To the side of us, Joseph gave a short laugh. "Like anybody I know'd believe me if I told 'em!" he said.

Kacey smiled a tiny smile and shook her head. "It just makes me worried about you," she said, putting her arms around my neck, "but I don't want you to have any more problems than you've already got, so I'll keep my mouth shut. I promise."

I sighed in relief and put my arms around her waist. I would've been happy to stay there for a long, long time, but suddenly Papsi's voice boomed over the auditorium sound system,

153

"Hey, you lovebirds and chaperone, it's closing time! Let's go home! You kids've got five minutes to leave before I shut off all the lights."

Maybe if he'd shut them off immediately I would've seen the cause of another box falling over backstage across from us. But even my eyes weren't good enough to see into the blackness beyond bright stage lights, and my mind was too filled with happy thoughts just then to suspect that more trouble was coming.

Chapter Fifteen

I woke up early the next morning because I wanted to see if I'd gotten a reply to my long e-mail to Patrick from the night before. I'd told him everything: the blood-in-a-bottle, Joseph's offering an arm, Kacey's wanting me to prove I had no reflection, the telekinesis. I'd already told the whole story to Mom before I'd started the e-mail to Patrick -- and she'd been superrelieved -- but I still wanted his feedback, too.

Blue light from the screen filled my room as the computer warmed up and I found a white polo shirt and some jeans to put on after my shower.

Within about five minutes, I was reading Patrick's reply:

Eric,

That's brilliant! It sounds like your timing was very good.

I hope to meet your friends fairly soon; I just need to work out a few more details before I visit your town. Do you think they'll be able to accept a *second* vampire?

You'll be happy to know there's been no sign of your father about Edinburgh lately, but Sharon's asked me to give you a warning to avoid tall young men who dress in western clothing. She said she'd 'seen' a problem arising between you and such a fellow. I can only guess it's her second sight working, so do take care.

Cheers,

Patrick

So Sharon wanted me to watch out for cowboys? Well, she must've seen the past and not the future. I'd already had a problem with a cowboy: Tobias. That certainly must've been --

Wait as second. I read the e-mail again and blinked hard. But it didn't change. Patrick? Here in Emma? Whoa! Maybe he and Mom were closer than I'd thought. And I planned to find out.

"No, he's *not* going to stay with us," Mom said, handing me the milk bottle. She was actually blushing. "Have I *ever* had a man stay with us before?"

155

"No," I answered, "I've never even seen you date anyone before Patrick. I just figured --"

"You just forgot that I told you I learned my lesson from your father about what can happen to a woman who's too trusting," she said. "And, no, I haven't dated since then. Until now. And this one is completely G-rated, I assure you."

I rolled my eyes, a little embarrassed. I hadn't actually been thinking about what they'd been doing -- uh, *physically*. I was only wondering if they were in love or just kind of buddies.

Mom waved her cereal spoon in the air at me, but she was smiling. "Well, you brought up the subject, and you'd better remember what I've told you, now that you've got a girlfriend, mister," she said.

Now I started blushing. "Mom," I whined, "She's not really my girlfriend. And I've only kissed her twice. Actually, *she's* kissed *me*, is more like it. That's all. I promise."

"Besides drinking her blood," Mom said.

"I drank Joseph's blood, too. And Kristen's. And some goth guy's. And I wanted to drink Michael's and Mr. Wendall's and Brendan's," I said, pouring the milk on my cereal. "Craving blood doesn't have anything to do with hormones!" That was one thing I'd learned in the past few months. And it was a relief to know it.

"Okay," she said, winking so I could be sure she'd been teasing me. But then she frowned a little and sighed. "But I do worry about your drinking that drugged-up boy's blood," she added.

"Why?"

She stared at the kitchen blinds for a moment. Then she explained slowly, "You can get HIV from sharing heroin needles and from infected blood. The virus isn't supposed to be able to survive the gastric acid in your stomach, but I still worry...."

By this time, the cereal in my bowl looked about as appetizing as wet cement.

HIV? I hadn't even thought of that. But if that white-haired vampire wannabe had been shooting heroin like Patrick thought, then there was a *chance* he'd been sharing needles, so there was a *chance* he might be HIV positive, which meant there was a *chance* the virus could've gotten into my own blood stream through my digestive system, even though my super saliva meant I had no wounds in my mouth.

Oh, crap.

I must've looked like I'd just had a narrow escape from a passing truck or something because Mom jumped up from her seat like it'd just ejected her and came to put her arms around me.

"Oh, honey," she said, "I shouldn't have said anything yet. It'll just worry you now. Look, I'll call the hospital in Salt Lake and we'll get you tested. I'll -- I'll tell them you got bloodied up in a fight with the boy. I don't think I'd better mention you drank his blood."

She kissed me on the cheek. "And maybe vampires can't get AIDS anyway," she added. "You have such odd blood and saliva."

Oh, yeah. Something that had been frozen inside me for the last few minutes started to thaw a little.

My blood had always puzzled nurses when they took samples. One had even muttered something about not knowing what type it was.

And I knew my saliva healed wounds and numbed skin. Maybe it killed viruses, too. Come to think of it, I'd never been sick with colds or flu that I could remember. When I got sick, it was always because I wasn't getting enough blood or because I'd been out in the sun.

I sighed. Well, I'd certainly have a lot of stuff to research when I got to university level.

"But, speaking of weird blood," Mom said, rubbing my shoulders, "Patrick, who *isn't* staying in this house, but who *is* coming to Emma, may know more about vampires' disease resistance than we do."

I nodded. That was true. I'd never asked him about that. Okay. Don't worry without a reason.

But I only half-listened to my own advice. And it was really hard to finish my cereal.

"Are you all right this morning, Eric?" Ms. Nielson asked me across the otherwise empty classroom. "You seem rather preoccupied, and you are here a good ten minutes earlier than usual."

I had jumped in my seat when she spoke and was now staring at her dazedly. "I, uh, just wanted to read over the first draft of our research paper that's due today -- before I hand it in, that is," I lied.

157

"Then why are you merely staring at the cover of your geometry book?" she asked. "Unless you did your paper on Euclid?"

"Uh, no. Bram Stoker, actually," I said, fumbling to pull my research paper out of my binder.

"Ah, then perhaps I might suggest that you need a good night's sleep tonight," she added, walking toward the filing cabinet, "as you seem a bit confused."

"Uh, yeah," I said, shuffling through the paper and pretending to scan for typos. At least she wasn't going to ask me what I was thinking about. Nielson was pretty cool, but I didn't exactly feel like telling my English teacher that I had just discovered the possibility that I might be HIV positive. If there was anything that could possibly be worse than having the school "officially" find out I'm a vampire, it would be having them find out I had HIV issues. Great. A vampire with AIDS. Why couldn't I just have acne like a normal teenager?

"Well, I think Kacey sounded like a sow giving birth," I heard Becca say. I looked up and saw her walk in with Rudy, Scott, and Britni.

"But 'Swamps of Home' is *supposed* to sound like that!" Britni protested. She sounded a little disgusted.

"What's a sow?" Scott asked.

"It's a pig, you a--"

"Watch your language, Rudy!" snapped Ms. Nielson.

"-- animal!" finished Rudy, looking smug.

But Nielson wasn't through yet.

"Are you accustomed, Becca, to hearing sows give birth?" she asked.

Becca placed her books in a neat pile on her desk. "We raise cows on our farm, Ms. Nielson," she said, smoothing her skirt under her and sitting down, "not swine."

"Then I suggest you keep your analogies to the bovine variety," said Nielson.

"What?" asked Scott.

"Cows!" both Rudy and I shouted at him at the same time.

Britni giggled, but Becca didn't.

I was glad Kacey hadn't heard Becca's remark; it was way more rude than what Becca'd said to her at the dance, and I didn't want Kacey to cry again -- even though she'd obviously been trying her best lately to be nice to Becca in spite of everything. Joseph had been right in saying that Becca was being a sore loser about the role of princess.

"Hey!" Joseph suddenly slapped a hand down on my desk, taking my attention away from Becca. I hadn't heard him enter the room.

"Look at this!" he demanded excitedly, turning his arm palm up.

"Look at what?" I asked him. There was nothing to look at. It was an arm.

"Not a mark or a bruise," said Joseph, half-whispering now. But he didn't have to. No one could've heard him over Scott, who was yelling "Bovine!" repeatedly at Rudy with all the delicacy of a small freight train.

"Of course not," I said in a fake-sophisticated voice. "I don't leave marks."

"That's way cool," Joseph said, and he wheeled around to get to his desk.

That's when it hit me. If I'd gotten HIV from the goth guy, then I could've passed it on to anyone I'd bitten since, from my saliva to their blood. That meant Kristen. And Joseph.

Joseph. My best friend. Somebody who believed me about being a vampire and still liked me. Somebody who already had to deal with life without legs, and now he might have to deal with life with AIDS as well. Because of me.

Sick.

For the first time since I'd gone to Scotland, I hated myself again.

And things didn't get much better. We had a pop quiz in geometry, and I didn't know the song "Normandy" as well as I thought at rehearsal that night.

On Thursday, I got an e-mail announcing another paper -- this time on Taoism -- in my Chinese philosophy class, and Kacey was really sad and quiet that night -- except on stage, where she was as loud and obnoxious as Mr. Twiller, the drama teacher, wanted her to be. I figured she'd been hearing about what Becca had been saying, but I wasn't sure what to do about it. I thought about hypnotizing Becca to get even, making her act like a cow. But I wasn't sure I knew how.

Early Saturday morning, before the sun got too bright, Mom drove me to the University Medical Center in Salt Lake for a blood test. The nurse had to mix a thinner with my blood sample to keep it from coagulating in the tubes, but she said that wouldn't affect the outcome of the test. She told us we'd get the results by next week.

Mom helped me do some research on Taoism in the big, white library on the University of Utah campus -- to keep me out of the sun, too -- and then we went to see *Avengers of the Night* at a movie theater, but I still felt like I had a rock over my head, just waiting to drop.

By Monday morning, as I filled my juice bottles with warm cow blood -- after I'd filled a wheelbarrow with warm horse poop -- I was really wishing I could be somebody else. Anybody else. I mean, what could be worse than being a half-vampire who might be HIV positive?

Okay, well, other than being Scott, I realized in first period. But I still spent the day feeling sorry for myself.

Practice went okay Monday evening. I had my part down flawlessly for "Normandy." I forced myself to think about the music and not the blood test and what I might have to tell Joseph. And I remembered to get a drink from my lunch box when Michael's moles started making me think of strawholes.

Joseph had to stay much later than the cast and orchestra now. Papsi and Mrs. Jacobs, the art teacher in charge of stage crew, had all the crew members sawing, hammering, painting, and wiring like crazy. Tools, cords, boards, and paint cans were all over backstage, so I had to navigate carefully when I went looking for Kacey.

"Actually, I think she's in the bathroom," Britni told me, so I started toward the stage door, leaving Britni to finish getting a backrub from Joseph, who was supposed to be painting one of the royal thrones. But the can of lavender paint was still sitting without its lid on a rolling cart behind some chairs. Personally, I couldn't see how Joseph would be able to maneuver his wheelchair through all the clutter to get it.

I was about to reach over and get the can for him, when Becca suddenly came through the doorway.

"Looking for your tomboy princess?" she sneered at me.

I wanted to leave ASAP at this point, so I ignored the can and cart and walked past her. "Better than looking at you," I retorted.

"Really, Eric," she said, "I thought you had better taste."

"Glad I don't know what you taste like," I snapped. Her blood was probably as sour as her personality. But hey, if I did get AIDS, I could always threaten to bite her. That might keep her away.

I turned back to look at her. She was standing right next to the stack of chairs, looking very clean and proper in a white sweater with her long, blonde hair loose over her shoulders. Too clean and proper for someone who was talking dirt like this.

"You know why Kacey got the lead, don't you?" she asked. But she continued without waiting for me to answer, "She got it because Cook and O'Flannery knew she'd talk you into playing the piano for the orchestra. It was you they wanted, not her."

This was too much. It was time to get even.

I focused my eyes on the cart behind her.

Slowly, I told the cart in my mind. Very slowly. Don't let it be obvious. Roll forward.

I hoped Britni wouldn't notice the cart moving or I'd have some lying to do later.

Becca was still giving her monologue. "And so we got a princess who's not even any good! I think you should both just drop out and let the rest of us put on a decent show!"

The cart was right behind her now. Right between her and the only clear path to the outside door.

I focused my eyes on Becca again. "You know what I think?" I asked her.

"I can just imagine."

"I think you can't handle the fact that she makes a better princess than you do," I told her calmly.

"She does not! I could do better than that cow!" she yelled, putting her hands on her waist. I could see Britni and Joseph watching now, and Alexis had joined them, her face turning dark with suppressed laughter.

Keep calm. Becca'll get angrier if I don't react.

I shrugged my shoulders. "But if they'd put you in as the obnoxious princess who can't sing, it would've been typecasting, and Mr. Twiller says he never typecasts," I said in a bored tone.

Alexis lost the battle with laughter here, and she kind of snorted. "Oh, sorry," she called over, still laughing.

"I'm not!" Joseph shouted. He still had his hands on Britni's shoulders, but she was pressing both of her hands over her mouth.

"Oh, you people are *so* pathetic!" Becca announced. And she turned to leave quickly. Too quickly. Right into the cart.

It was a beautiful moment. She grabbed at the cart to keep her balance, and, in the process, jerked it so that the paint can fell over, right onto her chest. So much for her white sweater.

She screamed. Joseph started clapping and whistling. Alexis gasped. Britni tried to stand up from her cross-legged position on the floor, but she fell over and began laughing. I just watched. And smiled. This was the best moment of my whole crummy week.

"What the crap is going on?" Rudy half-yelled from the doorway behind me. And Kacey was behind him, trying to see. I wondered if she'd heard what Becca had said.

Becca had set the paint can upright again, but she was dripping.

"He did this to me!" She moved a sticky hand in my direction, splattering paint drops everywhere in the process.

I shrugged. "I didn't touch her," I told Rudy truthfully. "She walked into the cart and tipped the can over onto herself."

Rudy stepped up by me and surveyed the mess.

"Aren't you going to do anything?" Becca whined at him.

Rudy folded his long arms across his chest. "Nyah," he told her, "you look pretty good in that color."

I laughed.

Kacey just stood there, looking like she wanted to laugh and cry at the same time.

"Kacey, she was probably dissing on you again, got carried away, and bumped into the cart," Rudy told her over his shoulder. "Frankly, I'm sick of hearing her whine about you. This serves her right."

Becca snatched some newspapers off one of the stacked boxes nearby and started trying to wipe off her sweater. "You people make me sick!" she said.

Then she turned and pointed a lavender finger at me. "I know how you did this, Eric Wright," she said, "and I'll get you back for it!"

"And your little dog, too!" Rudy shouted after her as she stomped around the cart and out the opposite door.

Chapter Sixteen

Mom had to leave for Arizona on Tuesday morning to scout out possible locations for a chain of dry cleaning stores, so I was the only one home to answer the phone during the day -- when the medical center was most likely to call. That meant I'd be the first one to hear whether or not I was HIV positive.

So every time a telephone solicitor called for the rest of the week, I got an adrenaline rush and a dry throat. But that's all that called: Ken's Carpet Cleaning, Steven Hampsterman for city council polls, and dog obedience lessons. No medical stuff.

I was starting to understand how old Pavlov-buddy had conditioned all those dogs to react every time they heard a bell ring. Just call me Rover.

Wednesday morning started off with an e-mail from Patrick:

Eric,
Your mom wanted me to tell you the good news personally: I'll be in the States by Friday. If my car hire goes smoothly, then I'll reach the quaint little town of Emma about 90 minutes past sunset. I'll be staying on a street called 300 East. So, I'll visit you by Saturday, at the latest.
Cheers,
Patrick

That was good news. And Mom was supposed to be home by Friday, too, so we could go over to the motel and --

Wait a second. The J-Bar Seven was the only motel in Emma, and it was on Main Street, not 300 East. I passed it every single day on my way to Patrick Henry Junior.

So where the heck was he staying? Maybe he had the wrong address. Maybe he had it mixed up with our address on 300 South. Yeah, that had to be it. Guess he just couldn't deal with all the logical street names around here. After all, the way they named streets in Scotland, 300 East and 300 South would probably just be the same thing anyway.

So the day started off pretty well. Too bad it didn't stay that way.

The bell had just barely rung for first period to begin when Mrs. Engles appeared in the doorway and had a quiet conversation with Ms. Nielson, who then informed Kacey, Joseph, and me that we'd be paying a visit to the office.

My stomach started to dance the polka. Scum. What was this about? Another security video problem? Becca and the paint can? Were there security cameras on the stage? Oh, no! Had I been taped drinking Joseph's blood?!

The three of us were moving in dead silence behind the bony Engles with her slick, black hair, navy blue suit, and chocolate-colored skin. If she'd stuck one hand out in front of herself, pointing toward a bleak future, she might have passed for the Ghost of Christmas Yet-To-Come.

Obviously the Inquisition was going to get all three of us. I looked to my right at Joseph. He was frowning as he pushed his arms in an easy rhythm to propel himself on the smooth linoleum. What if he got suspended over this? Great. I might have given him AIDS and now I might have caused him a suspension.

And what if he caves in and tells them I drank his blood? That I confessed my vampire DNA? That I moved the juice bottle and the cart without touching them? That --

Joseph looked up at me and gave a twisted smile.

My stomach slowed down to a Viennese waltz tempo. Nyah. He'd never rat on me. Even if I did get him suspended.

But Kacey?

She was walking on the other side of Joseph, head down, books to her chest, and a flushed look about her cheeks. Was she mad? At Engles? At me?

Would she tell? Did she even believe what I'd said? Would she make them think I'd been trying to frighten her? What if that's what she really thought?

I desperately willed her to look at me, but she wouldn't. And telekinesis wouldn't work on a head attached to a very determined human body; that much I knew.

I just wished I also knew what she was so determined about right then.

Kacey was ushered into Engles' office and Joseph into Wendall's. I got stuck with the grouchy secretary while I waited. And waited. And felt my stomach go back into whirling dervish mode while I imagined what might be happening to my friends. And what might happen to me.

Gyah! What if I tried to bite Wendall again? What if I succeeded and got caught? I'd be expelled, for sure. Maybe even arrested. Swell. I'd have to call Mom in Arizona and tell her what I'd done while the cops listened and laughed. Student attacks principal's head. Great.

But it turned out I didn't have to worry about that. Apparently Engles thought Wendall couldn't handle me, so she insisted on doing the interrogation herself.

Kacey was directed out of Engles' office and into my chair by the secretary. She didn't make eye contact with me, but I hardly had time to worry about that, as I was ordered into Engles' office, which was green-tiled like Wendall's, but was minus the motivational posters -- it had a large cork bulletin board covered with a huge calendar and memos instead.

"Have a seat, Mr. Wright," Engles said, pointing to a hard wooden chair near her desk. I sat obediently, feeling rather nauseated.

"Let's see if your story contradicts that of your friend Miss Wolton," she said, running a hand along her slim skirt and sitting down on the leather chair at her desk. "Your classmate, Rebecca Clyde, has accused you of dumping paint on her after play practice on Monday night, and --"

"I never touched the cart; Becca walked into it," I interrupted her. "Joseph, Alexis, and Britni all saw it happen."

"Your friend Mr. Mitchell is already talking to Mr. Wendall, as you know," Engles answered.

"Then he'll also explain that Becca's been spreading a lot of rumors ever since she got pissed off that Kacey got the part that she wanted in the play," I said. "Becca's been telling a ton of lies lately, and a lot of people can back me up on that."

"And how do you explain her claim that you've been trying to start a Satanic cult?"

I choked. This was unreal!

"A *what*?!"

"You heard me, Mr. Wright."

"I am NOT a devil worshipper!" I half-yelled at her. I was leaning forward in the chair now, feeling like I was ready to pounce. What kind of crazy garbage was this? How'd Becca get devil worship from spilled paint?! And how many people had she told?

165

Ms. Engles calmly went on. "Miss Clyde has stated that she saw you sucking at Mr. Mitchell's arm and heard you claim that you drank his blood," she said.

"How'd she --?!" I stopped myself before I blurted out "see that" -- but then I did see that. Right as I was realizing what those falling boxes backstage must've meant and wondering exactly how much Becca had seen and heard, I saw it there, stuck on top of Ms. Engles' computer monitor. A small mirror. Little pinpoints of deep red were glowing from my pupils in it, just behind her head. My blood felt colder than the snacks I'd been carrying in the lunchbox.

I closed my eyes and took a deep breath. Please, God, don't let her turn around. This is bad enough already, and I don't know how I'm going to get myself out of it. Don't let her turn around and notice me in that mirror. *Please.*

I had to take control of this situation. Fast. I opened my eyes and stared straight at Engles. Look at me, I thought. Not behind you.

"Ms. Engles," I said firmly, "Becca Clyde is angry and jealous of Kacey. I've heard her say a lot of ugly things lately, and it sounds like she's saying more ugly stuff now."

Calm. Maybe hypnosis tones will work. Try it.

"I'm not into Satanism and neither are Joseph and Kacey," I said, wishing the hypnosis would calm my own stomach, and forcing myself not to glance at that mirror. "And accusing someone of drinking blood sounds pretty crazy to me," I lied.

Crap. I hope she doesn't decide to search the lunchbox in my locker, or she'll find blood, all right.

Either I was too nervous to get the hypnosis to work, or else even vampire powers were useless in calming superwoman here, because Engles just wasn't easing up on her hawk-like fierceness.

"Mr. Wright," she said, with absolutely no less intensity than before I'd tried the hypnosis, "answer this question straight: Did you or did you not attempt to drink Mr. Mitchell's blood?"

Great. I could lie or I could evade the question. Either way, I'd be acting like a politician. The thought was not a pleasant one.

I looked Engles straight in the eye. Stay calm. "If Joseph's been bitten, he'll have a wound, possibly an infected one by now, right?" I asked, choosing the evasive technique as the lesser evil. "Why don't you have a look at his arms?"

"You didn't answer the question, Mr. Wright."

Geez. This woman should work for the CIA. "I don't need to," I said. "Joseph's skin will show whether or not Becca's lying."

She looked hard at me, but I didn't look down. I didn't dare show how scared I really was. My spit had dried up and my stomach was heaving nearly as much as it had been that night in Scotland.

After what seemed like twenty minutes, she spoke. "All right, then," she said, "let's go to Mr. Wendall's office."

And she turned around to grab her keys off her desk.

NO! My arms and legs started to tingle, like I had Fourth-of-July sparklers in all my capillaries. Adrenaline was surging through my body at an incredible rate.

Her eyes caught the mirror, and for just a split second I saw their reflection, wide in incomprehension. She was going to realize that bizarrely-veined, evil-eyed thing in the mirror was me. Then there'd be more questions. She'd take me to a bigger mirror to prove it. And then -- ugh, I didn't even want to think about the rest.

Desperate and feeling incredibly sick to my stomach, I did the only thing a vampire could possibly do to save himself at this point.

I stood up.

So all she could see was the reflection of my green polo shirt. Which did not have vampire DNA and looked perfectly normal in the mirror.

It worked. She shook her head slightly and stood up, raising one eyebrow as she glared at me. I nodded toward the door to let her know I had manners enough to let her go first, and she went. I followed her down the short, narrow hallway the best I could without collapsing. My stomach was still dancing, and it felt like my heart had now joined up as a partner. And it wasn't a fox trot they were doing, either.

She knocked on Wendall's door and then went in. Joseph was parked in front of the desk. He looked so confident he was almost cocky.

Yeah, sure. You got Wendall-the-Marshmallow. I got the kindred spirit of McCarthy and his communist witch hunts. Like that was fair.

"Well?" asked Engles, no nicer to Wendall than to me.

Mr. Wendall stood up and frowned, the big artery on his temple bulging slightly. "Joseph, here, claims that Rebecca most likely misheard one of his and Eric's conversations about the novel *Dracula* they were reading for English class," he said.

"Actually, what I said was that Becca's lying enough about one of our conversations to make her tongue burn off," Joseph said. Yup. Cocky. I would've laughed if I hadn't been so frickin' scared. After all, Joseph didn't have to worry about his reflection in a mirror or what the administration might find if they searched his locker.

Engles ignored him. "Miss Wolton would only state that Mr. Wright was not standing near the cart when Miss Clyde got paint on her sweater and that she -- Miss Wolton, that is -- did not know what would make Miss Clyde claim that she and these boys were studying Satanism."

I grinned slightly now. Kacey had lied to protect me. Cool.

"Ms. Engles," I asked, feeling slightly braver, "could we check Joseph's arms to prove there are no bite marks?"

Joseph glanced at me and smirked. He knew what I was doing. And he *never* has a problem with showing off his arms. Since he pulls his body weight and that wheelchair around all day long, he has the biceps and pects of a full-grown athlete. I'd be jealous, except that I have legs, so I guess it's fair.

Obligingly, Joseph held up both forearms for the adults to inspect. His constantly-used muscles bulged as he did so, but the only marks of any kind were the usual calluses on his hands from rubbing them on the wheels all day, every time he needed to move. No teethmarks anywhere. Of course.

I smiled again, a little broader this time.

Engles and Wendall both reluctantly conceded that there was no evidence whatsoever that I had bitten Joseph. I sighed. The witch hunt was over. For now.

I felt drained and weak by the time they let us go back to class. Kacey wouldn't even look at either of us, so that didn't help. And I still didn't know how many people Becca had told this story to.

But I was too tired even to be mad at her. All I wanted to do was go home and sleep, but I couldn't. I had English and geometry to get through, then I had to go home and revise the paper on Stoker and write one on Taoism for my online class.

Maybe all the homework would take my mind off HIV and Engles and what Becca had seen and why Kacey wouldn't look at me. Or maybe not.

Chapter Seventeen

The paper on Taoism turned out to be a lot harder than I expected. I worked on it Wednesday. And Thursday. I had to read three books and go to more websites than I can even remember to get the information to prove my point.

I worked like a diesel engine pulling a mobile home up a canyon road, but I still had to spend all afternoon Friday typing it up to e-mail to the community college before the five o'clock deadline. So I missed my nap and was less than thrilled about shoving the music score into my backpack and running -- under the shadows of buildings and the big trees in front of the library, of course -- back to school for rehearsal.

I knew I was going to sound crappy. I hadn't had any extra time to practice all week -- just at evening rehearsals. And what kind of a slave driver was Mr. Twiller to hold practice on a Friday night, anyway?

Oh well, at least all my friends were at rehearsal, too. Not that it mattered with Kacey, though. She'd been avoiding me for two days in English and at play practice, and I hadn't had any time to text her in the afternoons because of all my homework. Maybe I could talk to her during a break tonight.

Missing my nap really started to make a difference by about 7:00 PM, when we'd been going over the dance number for "The Old Soft Shoe" for about thirty minutes.

Everyone else except the orchestra and Rudy, who played the jester and had this as his solo number, got to take a break. But we played it over and over again because the big oaf couldn't dance. Seriously, he looked like a rag doll having a spasm: arms, legs, head, all flopping out sporadically. Only he had to be the tallest rag doll ever made. A 6'7" rag doll would scare any little kid.

But when I caught myself staring at how the stage lights highlighted the tendons in his neck as Ms. Cook walked him through one section for about the hundredth time, I knew I'd better get out a blood bottle before I embarrassed myself by drooling.

Not that cold blood sounded any tastier than usual, mind you. It's about as exciting as room-temperature milk. But, given the choice between Rudy's neck or cold blood that made me think of snakes, I opted for the second one.

Fortunately, just at the same time, O'Flannery insisted on a break for the orchestra, too, so I grabbed one of my black bottles and climbed the stairs to the stage, hoping to find Kacey or at least Joseph.

The door from the stage to the parking lot was open, and I could see flood lights streaming through it. Thinking Joseph might be out there painting scenery, I headed that direction.

But, just before I walked around a big piece of lattice with a bunch of plastic vines wired onto it, I heard something that made me stop.

"So, are you sulking because you're pissed off at Engles and Wendall for treating us like criminals or because you're mad at Eric for telling you things you didn't want to hear?"

It was Joseph's voice, no doubt about it. And he could only be talking to Kacey, who was taking way too long to answer him.

There was a sound of shuffling feet on the newspapers spread out to catch spilled paint. "I'm not sulking," Kacey's voice answered. There was a snort from Joseph, which she ignored and said, "But I'm mad at all of 'em."

Okay, so I wasn't being particularly honest by deciding to stay hidden behind plastic plants and eavesdrop, but there was no way I was going to miss this conversation.

Silence followed for a second or two, then Joseph asked, "Will you hand me the other paintbrush?"

There was another crackle of stepped-on newspapers, and then Joseph's voice went on. "I think Eric *had* to tell us that stuff," he said. "He'd been hiding it for so long; he needed to know that we'd still be his friends even when we knew what he really is."

Kacey's voice went really quiet now, and I had to hold my breath just to hear her.

"You talk like you believe him," she said.

Joseph made a disgusted grunt. "Let's see," he said, kind of too loud -- and I glanced around to make sure no one else was close enough to overhear -- "he can't be in the sun, always looks like he's been photoshopped in pictures, can move stuff without touching it, gets sick when he tries to be a vegetarian to please you, and drinks my blood without gagging and without leaving any kind of mark." There was a pause, and he added in a loud, sarcastic whisper, "If Eric's not a vampire, then how the heck do you explain all that?"

He made it sound so simple, so ordinary.

"Maybe he just wants attention," Kacey suggested. My stomach twinged.

But Joseph sounded very serious when he answered her. "Look, Kacey," he said, "being a freak isn't something you want people to focus on. I hate it when strangers stare at where my legs *aren't*. It's like they can't see I'm still a person; all they see is the wheelchair or that I'm missing major body parts."

Kacey sounded defensive when she protested, "You're not a freak, Joseph!"

Joseph's answer was sharp and clear. "Neither is Eric," he said. "But people can make you feel that way when you're different."

"Eric's not in a wheelchair." There was more tension in her voice when she spoke this time.

"But I don't have to drink blood, and my picture can be in the yearbook without scaring anyone. And at least no one's ever treated me like a demon just because I don't have any legs."

"It's not the same, and you know it!" She sounded half-angry now.

"Why not?"

"Well," she hesitated, "*you're* for real." Crap. She thought I was making this up?

"How do you know he's not?" Joseph fired back at her.

"I don't believe in vampires or ghosts or witches!" she said.

"Then how come you asked Eric if you were going to turn into a vampire when he told you that he'd bitten you?"

Kacey didn't answer, but Joseph had apparently made her even angrier because there was a rattle of newspaper, and I flattened myself against the lattice as her footsteps came closer to the door.

"Kacey, wait!" Joseph called, and I heard his wheels crunch over the newspaper, too. "Do you believe that Eric believes he's telling us the truth?" he asked her quietly.

She didn't respond for about five seconds, but finally she said, "Yeah, I guess so." She sounded a little deflated.

"Then don't give up on a friend just because he believes something you don't."

Joseph had to be about the coolest friend anyone could ever have.

There was more rustling of newspapers and a sigh. "I never said I was giving up on him," Kacey said. "I just don't get what's going on."

"Then at least you could treat him like he's still your friend until you figure things out for yourself."

Kacey didn't reply. She just came through the door so fast that I didn't have time to move. But obviously her eyes hadn't adjusted to the backstage darkness after the floodlights, because she didn't even see me. Or the piece of plywood she stumbled on while walking to the door that led to the hallway.

I watched her go and then remembered I needed to drink the blood in my plastic bottle. Which sucked -- figuratively and literally.

Kacey didn't believe in vampires. So she didn't believe I was telling her the truth. I should've been mad, I guess, but who could blame her? My mom hadn't believed what my dad had told her until a couple of months after I was born.

At least Kacey still wanted to be my friend, but if it turned out I really was HIV positive, I wouldn't tell her; she wouldn't handle that news well. I'd only tell Joseph. I'd *have* to tell Joseph. Crap.

I trudged back down to the orchestra pit -- which wasn't really a pit, but just the floor space between the stage and the seats in the auditorium. I put my empty blood bottle away and began to play the Billy Joel song I'd learned for the dance concert. I ignored the chatter of the other people coming back to their instruments until I felt Michael give me a soft punch on the arm.

"Hey, what's up?" I asked, trying to sound like I felt normal. Which I didn't.

"My brothers and I are having a party for the orchestra at our house tomorrow," he said. "Can you come?"

"What time?" I asked, glad that Michael didn't seem as much like food to me anymore. I'd fit in a lot better at the party now that I wouldn't be thinking of the host as part of the refreshments.

Michael grinned. "I know you're allergic to sunlight," he said, "but you're in luck; Rich has to work tomorrow, so we won't start until about six."

"Okay. I'll ask my mom when she gets home, but she'll probably say yes," I said, smiling.

So Michael and his brothers didn't think I was a freak because I couldn't go out in sunlight. And they must not have heard Becca's stupid rumors, either. That was definitely cool. Maybe she hadn't spread them very far. I hoped.

"Hey, Michael?" I called to him, twisting around on the piano bench.

He looked up from adjusting the strap on his saxophone. "Yeah?"

"Thanks for the invite."

"No problem," he said and gave me a thumbs up sign.

Practice didn't end until nearly nine, and by then I felt more like a zombie than a vampire. My eyes were like a couple of marbles in my head, and I stared at things without seeing them. That's what happens to me when I've missed four hours of sleep.

And apparently, I wasn't the only one who'd noticed.

"Eric," said Mrs. O'Flannery, leaning her short, round body against the baby grand, "do you realize you never once turned on the music light tonight?" She patted the little lamp above the music holder.

Oh, crud. I'd forgotten. I don't need it, of course, because I can see so well in the dark, but I didn't want to give O'Flannery even one reason to suspect there was any truth behind the rumors she might've heard in the staff room: that there was a dangerous freak in her orchestra pit. Even though it was a *half-Irish* dangerous freak, which probably would've made a difference to her.

"Oh, sorry," I told her. "I just forgot." Well, that was the truth, anyway.

She looked at me hard. Although she seemed like the sweet grandma-type, I could tell it would be difficult to fool her about anything.

"I'd have thought you had your music all memorized," she said accusingly, "but you turned pages with the rest of us."

It was like she was daring me for an explanation, so I gave her one. "Well, I see better in the dark than most people," I told her. "I guess it has something to do with my allergy to sunlight."

She raised one eyebrow and tilted her head. "I guess," she said, and began to stack music on the piano. She had the attitude of a teacher who knows a kid has been cheating but she can't prove it.

175

I wondered how much discussion about Satanic cults she'd heard. Still, if it was *just* teachers.... Well, teachers usually weren't the ones who over-reacted about such things. At least I'd never had a teacher freak out over me before. And I didn't want it now, either.

Anyway, I certainly didn't want to hang around for any more of *that* conversation, and there was no one else I knew well enough to talk to in order to avoid more of her questions. Michael, Jeff, Rich, and Kathy had already gone.

I looked up on the stage in hopes of seeing Kacey or Joseph, but it was deserted except for Papsi, untangling a bunch of electrical cords by the backdrop, and Becca, walking off stage and looking way too smug about something.

I knew I should probably confront her about all the stuff she'd been saying, but that would've meant explaining away what she must've seen the day I drank Joseph's blood. And I was so tired. I'd do it later.

So I swung my backpack over one shoulder and went toward the stage door that led to the parking lot. Joseph had been painting out there earlier; maybe I could still find him.

The floodlights were off now, but I could see all the pieces of scenery just fine as I stepped through the door.

Maybe if I hadn't been so tired I would've been able to react faster than I did. But I was, so I couldn't. Or something like that.

Anyway, one second I was stepping onto the newspaper drop cloths taped all over the place under the now-lavender thrones and a big bunk bed frame, which was half-painted and surrounded by dirty brushes and opened cans of red paint. And the next second I was five feet away, behind the dumpster, without my backpack, and with one huge, hairy arm across my chest and one huge, hairy hand over my mouth.

My head reeled for a second or two. What the --?!

But wait. The hand smelled too much like cow for my taste, and the breath that was coming from over my left shoulder smelled way too much like that beer I'd once nearly puked over.

Hmmm. Cows and beer. Had to be Tobias. Well, nothing to fear in the intellect department anyway. But I felt like I was about to wrestle with King Kong. Oh. So *this* was what Sharon had been trying to warn me about.

"Just hold still, you bastard," he told me. I wondered if Tobias somehow knew I really was illegitimate or if he just liked

176

the word. Probably the second choice; I doubted he even knew what a bastard was.

Maybe I could talk him out of whatever he wanted. I started to open my mouth a little, but suddenly his left hand shifted to under my jaw with three fingers digging into my nose and eyes, clamping my mouth shut.

"Now, just listen up and don't try to say nothin'," Tobias said. "My sister heard you tellin' some mighty strange stuff to some of your friends a while back. And she don't believe in fairy tales no more, but she don't like you tellin' the principal she was lyin'. And I don't like it neither."

I wanted to snap back at him that his sister was another word that started with a "B," but I couldn't. Which was probably just as well.

"Now," Tobias continued, "Becca ain't told no one but the principal and that lady yet, and she's willin' to tell them folks she made a mistake and let things be, *if* you cooperate here." He pronounced the word "cooperate" very carefully, as if it had too many syllables in it for everyday use.

For a second I felt hopeful -- Becca hadn't told anyone but Wendall and Engles!

But Tobias still wasn't finished, "Or, she can tell your neighbors and the rest of Emma City that she saw you drink a kid's blood. People in Emma don't like no vampires or Satanists, and they'll be makin' life hell for you and your ma if me and Becca keep tellin' what she saw, so you'd better shut up and listen to me good. You hear?"

Then there was a click as Tobias moved his right thumb, and I felt something sharp and metal against my chest. It wasn't exactly a wooden stake, but I knew it could do some damage anyway.

Oh, crap.

Chapter Eighteen

I was so tired I couldn't think logically at first. My left brain was out to lunch somewhere -- Zimbabwe, I think -- and my right brain was busy visualizing possibilities: like Sophie Jackson screaming at me for trying to eat Brendan, Kacey telling her brothers I'd attacked her and drunk her blood, and Michael -- wearing a turtleneck -- telling me he didn't want me anywhere near his house or his party.

Oh yeah, *and* I had a switchblade making an interesting indentation on the placket of my polo shirt, right over my sternum. Something about that tends to drive your reasoning powers away, too.

"You're scared now, ain't you?" Tobias said, prodding me a little with the knife. "Your heart's racin' like a jackrabbit's before I break its neck." That was an unappetizing simile, if I'd ever heard one. Whatever was on his mind, I wished he'd hurry and tell me; I was obviously going to get the bad end of the deal anyway.

"All right," he said, apparently guessing my thoughts, "here's how it is: you stop dissin' on my sister, you drop outta this play, and you make your girlfriend drop out, too, so my sister can be the princess like she wants."

I tensed. Was he nuts? Nobody *made* Kacey do anything! And what made him think Mr. Twiller would put Becca in even if --

"Cuz if you don't, then me and Becca will go to the *Emma Ensign* reporters about how you're startin' a cult and gettin' your friends to let you drink their blood. *And* she's gonna post it all on her friendsite page for school. Then everyone'll know, not just that fat man and the black lady."

And there'd be reporters around the house. And they'd find out from Hank Jackson that I get blood from his animals. They'd put it in the paper, and then there'd be whispers behind my back in the halls at school. And people would stop talking when I came into a room. And Kacey's parents wouldn't let her anywhere near me. And the women at church would gossip about my mom. And we'd get dirty looks when we went into Al's Grocery Mart or the Gas-n-Go. And kids at school would treat me like I had the plague. And I'd lose all my friends, just like every other time. And we'd end up moving. *Again.* Nooooooo!

Why had I been stupid enough to think I could tell *anybody* I was a vampire?! Patrick and Sharon had been wrong to talk me into it; nobody around here could handle this.

I felt sick.

This wasn't just about me this time, or even about me and my mom. It was about Kacey. And Joseph. They didn't deserve to get dragged into a newspaper scandal because of me. But Kacey *did* deserve her part in the play; Becca wouldn't be anywhere near as good.

So what was the right thing to do?

Maybe I could convince Mom to take me back to Scotland for a while until people forgot about this. Or maybe we could just move to Scotland. But I'd miss Joseph and --

"That's enough decidin' time," Tobias cut into my thoughts. "Just nod your head to say you agree to our deal. You got away from me last time, but you won't get away this time."

Last time? Oh yeah. The blood drive when I'd run off before he could --

Wait a sec. I'd *run away.* Just like Mom and I had pretty much run away from every place where people had given us trouble. Just like my dad had run away from my mom after he'd tricked her and gotten her pregnant. Just like my dad had run away rather than talk to his own angry cousin in the kirkyard.

Crap. I didn't want to be like my dad. Especially since I'd barely stopped having to be ashamed of what I am.

Very suddenly, my left brain and all its logic returned from Zimbabwe. I took a big breath -- which reeked of cow, as Tobias' hand was still over my nose -- and I shook my head side-to-side.

No. I *won't* do what you want. I'm *not* going to run this time.

"What the f---? You little bastard, I'm gonna make --"

"Eric?" It was Kacey's voice. Tobias shut up immediately.

"Look, there's his backpack. Eric, are you out here?" That was Joseph now.

Yes! Help was here!

I lurched to one side, throwing Tobias up against the dumpster with a crash.

For a few seconds, the hairier Clyde sibling lost his grip on my mouth, and I yelled to my friends, "It's Tobias! He's got a knife!"

Then I felt that knife slash across my left bicep and my chest as I twisted and fell face up onto the asphalt behind the dumpster, with a Sasquatch of a cowboy over me, sitting on my stomach, trying to grab my arms with one hand and slashing wildly with his switchblade in the other -- and grunting.

My left arm hurt like crazy and my chest did, too -- and in the middle of a fight I didn't exactly have time to get any of my medicinal spit onto the wounds. I sniffed. Bitter blood. That was mine. Not good. Still, it'd take a lot more than this to make me bleed to death with my abnormally-quick-to-coagulate blood.

Tobias must've outweighed me by a hundred pounds. There was no way I could throw him off of me, but I had to do something until Kacey and Joseph got some help. If they were getting help. I didn't even know where they'd gone.

I punched Tobias in the stomach as hard as I could, and he swore, then punched me in the jaw with his left hand. But my mouth was open, and his hand jammed across it. Right into my extra-sharp cuspids. I was in pain, but he started howling. And blood that was not my own spurted into my mouth. Cool. Bonus points for me.

I barely had time to swallow his blood before Tobias swung at me again with the knife, but I moved the only way I could think of: I sat up to head-butt him in the gut just as he tried to stab me, so the blade slashed over my left shoulder. It burned like fire, but it wasn't deadly. Still, now I had an aching jaw and wounds all over the left side of my body, all throbbing with each heartbeat.

I started to shove him with my right arm. How much longer could I keep him from doing serious damage to me?

Suddenly, his body arched backwards away from me, and the knife flew out of his hand.

What the --?! Kacey?

"Don't you *dare* hurt him again, you creep!!" she shouted. She'd whipped his head back by the hair at a sharp angle. Guess she'd learned a few things from dealing with all those older brothers.

I didn't have time to analyze her fighting techniques any further just then, but I did know enough to pull my legs out from under Tobias and roll toward the outer wall of the auditorium about four feet away while she was kneeing him in the kidneys.

From there I watched Tobias stand up, with Kacey on his back, her legs wrapped around him and kicking, and her left arm as tight as she could hold it around his neck, choking him enough that he could hardly spew out obscenities at her.

Clearly, she was not a girl to mess with.

I struggled to stand up and help her, but Joseph was faster.

I bet Tobias didn't consider a legless, 3'5" fifteen-year-old much of a threat. But he didn't know Joseph. How strong he is. And how fast.

So, as I staggered to my feet, oozing blood and in a ton of pain, and Tobias, whose switchblade was now on the ground somewhere, tried to pull Kacey loose from his neck, Joseph nimbly slipped out of his wheelchair, did his strange chimpanzee run on his hands until he was between Tobias' feet, then plopped down on the ground and clamped the cowboy's legs together by wrapping his arms like a human vise around them.

Kacey screamed as Tobias went over head-first, and I winced as her arm took part of the blow. But the whack of bone hitting asphalt sent a memory through my brain: the plastic frog whacking the kid's skull on the airplane. Suddenly, I had an idea.

"Get off him, Kacey!" I choked out, as soon as Tobias had hit the ground. Joseph was still between his feet, struggling to get on top of the cowboy.

But I didn't have time to watch whether Kacey moved or not, I was fighting the only way I still could: telekinesis. Holding my right hand against my burning left arm and breathing way too hard, I stared just above two gallons of red paint, willing them upward from the newspaper next to the bunk bed.

Up. That's right. Now over here. Farther. A little more. To the cowboy.

Grunting and a yelp came from Joseph. But I stayed focused and moved the cans over to where Tobias lay, face up now, flailing to kick Joseph off.

And now... dump!

Splot! Right over Tobias' head. Fortunately, Kacey had jumped off him and was just standing up.

I guess it's pretty hard to breathe under two gallons of red paint. And I'm sure it's hard to see anything. Tobias was gasping and sputtering, trying to wipe paint off his face, and still bleeding rather nicely from his left hand, as Joseph let go and scuttled away.

But now what? I could hardly stand up any longer; the pain in my arm, shoulder, and chest was so bad. I couldn't possibly defend myself physically at this point. And I had blood -- my own and Tobias' -- all over my face and shirt.

I looked over at Kacey; she was shaking -- probably from the effort of trying to bring down that ox -- and rubbing her left arm. And Joseph was massaging his stomach with one hand, his glasses bent at a weird angle on his nose, which was bleeding.

Breathing now was requiring severe effort on my part. I wasn't sure if I even had the strength to run away. But maybe Joseph and Kacey could go and get help. Maybe. Please?

For about three seconds, we stayed almost frozen like that, all of us waiting for something.

Then that something happened.

"Hey, what on earth are you kids doing to make all that noise out here?" Papsi's voice bellowed through the doorway. "It sounds like World War III. Do you want every homeowner on this street calling to report --?"

He flipped on the floodlights, and I winced, squinting my eyes nearly shut behind their blood-sticky lashes.

"Holy sweet prophet Elias!"

Papsi's voice had dropped as close to a whisper as I'd ever heard from him before.

Chapter Nineteen

It was nearly 2:00 AM on Saturday by the time Mom and I got to leave the University Medical Center and start for home.

I'd been more alert when Papsi had asked me for Mom's cell phone number -- right after he'd called 911 -- than I was now. Patrick was right; I'd make a lousy drug addict. I'd puked over the blood of a heroin user, and now the legal narcotic pain-killers from the hospital were making my brain act like it'd been spammed with the pop-up ad virus from Hades. Images of police, Kacey crying, an ambulance ride, the emergency room, Papsi sitting with me until he suddenly morphed into a very worried-looking version of my mother, nurses with syringes that made me think of barnyard animals, and enough stitches to make me feel like something created by Mary Shelley were all dancing around in my head. I was surprised the Sugar Plum Fairy wasn't there, too.

Dazedly, I stared at the windshield and vaguely formed the thought that I'd rather have the pain and still be able to think straight. Ugh.

Mom didn't say too much, but she kept reaching over and patting my leg or squeezing my hand about every two minutes as she drove us up Parley's Canyon toward Emma City. Even with my confused brain, though, I could still understand the salty, white streaks on her cheeks. I'd been in no danger of dying, but no mom wants to see her kid get sewn back together like he's Great-Grandma's quilting project. My wounds hadn't been too deep, but they were long, and I hadn't been able to heal them with my saliva in time, so the emergency room doctor had gotten plenty of sewing practice tonight.

As we turned onto our own street in Emma, Mom said, "Now, you just stay put until I can help you into the house. I'll come back and get my suitcase afterward."

Suitcase? Oh, yeah. I'd almost forgotten she'd come straight to the hospital from the airport.

"It's okay, Mom," I told her, feeling like I had peanut butter all over my tongue. "My legs are fine. I can walk."

"Oh, really?" she said, smiling over at me. "You can't even talk normally. I'm not letting you walk into something."

"Do I sound that bad?"

"Yes, actually -- But what in heaven's name?!"

I strained to sit up a little and see what she was talking about. There were two vehicles parked in front of our small, gray house. One was familiar: a rust-eaten 1968 Ford pickup belonging to Kacey's brother Phillip. Vaguely, I wondered why he'd parked it a street away from their home.

I didn't recognize the other car at all. It was small and dark green with Joe's Rent-A-Car stenciled across the rear window. Maybe the Jacksons had company.

Obviously the narcotics had affected my brain speed. I may as well have just shipped my brain back to Zimbabwe for all the good it was doing me right then.

As we pulled into our driveway, lights came on in the cabs of both the pickup and the green car. Then, as I stepped out of our car and leaned against it so I didn't fall over, I saw Phillip lifting an empty wheelchair out of the back of the truck and Kacey running toward me. Her left arm had a bright red cast on it.

"Oh, Eric!" she said, way too loud. "I've been really worried! I begged Mom and Dad to let me come over and wait for you. And Phil was cool enough to take my side of the argument."

She was standing close to me now, but she looked scared to touch me.

Actually, I didn't blame her. They'd washed the blood off my face and arms in the emergency room, but they'd also cut my shirt off, so I was only wearing my jacket over one shoulder because of the pain in my left arm, and that didn't hide my Frankenstein stitches -- covered with sticky, clear antibiotic gel and medical tape edged with stray flakes of dried blood -- or my glow-in-the-dark white chest, which was currently covered with goose bumps in the cold night air. (Look, vampires *don't tan*, okay?)

I reached over -- with my right arm -- and took her hand, which was not covered by the cast.

"Thanks," I managed to say. Okay, so it wasn't very eloquent, but she smiled anyway.

By then Joseph was wheeling up to us, and Phillip wasn't far behind him. "Dude, how many stitches?" Joseph called out to me.

"Fifteen in my arm, twenty-eight across the chest, and nineteen on my shoulder blade," I said, with effort. Kacey squeezed my hand hard.

"You rock!" Joseph said, smiling broadly. I noticed he wasn't wearing his glasses.

"How about you guys?" I asked them.

"Glasses are broken, but the nose isn't," Joseph said, still grinning.

"I've got a stress-fracture; it's not too bad," Kacey said. "But the cops asked us about a million questions after you left in the ambulance, and I bet they'll be around tomorrow to ask you a million more!"

"Yeah," Phillip said, putting his arm around his sister's shoulders, "but Tobias is gonna be in the slammer for sure. He's eighteen now, so no juvenile DT for him. That punk's been bullying people for years, but he's never actually tried to *stab* anyone before. This time he's gonna get what he deserves."

I was still having trouble remembering which plane of existence I was on, but somehow I managed to say to Kacey and Joseph, "Thanks for helping me out tonight. I would've been pretty dead without you guys around."

Kacey smiled, then squeezed my hand again and sniffed. "Hey, it's cool," Joseph said and nodded.

After two or three incredibly long seconds of silence from all of us, during which my narcotically de-pained brain cells were reworking my struggles with Tobias into Obi-Wan Kenobi's fight with Darth Mal, Phillip suddenly said, "So, who's the guy talking to your mom?"

Huh? I looked in the direction Phillip had turned, and there, by our old white VW, was a man who looked like he should have Tiny Tim on his shoulder.

"Patrick!" I half-yelled, and started toward him. But the driveway lurched precariously under my feet, and Kacey grabbed hold of my right arm with both her hands. The roughness of her cast scraped against me.

"Whoa! Be careful!" she said, sounding a little too much like my mom.

But twenty minutes later, we were all inside the kitchen, and Mom was fixing cocoa. Well, everyone was inside but Phillip, who'd just gone back out to get my mom's suitcase and my backpack out of the car and to take the stuff to our bedrooms, which was definitely cool of him.

"So tell me," Patrick said, opening various drawers until he found the one with spoons in it, "why did this chap attack you?"

"Because his sister had overheard me telling Joseph and Kacey here about my being a half-vampire," I said, slowly and carefully, trying to get my tongue to work right.

"Becca is such a --" Joseph started, but Kacey cut him off with a glare. Mom gave a short laugh as she poured cocoa into the cups Patrick had managed to find.

"And he threatened to expose you if you didn't give in to his demands?" Patrick asked.

I nodded. "To the *Emma Ensign* and our school's social media site," I said. Mom winced.

Patrick frowned. "To the local newspaper and all over the internet? Quite a threat," he said. "What did he want you to do?"

"Convince Kacey to drop out of the play so Becca could have the part."

"And you told him he could bugger off?" Patrick suggested, handing me a cup of cocoa.

I tried to laugh, but it hurt. "Kind of," I said, grimacing a little.

"The boy had a switchblade, and he gave Eric three nasty slices before these two came on the scene," Mom filled in for me, nodding toward Kacey and Joseph. "I'm just glad Eric has such good friends and that his geometry teacher was able to handle the situation, especially after Eric grew delirious and babbled on to him about being a vampire before I made it to the hospital."

Holy crap! I'd told Papsi?! What on earth would he think?!

I opened my mouth to ask, but Mom interrupted me with an explanation. "Fortunately, Mr. Papinikolas told me there were some things he'd rather not know about," she said, raising her eyebrows at me, "and that he was just going to assume you were in a state of confusion -- although it was clear to me that he'd heard enough to know there was more to it than that."

Kacey, who'd been looking more and more uptight as my mom explained, suddenly blurted out, "You told Papsi that stupid vampire story you told us?! Eric, how *could* you?!"

I hoped Phillip hadn't heard her, but I was too tired to remind her to be quiet.

"I didn't know I was telling him," I said. "But it's not a 'stupid story.' It's the truth."

Kacey rolled her eyes and looked at my mom, who nodded at her and smiled. "It *is* the truth, Kacey," she said calmly. "Eric really is part vampire."

Kacey's mouth dropped open a little and she looked like she'd been slapped. I guess she hadn't expected my mom to back me up on this. But she recovered fast, then turned to Patrick, scowled, and snapped, "What about you? Do *you* believe them?"

Patrick laughed really loud. "Oh, yes, my dear young lady," he said, once he caught his breath, "I *do* believe them."

But Kacey was unconvinced. "Why?" she demanded. "I mean, you hardly even know Eric. He's been my friend for two years. He showed me the mirror thing, and I don't know how he moves stuff like he does, but I can't make myself believe him. You haven't seen him do any of that, so why do you believe what they're telling you?"

Weird. But in some ways she was right. Kacey didn't know it, but Patrick actually never had seen me drink blood or use telekinesis.

Patrick stopped laughing and sighed. "I know Eric's father," he told her kindly. "He's my cousin, and he's a full-blooded vampire." He paused and glanced between Joseph and Kacey before adding, "And so am I." He took a sip of cocoa.

Kacey stared at Patrick as if she expected him to change into a bat immediately and flap away.

But Joseph was impressed. "Awesome!" he shouted, raising his arms above his head like he'd just made a touchdown. Mom smiled at him, then reached over and ruffled up his hair the way she often does to mine. Joseph didn't seem to mind, either. Not that I thought he would. Joseph likes the attention of women whether they're nine or ninety. I grinned at him as well as I could with my sore mouth. The painkillers were obviously starting to wear off now.

"What's awesome?" Phillip asked, striding into the room and picking up the cup we'd set out for him.

My grin was gone instantly.

What could we tell him? Phillip's a great guy, but I wasn't in the mood to confess my secrets about teenage vampirism to anyone else right now. Things had gotten way out of hand as it was.

But Mom, cooler than an icicle in January, said, "Tonight the medical center gave me the results of Eric's blood test after his tussle with the drug-user in Scotland. We'd wanted to make sure he hadn't been in contact with HIV-infected blood, but he had clean test results, so we're celebrating, Phillip."

"Hey, that's good." Phillip smiled at me, then gulped some of his cocoa.

No HIV? That rocked! I hadn't known Mom'd gotten the test results, but I could tell she wasn't making this up.

I wouldn't get AIDs. And neither would Joseph. Or Kristen. I hadn't given anyone anything. Whew.

Smiling the best I could, I leaned across the table to get a napkin -- and winced again.

Nobody said anything for a few seconds. Kacey was still staring at Patrick, who nodded reassuringly at her a couple of times. Joseph rolled his eyes and shook his head at her, then concentrated on his hot chocolate. And my mom kept switching between smiling at Joseph and Patrick and giving worried looks to me, Kacey, and Phillip. Only Phillip cluelessly finished off his cocoa in peace.

Finally Kacey spoke. "Maybe we should go soon," she told her brother. "I'm starting to feel strange." She paused and looked at me. "Kind of confused, you know?"

I smiled at her gingerly. Even though she wasn't too happy with the vampire stuff, she was still keeping it a secret. How cool was that?

Phillip picked up his own cup and his sister's and walked over to the sink, saying, "Yeah, I bet you guys are pretty tired. Let's get you home, sis." He put the cups down and then asked Joseph, "You ready to go, buddy?"

"Yup," said Joseph, maneuvering his wheelchair around the table, "but Kacey and I are going to come and see you tomorrow, Eric. Right, Kacey?"

His last words sounded like a command. He obviously didn't expect her to agree with him, but she smiled at me -- with my sickly white chest and everything.

"Yeah," she answered Joseph, "I think he's crazy -- and he's not the only one around here who is," she looked at everyone she wasn't related to and then rolled her eyes. "But he's still my friend," she added.

Joseph grinned and gave us both a thumbs-up sign. Kacey smiled at me guiltily, then walked toward the front door. I didn't even try to get up and follow. I hoped they'd all understand.

Mom walked them all out instead while I stared into space for a few minutes as Patrick put all the cups into the dishwasher.

"Eric," he asked me, "whilst you were fighting with this boy tonight, did you ever feel the urge to attack him with your teeth? To bite him in anger?"

What a crazy idea! I hadn't even been hungry. Why would I want to bite somebody when I wasn't hungry?

"No," I told him, still staring into space, "but when he punched me on the jaw, his hand went into my teeth and got sliced." I smiled a little, remembering. Then I yawned, which made my mouth hurt again.

"So you never thought of biting him?"

Duh. Isn't that what I just said? "No," I told him.

There was silence for a second or two, so I carefully shifted myself to look at Patrick. He was smiling at me and leaning over the top of the counter on his elbows. "You're not one bit like your father, Eric," he said.

Oh. So *that's* why he'd asked. My creepy, violent, druggie dad would've attacked and then run. And I hadn't done either. Cool. I really wasn't like my dad. Not in anything.

I smiled at Patrick.

"Sean might be in jail by now, you know," he told me. "I did a bit of asking about until I found the goths you met in Fleshmarket Close that evening, and they informed me that 'the Master' had been questioned by the police for alleged possession of heroin and cocaine. I thought you'd like to know, just in case he had suspected anything about who you might be. He ought not to be out looking for you for a few years, at any rate."

Wow. I hadn't even thought of that. What if my dad had come looking for me here, in the US? Ugh. That was even a worse thought than Tobias' threats. I shuddered a little and went back to staring at the table. I was just too tired to be a good conversationalist tonight.

But Patrick wasn't quite finished yet. "Your mate Joseph is quite a brilliant chap," he said, "and I believe Kacey is trustworthy, even if she is skeptical." He chuckled a little.

"Yeah," I said, "I think you're right."

191

"And I'll chat with her a bit more tomorrow evening -- after I get settled into my flat -- and we'll let her ask questions and get to understand us a bit better," he continued.

Wait a sec. *Flat.* That means an apartment. People *live* in apartments. They don't get them unless they're staying. Not just visiting.

I turned around fast, and the sensation of ten thousand paper cuts went across my chest.

"Oh, crap! Ouch!" I said, sucking air over my teeth. When I could breathe again, I asked, "You're *living* here? You're going to stay?"

Patrick walked around from behind the counter and came back to the table. "Well," he said, pulling out a chair and sitting down across from me, "I start work at the community college computer lab in Park City on Monday evening, and it's a bit of a commute from Edinburgh."

"But why did you leave Scotland?" I asked. "Are you and my mom, like --?" I really didn't know how to finish, and it sounded pretty lame anyway, but I was too brain-dead to do any better.

But Patrick was smiling like Bob Cratchit again. "Your mother is a remarkable woman," he said. "And it's not every day a male vampire meets a non-vampire woman who is so sympathetic."

I snorted. Geez. He was right about that. I wondered if Kacey would ever really believe me.

"And I haven't discussed this with your mother yet, so I'd appreciate it if you'd keep quiet about it for a while," Patrick had dropped his voice almost to a whisper, and he kept glancing up at the kitchen door as he spoke, "but I am hoping that *sometime* in the future, I might be allowed the privilege of becoming your stepfather. What would you think of that situation?"

If I'd had the energy, I would've gotten up and tap-danced in a circle and set off the firecrackers I keep in my bottom desk drawer downstairs.

No HIV. I'd stood up to Tobias' bullying and won -- without acting like my dad. And with Tobias in trouble with the cops, nobody'd believe Becca if she told more stories about me; they'd think she was lying to defend her stupid brother. My hands hadn't been hurt in the fight, so I'd still be able to play the piano for the school musical. I had two awesome friends -- even if one of them did think I was living in a Bram Stoker fantasy world --

and Michael's party invitation proved I was making other friends as well.

And now, if Mom liked Patrick as much as I hoped she did, I might get a totally amazing stepfather, too.

Well, I summed it up for Patrick with all the eloquence my narcotically-numbed brain could muster. "Dude, that'd be way cool!" I told him.

Life was good. Even for a half-vampire.

About The Author

At age six, Lisa Shafer wandered into a room where a movie was being played at a church Halloween party and was horrified by a scene wherein the vampire's evil assistant slit the throat of the overly-trusting traveler and let his blood drip onto Dracula's dust to re-grow him. She slept with the covers over her neck for years afterwards.

Ms. Shafer's first vampire story won a prize in a sixth grade contest, and she's been writing about them in one form or another ever since. *Confessions of an Average Half-Vampire* is her debut novel, which means that, although it's far from the first one she's written, it's the first to make it out for public reading. Please visit her blog at http://lisashafer.blogspot.com to learn more about her other books, including the sequel to this one, which is entitled, *All In The Half-Vampire Family*, and which will be available to readers in 2012.

When she is not writing about vampires, Ms. Shafer is generally found grading persuasive essays written by her students, chasing the dust bunnies that grow magically everywhere in her house when she's not looking, and planning trips to Scotland. Her bad habits include staying up way too late at night to read and eating way too much chocolate.

Bonus Section:
A Few Drops Of Fresh Blood
From The Sequel,
All In The Half-Vampire Family

"Kacey," I said, rubbing her back a little, "I can't be a non-vampire, but I *am* still your friend, you know."

Joseph took her hand again and said softly, "And you always liked Eric before you knew he was a vampire, so why should knowing it make any difference?"

"But I --" she hiccuped. "I don't want to deal with all that weird stuff!" She gave another hiccup that ended in a kind of burp, but she ignored it. "I just want to be with a *normal* Eric!" Hiccup. Sniff. "Or an Eric with porphyria." Big sniff. "Seeing him move stuff around and talk about needing blood --" Hiccup. Sniff again. "It doesn't fit with anything we've ever learned in school or church. I want it to --" Huge sniff. Little sob. "To go away so it won't be a problem anymore." She stopped talking and wiped her nose with the hand Joseph wasn't holding.

I could see I was going to have to do the hypnosis bit again.

"Kacey," I said, in a gentle but self-assured tone, "I don't really want to be like this either. And Joseph can't be all that thrilled with being 3'5" tall and not having any legs. But neither one of us has a choice. Sometimes that happens in life. It might even happen to you; you might get some disease or something and have to deal with it. Ignoring weird stuff won't make it go away."

I kept rubbing her back lightly. Her head was still down, but she wasn't crying so hard now. Joseph mouthed "Keep going" at me.

"And I know being a vampire isn't anything they talk about in science classes or Sunday School," I said, "but that doesn't mean it doesn't exist. Some day I'm going to study genetics and figure out why we have freaky reflections and stuff, but right now, Patrick and I are just one of those things that nobody's explained yet."

Slowly, the hypnosis began to work. But it was working on me, too.

See, hypnosis is what I do to animals every time I'm going to stick in a needle to draw their blood. So my saliva glands were working overtime, and my stomach was growling, even though I'd had extra blood before going to the movie -- just in case I got hungry watching fake vampires drink fake blood. Hey, I watch *a lot* of horror movies; I *know* I need more than popcorn.

Plus, I knew what Kacey's blood tasted like. I'd had it before. Human blood is so much sweeter than animal blood, and hers was good. So was Joseph's, but I hadn't been focusing on Joseph, so it was Kacey's blood I wanted now. Right out of that carotid artery where I'd drunk it last February.

Drool was slipping out of the corners of my mouth, and I stopped rubbing Kacey's back to wipe it away.

She looked at me dazedly. "You're drooling," she said, then frowned again.

I sighed. "I'm hungry," I said. "For blood. I can't help wanting it when I try to calm someone with hypnosis. That's why I bit you before."

"*Said* you bit me before." Okay, so she'd stopped crying. But she obviously still didn't like the vampire bit.

"You saw the bruise," I told her. I'd gotten carried away that time and drunk so fast it bruised her neck. Normally, a vampire bite leaves no mark at all.

"That doesn't prove you actually *drank* my blood," she countered.

I couldn't answer her; I had to wipe spit off my chin. Why did this always have to happen around girls? Having spit all over my face is just not studly.

It was Joseph who spelled out the obvious for her. "I felt it when he drank my blood. Why don't you let him drink yours now, while you're awake?" he asked her. "Then maybe you'll know he's telling you the truth."

My heart began to beat faster. I hadn't had human blood in weeks, not since Tobias had tried to punch me in the face during our fight and had sliced his hand open on my teeth. Joseph's idea sounded great to me.

Kacey said nothing. She just stared at me.

I leaned forward until I could smell her skin and the salt from the drying tears on her cheeks. I ran one finger down her carotid artery, and I could see it pulsing now. She didn't flinch, even though my mouth was only about two inches from her neck.

This just didn't seem like Kacey. But my stomach was past caring.

Hesitantly, I put my lips over the thin skin covering the artery and licked over the area to numb it with my crazy, medicinal saliva. Kacey jerked back and slapped a hand over her neck, her eyes wide.

Dang it.

"I wanna go home," she announced, standing up, but keeping her hand over that tasty artery.

Saliva was practically gushing into my mouth now. I gulped. How could I walk her home without biting her after this? Sure, I could slip over to the Jacksons' for a visit to their cows once I got to my own street, but could I last the five blocks?

Nope. I'd have to run for it and let Joseph be the gentleman and take her home.

I quickly turned to stand up and found myself looking directly at Patrick. He was standing motionless on the sidewalk about ten feet away from us.

Uh, oh. Not good.

He'd obviously been sent by my mom to make sure we were all on our way home, but he had a pinched look around his eyes. I could immediately tell two things: 1) he had watched the entire almost-blood-drinking episode, and 2) he was *not* full. Now I was more than a little worried.

"Hey, Patrick," Joseph called to him. "Are we out too late? Were you sent to hunt us down?"

Ouch. Poor choice of words, there. Joseph, I knew, could not see in the dark. He couldn't see the beads of saliva forming in the corners of Patrick's mouth. I'd never seen Patrick in an attack of bloodlust, but he'd admitted to me it still caught him off guard once in a while. Guess now was one of those surprise moments.

Shaking slightly with my own bloodlust, I jumped up from Kacey's side and went to him quickly. Wiping spit from my mouth then grabbing his arm, I said softly, "Are you gonna be okay?"

Patrick shuddered. He kept staring at Kacey. "I wish I'd not seen that," he said. "I need to escort you three home, but.... Do you have your backpack with you, Eric?"

Not wanting to look like a total social outcast, I'd left it -- and all my blood snacks in it -- at home while we went to the movie.

"No," I told him. "Can you make it to the Jacksons'? We could get one of the cows pretty fast." I swallowed another huge mouthful of vampire saliva.

Patrick said nothing. He just stared at Kacey. It was almost scary, but she was still calm from the hypnosis and just stared back at him.

Great. Patrick hadn't had human blood in *years*. He'd told me so. But now he'd stumbled on me trying to drink Kacey's blood, and I'd caused him to crave it again. And just when I was fighting like crazy not to want it either.

"I'll be all right," he said, after about a minute. But he was shaking worse than I was.

Kacey walked over to us on the sidewalk, still apparently fascinated with Patrick's struggle for self control. "What's wrong?" she asked.

Patrick shuddered and forced himself to stare across the street at the J Bar-7 Motel, home of the ugliest turquoise doors in the West. I kept a grip on his arm. I knew he would never, ever attack anyone, but I wasn't so sure about myself just then.

But Joseph had had all he could tolerate. He climbed back into his wheelchair and glared up at Kacey.

"'What's wrong?'" he said. "*You're* what's wrong! You pull a crying fit so Eric will try to calm you down. Then, when he does what every vampire does before drinking, you get upset when he gets hungry! And Patrick saw it all, so you've caused two vampires to suffer -- just so you could have Eric's attention!"

Wait. Was *that* what she'd been doing? Manipulating me? But --

I felt Patrick's muscles tense under his jacket. "I'm sorry," he said. "Just give me a moment, please. I haven't had any blood today."

Whoa. *Big* problem. No wonder he was salivating.

Kacey's mouth went into a tight line, and she turned and marched off toward 200 South, where she lived. Part of me wanted to go with her, but the rest of me knew that would be a *very* bad idea. My heart was pounding, and I could hear that Patrick's breathing had gone all ragged.

"I should see that she gets home safely," he said, then caught his breath and continued, "but I'm not able just now."

"She'll be fine," Joseph said. "This is Emma City, not New York." He paused, then added, "Hey, does this bloodlust thing hurt? You guys look miserable."

"It's like hormones and hunger pains all at the same time," I explained. "It hits the stomach, the saliva glands, and the brain all at once."

Still staring at the motel and breathing hard, Patrick gave half a laugh. "Especially the brain," he said. "It's difficult to think of anything else when the craving hits. I suspect this might be how a drug addict feels." His voice sounded a little slurpy with drool.

"I bet it's worse for Patrick than for you," Joseph said to me. "He's full-blooded, and you're just half. It's got to be a stronger feeling for him."

Worse than what I felt? Ugh.

Patrick tensed again, and I gripped his arm harder. He was really struggling with himself. I figured Joseph was right. I'd never seen Patrick less than perfectly in control before.

"Let's go to the Jacksons'," I begged him, tugging gently on his arm.

"Wait," Joseph said, rolling his chair a little closer, "Kacey's gone, but you guys can have some of *my* blood."

My heart started beating harder.

"Don't joke, please," Patrick said softly.

"I'm not joking," Joseph said, staring at Patrick's back in the dark. "Eric drank my blood once before. I'm not scared, and you guys both look pathetic. Let me help you out."

Patrick was almost frozen. I felt really sorry for him. Joseph was right, as usual. "Patrick, he's serious. You'd better drink," I said.

"I don't like to battle with my self-control like this," he said.

"What about you?" Joseph asked me.

"I -" This was so hard to say. "I don't think you should lose that much blood. I'll -" I had to stop and swallow, "find a sheep in a couple of blocks."

Joseph half-closed one eye and raised the other eyebrow. "Okay, I guess," he said, then added, "Patrick, the offer's still good."

"You know, Joseph, that it will make you lightheaded for a few hours?" Patrick asked, still looking away.

"Yeah, that's fine." Joseph sounded confident.

Carefully, I let go of Patrick, and he turned and knelt swiftly at the side of Joseph's wheelchair. Joseph put out his arm, just like he'd done for me in March.

But Patrick shook his head. "The neck will be faster," he said. "If I may...?"

I gulped hard.

Joseph looked like he was going to laugh, but then moved his body toward the vampire at his side. "Go for it," he said, grinning. He looked at me and added, "This is weird."

And it *was* weird. I watched as Patrick put his right hand on Joseph's left shoulder to brace himself, then licked over his right carotid artery. It was the first time in my life I had ever seen another real vampire bite. It was like watching myself from a distance in a dream.

But as Patrick bit down, I felt saliva overflowing my mouth again, and I had to look away. I had to watch analyze those awful doors on the motel -- although images of pulsating blood vessels danced across them -- until Patrick was through.

Less than a minute later, I heard Joseph announce, "You can look now."

But I could only do it for a second. Joseph rubbing a hand over his neck and Patrick wiping off his mouth -- it was too much.

I ran for the barnyard as fast as I could.

Made in the USA
Lexington, KY
01 March 2012